Venus ran behind the complex, broke a window in Gina's bedroom, opened the window, c_____ _side. From the bedroom, where Gina lay _____ ___ __h fear, Venus heard the gun battle in _____. She grabbed Gina by the arm and dra___, ___ _ window and across the parking lot __ ___ ___ed area.

They found the dark blue van in the parking lot. Inside, they found enough arms and ammunition to supply a small army. They found communications devices, and they found a bomb detonator. The thing that most interested Venus, though, was the English-Russian language grammar, bookmarked at "Important Shopping Phrases."

The three corpses carried no personal identification. There wasn't much to go on, but one look at their dental work was enough to tell Venus they weren't Americans.

★

"...the sky is the limit for talented Skye Kathleen Moody."
—*The Midwest Book Review*

D0181052

Previously published Worldwide Mystery titles by
SKYE KATHLEEN MOODY

RAIN DANCE
BLUE POPPY
WILDCRAFTERS

SKYE KATHLEEN MOODY

HABITAT

WORLDWIDE®

TORONTO • NEW YORK • LONDON
AMSTERDAM • PARIS • SYDNEY • HAMBURG
STOCKHOLM • ATHENS • TOKYO • MILAN
MADRID • WARSAW • BUDAPEST • AUCKLAND

To my mother, Donna I. Kelly,
an endangered species,
with love.

HABITAT

A Worldwide Mystery/February 2001

First published by St. Martin's Press, Incorporated.

ISBN 0-373-26375-9

Printed in U.S.A.

Acknowledgments

The author wishes to thank Betsy L. Dresser, M.D., director of the Audubon Center for Research of Endangered Species (ACRES) at the Freeport-McMoRan Audubon Species Survival Center in Louisiana, whose unique vision and groundbreaking research is today saving countless of Earth's endangered species.

The author appreciates the expertise, keen insights and generosity of her editor, Kelley Ragland, and literary agent, Pamela Ahearn, and the loving encouragement of her siblings and Gregory Browning Smith.

Any inaccuracy or factual errors inadvertently contained in the manuscript are entirely the author's responsibility.

Honor is like an island, rugged and without a beach.

—Nicolas Boileau-Despreaux,
1636-1711, *Satire*

ONE

BREEDHAVEN

ELMER POOLE found the human skeleton poking up out of shallow loam thirty feet above his boat launch on Helix Island, the uppermost-inhabited rock in the San Juan archipelago. Helix has no beaches, just steep, slippery shoals that plunge suddenly into the inky saltwater Haro Strait, where porpoise frolic and orcas dance and giant octopuses comb the deep. Tides rise and fall, periodically tossing kelp-wrapped debris onto the rocks, but usually the sea's largess slides right back down into the strait. The rocks are that precipitous, that slick. So the tide hadn't delivered up these human relics, which led to the logical conclusion that they must have been buried up here at the cliff's edge, where hard rains washed loose soil into the Haro Strait, gradually exposing them. Buried bones.

Elmer found the skull and bones right about where his deceased mother's parsley patch grew, stubbornly outliving her, on the steep southwestern shore of Helix Island, near a peach tree grown from a seed Elmer himself had sown in his childhood some seventy years ago. Elmer hadn't meant to dig up the ancient parsley patch—not to mention a bunch of bones. He'd only meant to stop the progress of a pesky wasp colony—what Elmer called yellow jackets—who had built their papery nest in a flinty crevice cliffside of the parsley. The wasps swarmed everywhere, even in his house, and were driving him crazy.

In themselves, bones didn't particularly disturb Elmer, even human bones. What got to him, though, was the skull. From the looks of the low forehead, the smallness of it, Elmer believed the remains were those of an ancient man who had lived on this rocky archipelago thousands of years ago, perhaps even before this mountain chain got submerged to form islands. From all appearances, Elmer had discovered a priceless piece of ancient history: "prehistoric San Juan Man."

Elmer had no reason to conceal his find, and the news spread fast. The *San Juan Register* sent a reporter over from Friday Harbor. The *Anacortes Crier* sent someone across from the mainland. A network television crew choppered up from Seattle, another flew down from Vancouver, British Columbia, and all the photographers made images of Elmer holding the skull of Prehistoric San Juan Man. Soon after the news broke, a delegation from the Lummi Nation arrived, declaring that any old bones found in the San Juan Islands belonged to the Lummi, and demanded their ancestors' remains. For five solid days, Prehistoric San Juan Man enjoyed celebrity in the form of media attention, curiosity seekers, prideful islanders, angry Lummi, and quibbling anthropology buffs. Then one dank, fogbound spring morning, a real anthropologist from the United States Fish and Wildlife Service landed at Helix Island, examined Prehistoric San Juan Man, and pronounced him Modern San Juan Man.

The USF&W anthropologist surmised that muscle and tendons, flesh and blood, had connected this skull and these bones as recently as six winters ago. To punctuate his findings, he showed Buzz Cone, the San Juan Islands sheriff, where a .38-caliber bullet had pierced the skull. What's more, DNA tests proved the bones belonged to retired sea captain C.Z. Blakey, the lowbrowed Puget Sound harbor pilot who had gone missing one cold December morning six years ago.

Just hours later, Sheriff Cone's posse showed up at Lois Blakey's bed-and-breakfast inn on the northern tip of Helix Island and arrested Lois for the murder of her husband. The evidence—besides the bones—consisted of an industrial-strength meat grinder the widow Blakey had recently sold to Hamburger Haven over in Anacortes, and a human tissue-tainted sausage-patty press that Lois had stored in the pantry at her B&B. Though no gun was found, circumstantial evidence pointed to Mrs. Blakey. The motive, claimed the arrest warrant, was the hefty pension Captain Blakey refused to share with Lois, who was hard up for cash to pay her creditors. Selfish, selfish husband.

An undercurrent of controversy rippled through the island after Lois Blakey was arrested on purely circumstantial evidence.
Some folks believed she did it. Others perceived Lois as pure
as driven snow. But Lois hadn't made any true friends on Helix,
and gradually the talk died down. The island settled back to
normal, having little else to bother with, except the summer's
overabundance of wasps, and, too, the pesky nuns, but nobody
wanted to talk about the Sisters of Mercy on the Rock. Not out
loud, anyway. The "Nun Question" was fraught with emotional
hand-wringing, and Helix was too small for feuds of any con-
sequence. Islanders know to keep the peace with their neighbors,
even when their neighbors happen to be nuns of a supremely
suspect habit. Nobody wanted trouble, except maybe Elmer
Poole, who had the temerity to die suddenly the day after Sheriff
Cone took San Juan Man away from him, leaving a last will and
testament so vindictive, so fraught with innuendo and bitter fin-
ger-pointing, that the islanders actually wondered if Elmer
Poole, not Lois Blakey, had murdered Captain Blakey. Apparently, Elmer was that blackhearted. Why else would Elmer Poole
up and die so suddenly and then announce from the grave via
his meticulously revised will, that he intended to break his promise to the islanders?

And what a promise. Years earlier, Elmer had vowed that,
upon his death, his four-hundred-acre estate, which comprised
the southern portion of Helix Island, the most naturally pristine
and coveted land in all the San Juan archipelago, would be gifted
in perpetuity to the Helix Island Preservation Land Trust. But
now Elmer had double-crossed the islanders, declaring in his
will that ever since Helix councilwoman Edna Furbank sold her
back five acres to the Sisters of Mercy on the Rock that he no
longer felt anybody on this island cared about preservation and
true sanctity. In Elmer's estimation, the nuns were a bunch of
repressed females with furtive underpinnings and land-grabbing
instincts. Elmer's punishment to his fellow islanders for Edna
Furbank's breech of the unspoken island covenant—*viz.*, no islander would ever sell property to non-native influxers, especially not the nuns—was the breaking of his own promise to
leave his land in the islanders' trust. Instead, Elmer stated hotly

in his last will and testament, this idyllic island paradise would be turned over to a very different private trust, and forthwith converted into a cockamamie endangered-species habitat.

"Oh, great," drolled Sleeper Sexton, the island's chief councilman, "just what Helix needs. A bunch of non-native antelopes chewing up our gardens and molesting our hens."

Other council members agreed with Sleeper, as did every Helix islander, including even the nuns over at Mercy on the Rock Cloister on the northeastern tip of the island. So when Dr. Hannah Strindberg arrived on Helix one tranquil spring morning and unloaded her first cargo of Japanese red deer, set them loose on Elmer's estate, the islanders watched warily, inwardly fuming at Elmer Poole's quashed covenant.

What really fried Sleeper Sexton, though, was all the construction work that went on over the fall and winter, the building materials and earthmovers taking up so much precious space on the ferryboats sailing to and from the mainland. Islanders often had to wait hours for another ferry, because the boat they wanted to board was filled up with Dr. Strindberg's construction crews. Then the rudest blow of all came early one spring afternoon, when Jean Teaweather, another council member, happened to drive by the old Poole estate and witnessed Dr. Strindberg nailing up a sign at the new entrance gate.

Breedhaven, it read. *Endangered Species Habitat: Managed by the United States Department of the Interior, Division of Fish and Wildlife. No Trespassing.*

As if any Helix Islander would want to.

JUST WHAT DID "Breedhaven" stand for? The islanders pondered this question for weeks, never once entertaining an idea of direct action—say, calling Dr. Strindberg on the telephone and asking her point-blank what Breedhaven meant. Islanders aren't forthcoming or direct with outsiders. A non-native does not merit candor.

Breedhaven. Sounded highly suspicious to Sleeper Sexton, and to Jean Teaweather, and to lots of other folks. The islanders' curiosity was piqued further on a brilliant spring midday, when the *Klikitat* docked at the ferry landing next to Mercy on the

Rock Cloister, and two limousines and four Lincoln Town Cars drove off the ferry, up the ramp, and onto Helix Island. Jean Teaweather and a few other islanders stepped outside the little dockside post office/grocery store to stare, and wonder what this tony vehicular invasion meant. Mrs. Teaweather, in her postal-clerk's apron, shading her eyes against a noonday sun, moved to the front of the gawking group, to better follow the motor-cade's progress.

When the sleek cortege reached the dusty main road, Mrs. Teaweather thought for sure they were headed for the Chekhov estate. Ten years earlier, before the crackdown on influxers, Larry Chekhov, the colorful Russian tycoon, had bought fifty acres of wooded waterfront property on the west side of Helix Island. Some said he smuggled drugs from there; others called Chekhov's land-grab an innocent investment. Naturally Mrs. Teaweather speculated that this bevy of limousines must be headed to Chekhov Meadows. She was obviously mistaken, for when the motorcade reached the turnoff to West Island, it flew straight past, heading due south on the main road in the direction of South Island.

Four properties made up the south end of Helix Island: Lars Hansen's small five-acre spread, Andy and Lynette Dorlup's twenty-acre blueberry farm, a forty-acre state park, and, occu-pying the entire southwestern portion of the island, the old Poole estate, the place now called Breedhaven. In Jean Teaweather's mind, it stood to reason that the limousine parade was headed not for Lars Hansen's, nor for the Dorlups' berry farm, nor to the lovely state park, but rather was hell-bent on Breedhaven. If Mrs. Teaweather weren't employed as the postal clerk, she would have climbed into her pickup truck then and there and followed that slick parade. As it was, nobody followed the lim-ousines to Breedhaven. The islanders had the patience and com-mon sense to wait for Sleeper Sexton to return from his job on the mainland, and then send Sleeper and two of his council members over to Breedhaven, to drop by, in a neighborly fash-ion, and in guarded, islander style, to check out Dr. Hannah Strindberg and her guests.

About seven p.m. Pacific Daylight Time—for this occurred in

June—Sleeper Sexton, accompanied by fellow council members Jean Teaweather and Morris Fluke, drove up to the locked gate at the entrance to Breedhaven. Sleeper stepped out of his pickup, ambled over to an intercom perched on the gate, and buzzed. Pretty soon, a voice identifying itself as Dr. Hannah Strindberg's came over the speaker system. Sleeper identified himself, apologized for not phoning ahead, and was buzzed in through the gate.

As they drove onto the old Poole estate, Sleeper, Mrs. Teaweather, and Morris Fluke marveled at the superb condition of the property. Not only had the estate's lands been meticulously restored, some dramatic improvements had been made. For example, on the northernmost edge of the property, several acres of marshy wetlands that had fallen into disrepair during Elmer's watch had been restored and were now stocked with wild birds, most of which the islanders didn't recognize but were nonetheless beautiful. "Exotics," Mrs. Teaweather remarked with a meaningful sniff. Farther along the road, the thick sylvan landscape appeared healthy and unfettered and everywhere the eye could see, native vegetation thrived. On the east side of the property, rolling meadows burst forth in red-flowering currant blooms and wild rhododendron. Obviously, the islanders' fears that Dr. Strindberg and her Breedhaven cohorts would defile this pristine, virginal acreage had been wholly unfounded, and while this discovery greatly relieved Sleeper, the sudden appearance of a rhinoceros on the near horizon startled and dismayed him. Non-native species couldn't possibly be good for the ecology.

Just as surprising was the newly constructed magnificent compound where old Elmer's decrepit, rambling family home once leaned precariously into the north wind. In its place stood three large natural-wood structures, and if Sleeper wasn't mistaken, the largest of the three was a sort of lodge. Sleeper fervently hoped that Breedhaven wasn't some sort of environmentalists' retreat center, for the last thing any of these islands needed was another so-called "ecology study center" where hordes of ignorant tree-huggers crawled over the delicate native vegetation and basically mucked-up the fragile ecosystem in the name of "understanding the environment." If so, Sleeper would have to go to the county council and complain. In the archipelago, there were laws against defiling the fragile ecology.

Sleeper saw the two limousines and four town cars parked outside the lodge and steeled himself for another tense confrontation with some land-grabbing developers, for Sleeper suspected that this Breedhaven operation, in spite of its supposed connection with the U.S. Fish and Wildlife Service, was nothing but a cover for government real-estate developers sneaking onto Helix Island to slice up the island's southeastern portion into tiny little lots they'd sell for a sweet profit, caring not a whit for the islanders' feelings about overpopulation and limited fresh water supplies. So when Dr. Strindberg opened the door, Sleeper immediately glanced over her shoulder, expecting to see a roomful of bloated government bureaucrats. Instead, Sleeper's gaze fell upon the visage of someone he'd always wanted to meet, but never in his wildest dreams had expected to: the extraordinary beauty and famous movie star Bella Winsome-Diamond, whose legendary legs caused men stronger than Sleeper to weep with joy.

Lady Winsome-Diamond stood just behind and to the right of Dr. Strindberg's thin shoulder, and the very sight of the actress caused Sleeper to breathe a sigh of relief, for everyone in the Pacific Northwest knew that the talented British import was no land-grabbing real-estate mogul or government dupe. On the contrary, Lady Winsome-Diamond was a Pacific Northwest native (if you tweaked the definition, which everyone did in Bella's case), who championed the cause of environmental integrity in the glorious San Juan archipelago. It was, after all, according to San Juan Islands legend, Lady Winsome-Diamond who once-upon-a-time had faced down a boatload of Japanese whalers when they trespassed on a fragile San Juan Island marine sanctuary. From the bow of her yacht, Bella had lectured the intruders, in perfect Japanese, about the seven distinct and fragile ecosystems that existed, layer upon layer, on the very spot the whalers proposed to defile with fresh whale blood and sake bottles. Reportedly Lady Bella had brandished her diamond rings to reflect sunlight into the skipper's eyes, until the ne'er-do-wells changed course and fled.

Sleeper immediately concluded that since this clustering of town-car society included Lady Bella Winsome-Diamond, the visitors must surely possess a lofty purpose. He therefore immediately dropped his sizable guard, and when Dr. Strindberg shoved a glass of champagne into his hand, Sleeper didn't protest. Instead, he sipped.

Half an hour later, Sleeper, Mrs. Teaweather, and Morris Fluke found themselves in the midst of a perky cocktail party, giddy from champagne, slightly bloated from rich canapés, and their fears very much assuaged. The suspicious gathering, it developed, was nothing more threatening than the first meeting of the Breedhaven Board of Trustees, a select group of wealthy Pacific Northwesters whose considerable fortunes would nourish what Lady Winsome-Diamond described to Sleeper as ''vital research into endangered-species reproduction, really the cutting edge in captive breeding programs,'' conducted by Dr. Hannah Strindberg. Nothing that threatened the island's natural ecology, Bella assured Sleeper; in fact, she pointed out, the preserve was surrounded by an electronic fence that guaranteed the imported exotic wildlife would not stray. As for the peculiar birds, Dr. Strindberg explained to Sleeper that these were all species that either were too fat to fly or naturally followed a migratory path over the islands, and so would not threaten the ecological balance. No nasty peacocks or unsavory flamingos, Dr. Strindberg vowed. Sleeper felt ever so relieved, and allowed Dr. Strindberg to refill his champagne flute.

Mrs. Teaweather, meanwhile, lingered near the hors d'oeuvres, where she made a most pleasant discovery in the form of Elmer Poole's granddaughter, Rosemary Poole. Although she had grown up since Jean Teaweather had last seen her, Rosemary was instantly recognizable as a Poole (the distinctive caterpillar eyebrows and shelf chin). Rosemary had spent her childhood summers on Helix Island at Grandfather Poole's home, and Jean Teaweather remembered her as a homely girl with a rather turgid disposition and slightly furtive manner. At twenty-four, Rosemary had transformed into a pleasant-mannered and rather sophisticated doctoral candidate, up from Stanford for the trustees' meeting. Yes, she was one of

Breedhaven's seven trustees, Rosemary told Mrs. Teaweather, and, in fact, when she finished up her dissertation next September, she planned to work here at Breedhaven alongside Dr. Strindberg.

"Feeding the deer?" asked Mrs. Teaweather, feeling smart behind an oyster canapé.

In spite of the hairy caterpillars, Rosemary had developed into a gorgeous creature with a flashy smile that slightly intimidated Jean Teaweather. "Not at all," laughed Rosemary. "I'm a biologist. I'll be studying captive breeding processes with endangered species."

"Is that right?" Mrs. Teaweather's brows knitted. She didn't know what to ask next, so she just smiled and tapped her champagne flute against Rosemary's, remarking, "Here's to your dissertation, dear."

Dr. Strindberg paid special attention to Sleeper's champagne supply, and his glass was never empty. By his third glass, Sleeper had fully acclimated to the chic surrounds and now he regaled Lady Winsome-Diamond and several other trustees with quaint island lore. Sleeper had never been quite so forthcoming with mainlanders, but somehow, the visitors seemed so convivial, so charming....

Besides Della, Sleeper held the rapt attention of a petite, nattily dressed trustee named Ardith Pierce, who told Sleeper she bred minnows for a pastime. "When you are the widow of a successful investment banker, Mr. Sexton," Mrs. Pierce quipped wryly, "you must create your pastimes."

Mrs. Pierce immediately took a shine to Sleeper, made flirtatious chitchat, and once even inquired about his marital status. A widower, with nothing to hide, really, Sleeper nevertheless skillfully dodged Mrs. Pierce's question. Some matters are just too complicated. But Sleeper had to admit he enjoyed Mrs. Pierce's playful come-on. No one had flirted with him in a very long time. She was cute, too. Perky.

Over by the lodge's huge fireplace, Morris Fluke had sunk deep into sofa cushions between Stan Rowe, the retired fish magnate, and Frances Faber, the Seattle socialite who was already insisting that Morris address her by her nickname. "Morris, dear, please, everyone calls me Fanny."

Morris's cheeks burned but he obliged.

Across from Morris, in a deep wing chair, sat Larry Chekhov, the flashy Russian tycoon. Renowned as a flamboyant benefactor of quirky causes (considered by some a drug-smuggling Russki Mafia boss), Chekhov lived in Seattle and rarely was seen on the rock. Chekhov impressed old Morris as an affable, easygoing lad, nothing at all like the eccentric firebrand portrayed in local gossip.

Seated beside Larry Chekhov—fondling his earlobe, if you want to get technical—was Tina Medina, the aromatherapy-products queen, a languid example of beauty infused with ambition. Morris was wallowing in this lofty company when Sleeper came over and said it was time to head out. Morris rankled. He wasn't ready. Sleeper had to snarl to convince him it was time to leave Dr. Strindberg and her illustrious guests. The trustees' meeting was about to begin.

WHEN THE ISLANDERS had said good-bye to Dr. Strindberg and Breedhaven's tony trustees, and were driving home along the dark road that traced the island's backbone south to north, Mrs. Teaweather, who had been silent since leaving Breedhaven, suddenly piped up.

"Mercy," said Jean Teaweather. "I think we three have just been thrown the old champagne curve."

"How's that?" Morris's voice sounded groggy.

Mrs. Teaweather tilted her head. "I can't exactly put my finger on it," she mused, "but I just get the feeling that something fishy's going on at Broadhaven. Something we should know about."

"Breedhaven," Sleeper corrected her.

"Oh yes, Breedhaven. What a curious name."

Fluke snorted. "I'll tell you what's curious. All that talk about breeding endangered species. Mrs. Faber—I mean, Fanny—told me they make embryos right there in the laboratory. That's what's curious."

Sleeper said, "Nothing curious about that. That's what they

do at Breedhaven. They save endangered species by reproducing them through surrogate mothers. That's what they mean by a captive breeding program.''

Fluke said, "What gets me is that granddaughter of Elmer Poole's.''

"I didn't notice anything strange about Rosemary," said Jean Teaweather. "Did you, Sleeper?''

Sleeper shrugged. "Nope.''

Morris snorted again. "Then maybe you didn't notice the girl's tattoo? The one on her back, across the left shoulder blade?''

"Sure didn't, Morris.''

"Nope.''

"It was a double helix.''

Mrs. Teaweather made a face. "You mean, Rosemary has a snake tattooed on her shoulder?''

Morris said, "Not a snake. A double helix is the shape of DNA. You know, the stuff sperm's made of.''

"Ick," said Mrs. Teaweather.

Sleeper said, "Huh!" and then he didn't say another word until they pulled into the post-office parking lot. When he had left Jean Teaweather and Morris Fluke at their vehicles, Sleeper leaned out of the pickup's cab and said, "Let's keep the champagne aspect of this little visit to ourselves, okay?''

"Sure, Sleeper," agreed Mrs. Teaweather. "That's probably a good idea.''

Morris Fluke grumbled disapprovingly. "We've got nothing to hide," he argued.

"Maybe not," said Sleeper. "But if the other council members find out we were drinking champagne, they'll accuse us of not taking our jobs seriously.''

"It's not like we get paid," persisted Morris.

But Sleeper was adamant. "I just don't think it's a good idea to mention the party atmosphere. Think how Edna would take it.''

Morris saw reason then. Edna Furbank was the council's thorn in the side. "I forgot about Edna," he said. "Sure, Sleeper, we'll keep the champagne aspect to ourselves.''

Jean Teaweather waved and drove away. Morris Fluke drove off in the other direction. Sleeper sat in the parking lot for a long time, listening to the rustle of the night breeze through the shore pines, and dreading the prospect of going home to face Edna.

TWO

DR. WONG

DR. RAYMOND WONG'S office occupied the third floor of a red brick walk-up on the shady side of Jackson Street in Seattle's International District. First you had to ring a bell, get buzzed in (no intercom procedure, trusting soul), then scale the steep wooden staircase to the top story where a dirty skylight leaked muddy daylight onto the tattered hall carpet. Turn left, walk twelve paces, reach door. A narrow wood sign painted in Chinese characters, translated underneath into English, read: *When you lose your song, call Doctor Wong.*

The hall was unheated, full of winter frost. Venus Diamond rubbed her small, delicate hands together and blew into them. She usually wore leather gloves in winter, but had misplaced them. Lately, she had misplaced a lot of things, including her *joie de vivre.* Her fingers ached from the cold and were chapped. She raised a limp fist and knocked on the door. While she waited for someone to answer, she stood in the cold dank hall staring at her hands, marveling at how unworthy they were to wear the big pear-shaped diamond ring, the thin platinum band below it.

Reptilian scales. Hands only a crocodile could love. Neglected hands. Like the rest of her. Depression wreaks havoc on self-esteem and daily grooming, and didn't someone once say that hands are maps of the psyche?

Dr. Wong opened the door. He didn't look anything like she'd expected. When her U.S. Fish and Wildlife colleague, Louie Song, had recommended Dr. Wong to Venus, suggesting she see the renowned therapist about her recent troubles, Louie had described Raymond Wong as "wizened," which had led Venus to envision a small, elderly, semi-bald Oriental man, a sort of Confucius in a business suit. What she got when the real Dr. Wong opened the door and appeared before her was a small shock, not altogether unpleasant, still enough of a jolt to cause her to stammer.

"I—I—I was looking for Dr. Wong."

He smiled. "I am he."

He was young, athletic, with smooth ocher skin and rich brown hair that fell carelessly across a broad, unlined forehead. His star-blue almond-shaped eyes had a penetrating, scrutinizing quality. He wore blue jeans with a Pendleton shirt, and deck shoes sans socks. He looked like an Irishman masquerading as a Chinese, or vice versa, a physiognomy that shrieked "melting-pot America." And, too, he had chemistry.

Dr. Wong led her through a dark cluttered hallway into a small reception area where a tiny Asian woman, almost exactly Venus's height and weight, helped Venus peel off her cashmere coat and beret. Tactfully averting her glance, the woman vanished with the cashmere. Dr. Wong pointed to a door, so Venus opened it and went in.

His office was tranquil, airy, full of softly curved furniture and gentle wall coverings. It felt warm, cozy, and a fireplace at one end spat out smoldering embers. The doctor waved a hand at the couch. Venus sank into its goosedown pillows and Dr. Wong eased into a big leather chair facing her.

"Tell me about your problem," he said in a kindly voice.

Venus jerked her thumb over her shoulder. "It's like the sign on your door says. I've lost my song."

Wong smiled and made a church with his elegant hands. "Go on."

Venus said, "I feel sad all the time. Even though my life is idyllic."

"How is it idyllic?"

"I have everything a person could want from life. A husband who adores me. And, of course, I adore him. We've been married fourteen months, but we still think of ourselves as honeymooners. We're very much in love. My husband is the most thoughtful, attentive, affectionate person. Yet I feel constantly lonely. Besides the perfect marriage, I have an awesome home, a sizable nest egg, everything a person could wish for on a material level, including a groovy new Aston Martin DB7. Have you seen the new model?''

Raymond Wong shook his head.

Venus continued. ''I'm thinking about driving it off a cliff. A high cliff.'' She made a crashing sound and added, ''I think I have seasonal affective disorder. You know, SAD.''

''Light deprivation?''

Venus nodded. ''It's been a particularly dark winter, don't you think?''

Wong shrugged noncommittally and said, ''Tell me more.''

She raked her crocodile hands through her fluffy blond hair. ''Just that. Seasonal affective disorder.''

''What other symptoms?''

''I cry a lot. Actually, it's more weeping and sniveling. But I do it in private. Never in front of people.''

''What else?''

''No energy. Zilch. I wake up aching all over and I can't even garner the energy to salute the sun.''

Dr. Wong smiled. ''Ah, so you practice yoga?''

''Did. Before the depression. Now I can hardly move, let alone stretch. I don't have the energy even for the simplest yoga postures. As for working out, I haven't seen the inside of a gym in two months. My body's turning to Jell-O.''

''Have you had a complete physical examination by a physician?''

''Yes, of course. My husband insisted that I go to the university for a complete physical, and all the blood tests and so forth. You see, I had malaria.''

Dr. Wong made a face. She couldn't tell if he was impressed or mocking her. He said, ''How exotic.''

''Don't mock me,'' she said bitterly.

Wong's blue eyes twinkled. ''I am fascinated.''

''Anyway, it's not malaria.'' She realized she was squirming among the goosedown cushions. ''The tests showed I have no physical ailment or infirmity. Other than the Jell-O, I'm fit as a fiddle. It's just plain depression. The physician said I obviously am suffering from SAD. It's pandemic in this town. Have you noticed?''

"Many of my patients are under the delusion that they are suffering from SAD. But in virtually all cases, light deprivation isn't the whole story. In every case of SAD that I have treated, I have uncovered other causes for the soul's darkness."

"Well, the only thing wrong with me is SAD."

Dr. Wong ran a finger across his lips and said, "If you are so certain about your diagnosis, then why have you come to consult me? Maybe you should just move to Arizona and be done with it."

She held up one of her croc paws. "Hey, I'm a native Seattleite," she said. "This soggy gray morass that tries to be urbane is nonetheless my home. I can't just walk away from here."

"Why not? Do you have a job that prevents you from moving to a sunny climate?"

She squirmed some more. "Actually, I'm not working at the moment."

Wong raised an eyebrow. "Do I detect a note of regret in your voice?"

"Oh, no. No, not at all. I love my new life. I haven't worked in eleven months, and I thoroughly enjoy the leisure of a kept woman. I mean, of course, a kept *married* woman." She smiled weakly, unconvincing even to herself.

Wong nodded, but from her perspective on the couch, his nod didn't signal agreement. More like affirming his own observations.

"There's another symptom," she said. "Lately, I've acquired this obsession with counting. I count the steps from my car to the front door, or from the bedroom to the living room, or the kitchen to the garage, or whatever. It's like a compulsion. In my head, I'm counting all the time."

Wong nodded thoughtfully.

"So, tell me," she said, testing him, "can you help me? My friend Louie Song says you can cure anything."

"It all depends. Do you really want help, or are you just coming here to please your friend, this Louie...?"

"Song. Louie Song. We work together. Or did, until I took my leave of absence. Louie's a real pal. He noticed I was depressed, so he suggested I come to see you. He said if anyone could deal with my brand of trouble, it was the legendary Dr. Wong.''

Dr. Wong placed his elegant hands on his muscular thighs and pressed. This action triggered some brain gate that caused him to stand up. When he stood, his knees cracked. "I can help you," he said definitively. "On one condition."

Here it comes, she thought silently. *He's going to prescribe some horrid herbal tonics and make me give up caffeine.* She decided to be honest. "I despise chamomile tea and all that it stands for," she said, "And I won't give up caffeine. That's non-negotiable.''

Dr. Wong smiled. "That won't be necessary."

"Oh." She made a face. "Then what's the one condition?"

"You must move out of your husband's home for the duration of my treatment.''

She laughed. She thought it sounded like a titter, and that bothered her. She laughed again, hoping for a deeper, vibrant sound, but it still came out titterish. She said, "That's rich."

"I do not mean it as a joke. I am serious."

She stared at him. "You're suggesting I leave my husband?"

"For the duration of my treatment."

She sprang to her feet. "This is absurd," she said. "We're both wasting our time."

The Asian woman brought out her cashmere coat and the beret, helped her into the coat. On the way to the door, Venus turned to Dr. Wong and said in an accusatory tone, "Louie put you up to this, didn't he?"

"Louie? The gentleman who suggested you see me?"

"Right. Louie Song. He has this big crush on me. Not bragging, or anything. Louie didn't want me to marry Richard. I'll bet he told you to advise me to leave my husband.''

Raymond Wong stepped forward. "I have never met this Louie Song," he intoned solemnly. "And no one has ever put me up to anything. I tell you to leave your husband because I cannot treat you while you are living with him. This is my own judgment of your condition. You may choose. But I cannot treat your malady unless you follow my orders to the letter.''

She stood in the frosty hall staring across the threshold at

Raymond Wong. "And just what is my malady, in your opinion, Doctor?"

Raymond Wong smiled and said, "Spiritual suffocation."

She yanked the door shut. The sign rattled.

SHE DIDN'T GO directly home, because there was nothing to go home for, and besides, the Ungaro runway show was on at Nordstrom's. The city wore its Christmas trimmings, and on the corner of Fourth and Pine, a cluster of carolers vied for space with an espresso cart. No homeless on this sparkling sidewalk. Venus elbowed through the fray, emerging with a double macciato and a sprig of mistletoe tucked in her hair. One of the carolers might have pecked her on the cheek, she wasn't exactly sure. Deep in her purse, her phone rang and she heard the muffled sound, but ignored it and crossed the threshold into Nordie's. A new dress or some sexy lingerie might perk up her mood.

Watching Ungaro's runway show, her mind kept returning to Dr. Wong's words: "You must move out of your husband's home for the duration of my treatment." She settled on a floral lace gown, bias-cut, slinky, and a navy-blue blazer with nautical brass buttons and white trousers. The sales associate stared at her credit card. "Venus Diamond. Aren't you one of Lady Bella Winsome-Diamond's kids?"

"No," she lied, as usual. "No relation."

The sales associate sniffed. "Too bad for you. That dame's got great genes."

"So I've been told," Venus mumbled, and beat a retreat.

Behind her, the clerk sniped, "She's a lot taller than you, too. And pretty."

On the way out, she paused at the NARS counter, tried six shades of lip stain and settled on No Virgin Violet, which the cosmetics consultant promised would survive Armageddon without fading. Venus said, "Maybe we should all just tattoo our lips and be done with it."

The clerk recoiled. "Then what happens when we change our wardrobes?" she asked rhetorically. "Besides, that would wreak havoc on the world economy. What kind of internationalist are you?''

AT THE STROKE OF NOON, she stood on the pier at Belltown Marina and watched her husband approach. As usual, she felt her pulse quicken, the chemistry kick in. Richard Winters kissed her No Virgin Violet lips.

"Nice flavor. But then, you always taste luscious.''

"Why are you so perfect?'' she said.

They walked along the pier to the last slip, where the eighty-foot *Lady Bella* Starcruiser lolled against the marina's wood pilings. Chuck, the vessel's chief engineer, appeared on the main deck. "Your mother left ten minutes ago,'' he told Venus.

Richard grinned. "Excellent timing.'' They stepped aboard. Chuck went ashore and tactfully disappeared.

The *Lady Bella*'s private stateroom had a queen-size solid-teak bed with a tangerine silk headboard and matching duvet. Underneath a silk mosquito net, the duvet had been pulled back, exposing fresh sheets. On the bedside table sat a bowl of fresh fruit and a bottle of Perrier. Chuck's thoughtful touches.

The boat rocked gently in the water. They made love in slow motion, and finished just before the ship's clock struck one bell. They showered, dressed, and stepped off the boat just as Chuck reappeared with a bag from Ivar's and a six-pack of Pyramid Blonde Ale. "Your timing's impeccable,'' Richard told Chuck.

"I might say the same for you,'' quipped Chuck.

The two men stared at Venus. Chuck faltered. "Timing's a male thing....''

"Really?'' she said coolly.

Richard walked with her to the Aston Martin, opened the door. She slid behind the wheel, rubbed her chapped hands, turned on the ignition and the heater. He leaned in, kissed her, said, "I don't know if I can trust you in this puppy.''

"I'm a great driver.'' Defensively.

Richard laughed. "I mean, the attention you attract. From guys. A radiant blonde at the wheel of a DB7 is every man's wet dream. See you at dinner, babe.''

She watched him cross the parking lot, slide behind the wheel of his Land Rover, and drive off. Some deep sadness over-whelmed her, an increasingly familiar emptiness. Was Richard changing, growing stiffer, more remote? Or was she the change-ling? It wasn't what he said that seemed different, but how he said it.

The DB7 roadster had 335 horsepower, a supercharged V8, five-speed transmission, racing-style suspension, and a four-hundred-pound handmade aluminum body. The Aston hugged the road the way her Harley used to, and when she put the top down, she could almost remember what it felt like to sail along Highway 101 astride the Harley back in the olden days. Back when she felt alive.

At a stoplight, a gull swooped down, landed on the Aston's hood. She stared at the bird until he morphed into Dr. Wong. She tapped the horn and the gull laughed raucously, then flew away.

THREE

THE ESSENCE

HER NOSE beneath the surgical mask had frostburn from so much exposure to liquid nitrogen, and when her face fully emerged from the flame-cold cloud, a smile crinkled the white gauze that covered Hannah Strindberg's lips, and Dr. Strindberg's cheeks now were as chafed as her nose. Larry Chekhov watched in fascination as Dr. Strindberg turned from the freezer, clasping the precious vial. Dr. Strindberg's nimble fingers, so pale, so white, encased in thin latex gloves, also bore pink stains at the tips. They showed through the latex, cold spots burnished by so much exposure to artificial coolant. These lovely, agile hands caressed the slender object she had drawn from the nitrogen coolant, a single glass tube, four inches in length, capped and sealed and labeled with typeface too small to decipher without his bifocals. Chekhov blinked over Dr. Strindberg's shoulder, tried focusing on the minuscule words on the test tube's label, but it was no use. Whatever Dr. Strindberg claimed that test tube contained, Larry Chekhov would simply have to take her at her word.

It was December, and a frigid wind whistled outside the lab window. Larry Chekhov, who lived in Seattle, hadn't visited Helix Island for several months, but he had heard reports that the islands were suffering a serious drought, and so decided to fly up to see how Chekhov Meadows was faring. Since he was on Helix, Chekhov explained to Dr. Strindberg, he had decided to drop by Breedhaven, to inquire how the exotic animals were taking the drought. As a Breedhaven trustee, he was gratified to discover upon his arrival that the situation was under control, thanks to the careful management practices of Dr. Strindberg, who had installed heaters in all the exotic species' feeding shel-

ters and instructed Gordon, the caretaker, to deliver fresh water
to the animals twice each day.

Since he was on site, Dr. Strindberg invited the Breedhaven
trustee to visit her laboratory. Chekhov beamed with anticipation
upon entering the hallowed ground where Hannah Strindberg
nurtured rare-species embryos, where she hormonally altered the
chemistry of less-rare creatures, and then implanted the embryos
of endangered species into the surrogate wombs. In this lab,
Hannah Strindberg's innovative techniques were making history,
and Larry Chekhov had a genuine interest in these great scientific achievements.

The temperature inside the laboratory was approximately sixty
degrees Fahrenheit, still warmer than inside the freezer chamber
where Dr. Strindberg kept the legendary collection of rare-
species embryos known among the cognoscenti as ''Hannah's
ark.'' Chekhov watched as Dr. Strindberg unlocked the chamber,
opened it, drew out a single glass vial, then shut and locked the
deep freeze's door. The last remnants of clouds evaporated in
the warmer laboratory air. Grasping this test tube, she crossed
the lab with Chekhov in tow, the single co-celebrant in her complex isochronal ritual. How many times had Dr. Strindberg performed this rite alone, with no other witness to breathe the sacred silence, to contemplate the sacrifice about to be offered?
Each time she raised the hallowed vessel up out of the deep-
freeze chamber and carried it across the laboratory to the centrifuge, a cell or two of the precious frozen essence died, sac-
rificed to science, offered up for knowledge. To preserve the
limited amount of rare ingredients, Dr. Strindberg didn't ordinarily remove this exact test tube from the chamber. Instead, on
most days, she extracted a similar tube filled with less-precious
frozen essences, and carried this minor cargo across to the spinner.

''Protect the essence at all costs,'' Dr. Strindberg had remarked many times in board meetings, so often that Chekhov
joked it was Strindberg's mantra. Now, whenever Breedhaven's
trustees gathered for their semi-annual meetings, everyone joked
that Dr. Strindberg's mantra should open each meeting like a

prayer, or a pledge of allegiance—"Breedhaven: Protect the essence at all costs."

Hannah wore a white lab coat, the mask across her mouth and nose, and a surgical bonnet. Chekhov wore a matching ensemble, because Hannah had insisted, much to Larry's annoyance. Chekhov despised the mask's pressure over his nose and mouth, felt claustrophobic and sissy in the bonnet and the gloves, but he understood Dr. Strindberg's canon on total protection, total sanitation. No one, especially not Larry Chekhov and his fellow Breedhaven trustees, wished to risk contaminating the essence.

At the centrifuge, Dr. Strindberg carefully uncapped the glass test tube, and with a tiny paddle scooped out a pinhead-sized amount of the frozen ingredients, no more than a sliver. She placed this sample in the spinner, turned it on. Chekhov watched through a microscope attached to the centrifuge, saw the particle wither, melt, until the frozen speck transformed into a tiny tear-shaped liquid droplet, a cloudy globule the shade of healthy mucous, almost white. Chekhov said, "In this vial you are holding, what is in there?"

"Oh, this is tissue from an ortolon songbird egg. Not yet fertilized. I'm just checking this to see that it's still healthy. We won't use this particular vial today."

Chekhov leaned in and studied the vial. Hannah said, "Ova don't completely liquefy." Chekhov nodded, as if he could concur with something he knew nothing about. Or rather, almost nothing. Everyone, after all, knows what ova are, and what they're for, at least every civilized, educated person. What the bush people of Africa and the jungle people of Borneo knew about ova, Chekhov couldn't imagine. But he understood that this fluid essence comprised one-half of the formula for creating life in a petri dish.

"Now what are you doing?" Chekhov asked.

"Marking my vial," Dr. Strindberg explained as she used a scalpel to scratch marks on the glass vial. "It's my way of identifying which samples belong to me. Each time I remove a vial from the chamber, I add another scratch. Just a silly scientist's security measure."

"I see," said Chekhov. "And this ova sample you just tested? Is it good?"

Chekhov immediately flushed crimson, sensing he had said something stupid. But Dr. Strindberg didn't smirk or display any other signs of superiority. Dr. Strindberg said, "It's healthy." That was Hannah Strindberg's diplomatic way of educating Breedhaven's trustees. When they said something stupid, like, "Is it good?" Hannah would reply with more technically correct language. It wasn't "good," but "healthy." Life is neither "good" nor "evil," not even "bad." Life just *is*. Hannah Strindberg worked patiently to educate her benefactors, and for this reason almost as much as for her scientific brilliance, the trustees supported her work.

Chekhov, more than any other Breedhaven trustee, believed that he had a clear understanding of Dr. Strindberg's *über*vision. Since Earth's wild creatures were rapidly running out of habitat due to human encroachment on their native territories, Dr. Strindberg concluded the only way to save Earth's endangered species was by reproducing them in petri dishes and surrogate wombs, and then transporting the resulting creatures to new habitats. Thus over the years she had been collecting and freezing endangered species' DNA, and now Breedhaven possessed a virtual ark of the endangered that one day, Chekhov imagined, would earn Hannah Strindberg a Nobel prize, maybe even make her rich.

Dr. Strindberg said, "Larry, please ask Ted to come in now."

Chekhov padded over to the laboratory door, opened it and called out to Dr. Vigil. A few seconds later, the respected geneticist appeared at the door and slipped inside, dressed to match Dr. Strindberg. Directly behind Ted Vigil, came in Rosemary Poole, the svelte young Ph.D. candidate who assisted Dr. Vigil, and whose svelteness considerably intrigued Larry Chekhov. In fact, if the truth were told completely and without leaving out any fine detail no matter how small, Chekhov actually caught his breath and gasped upon seeing Rosemary enter the laboratory. For even in the silly lab regalia, Rosemary Poole was a knockout. Chekhov, more self-conscious than ever about his own appearance, fervently hoped he didn't look too awfully nerdish in his own bonnet and gloves.

The lovely Rosemary Poole carried a plastic box labeled with the word *Sterilized.* In the box lay four fat felines: a gray Abyssinian, a Siamese, a marmalade tabby, and a motley mixed-breed. All the cats appeared to be asleep, or drugged. *Ah yes, of course,* Chekhov told himself silently. *The little felids must be anesthetized to keep them calm during the procedure.* He watched as Rosemary placed the box gingerly on a small surgical table near Dr. Strindberg, then backed off and stood directly behind Dr. Vigil. Chekhov felt his pulse quicken. Something excited him.

Dr. Strindberg said, "Today, I am checking on the progress of four female semi-domestic island cats who have been implanted with Borneo Bay embryos. After hormonally altering these cats so that they could accept another feline species' embryos, all four have successfully become pregnant and are expecting litters. The resulting kittens, should any of these litters survive, will be purebred Borneo Bay kittens."

As Dr. Strindberg worked, Chekhov studied Ted Vigil. His hair the shade of golden sand, his eyes Mediterranean blue, his physique carved by some Michelangelo gene, this Apollo even possessed two exquisite ears, so aesthetically pleasing, right down to the pearly lobes, that it seemed to Chekhov as he studied their curves, that the Grand Sculptor had finally hit upon the perfect human being. Yes, certainly Ted Vigil possessed exemplary physical attributes, Chekhov thought to himself, except for one unfortunate flaw: his hands. What Chekhov called "Bolshoi hands," narrow, pink, fishy things that might in another life have worn ballet slippers. Protective of themselves, these hands seemed to draw up at the wrist in protest against effort. Did their immaturity and reticence reveal something? *Surely,* Chekhov thought darkly, *these are hands that never voluntarily pitch in.* If Vigil's touch was light and graceful, any strength they might display was an accidental quirk of Nature, or an illusion that Vigil had perfected. Chekhov thought all of this to himself, gloating. And to himself, Chekhov thought that Rosemary Poole surely possessed enough intelligence and observational powers to see beyond Vigil's other physical attributes, to notice his unfortunate hands. Hands that Chekhov (silently, to himself) pronounced hopelessly coy.

Chekhov's voodoo diagnosis of Ted Vigil's pros and cons failed to consider that Vigil emanated a distinctly capable and, as many of his colleagues often remarked, brilliant aura. But this morning as he joined Dr. Strindberg and Chekhov in the laboratory, Chekhov noticed that the hunk seemed anxious, even a bit impatient with poor Miss Poole. Chekhov noted how Vigil brushed Miss Poole aside as if she were mere dust, and he noted Rosemary's coolness toward Vigil. *Perhaps they've had a collegial disagreement,* thought Chekhov, *or maybe Miss Poole did something to annoy Vigil.* Chekhov secretly gloated at the apparent chilliness between the two, because that just increased his own chances with Miss Poole. He was planning to invite her to lunch after the feline sonograms, or whatever it was that Dr. Strindberg was now demonstrating. Chekhov turned his attention back to the operation at hand, but Rosemary Poole never left his peripheral vision.

At first Chekhov thought he saw a bird flying past the window of the operating room, then he realized that the window looked into the lab building, not outside, and what he was seeing was a young boy standing in the corridor with his nose pressed against the window glass. Chekhov started to say something to Dr. Strindberg, but didn't want to break her concentration during the delicate procedure.

As if reading Chekhov's mind, Rosemary Poole whispered softly, "That's Luther Lufkin, an island boy. He wants to be a scientist. The mongrel cat belongs to him."

Chekhov nodded. Now he understood.

Rosemary couldn't see clearly because Vigil kept blocking her view. Ted was annoyed with her for having tabooed sex this morning, so of course he'd be hard to deal with all day. She'd been terribly distracted lately, trying to figure out how to afford a winter holiday in Bali. Her bank account was perilously low, and the trust fund Grandfather Elmer had left her would not be available to her until she completed a reading list Grandfather Elmer had drawn up, and her doctoral dissertation. What was a poor little rich girl to do? This sort of strategizing required considerable mental stamina, so at the crack of dawn, when Ted put his limp hand on her, she really didn't feel like exerting energy. She'd rebuffed his advances and now Ted was getting even, blocking her view so that later, when she had to write about the procedure, she would have trouble stating exactly what took place.

Rosemary stood *en pointe* and tried peering over Ted's shoulder. He was much too tall, so she leaned sideways and peeked around his broad biceps. As she did this, she noticed Larry Chekhov standing across the operating table directly behind Dr. Strindberg. Mr. Chekhov was peering over Hannah's shoulder, but he wasn't watching what Hannah was doing with the cats. Mr. Chekhov was watching Rosemary, and if Rosemary wasn't mistaken, he was lusting after her. Rosemary seemed to recall that Mr. Chekhov was a fabulously wealthy man, and that he often spent lavishly on his lady friends. And now that she noticed, Mr. Chekhov wasn't so bad-looking. Rosemary batted her eyelashes at Mr. Chekhov, and the Russian moneybags winked. Rosemary was pretty sure that she'd figured out a way to see Bali this winter.

When the feline examinations were finally completed, Hannah Strindberg pulled off her latex gloves and her face mask, and Chekhov noticed that she looked exhilarated. Rosemary Poole took the still-dozing cats away in the sterilized box. Ted Vigil followed Rosemary out of the operating room, and now Chekhov was alone with Hannah. As he removed the pesky scrub gear, Chekhov said to Hannah, "Most interesting, my dear. And when are the kittens due?"

Hannah smiled. "If we are lucky, all four mama cats will give birth approximately two weeks from today."

Chekhov nodded. "Tell me again," he asked, "just what sort of kitten will result from this artificial insemination?"

"Genetically pure Borneo Bay kittens. That is, if we succeeded."

"And if we failed?"

Hannah frowned. "Then, my dear Larry, I am afraid the very

distinctive and immensely curious Borneo Bay cat will be doomed to extinction.''

Chekhov whispered earnestly, "Then we mustn't fail."

Hannah removed her lab coat and placed it in the laundry bin. "Now our job is to monitor those four cats. We'll have to keep a close watch. We can't afford for anything to happen to them, for anything to go wrong."

Chekhov raised an eyebrow. "But what might go wrong?"

Hannah stared past Larry Chekhov. "I wonder," she said to no one in particular, "if the *Earnest* is ready."

Chekhov frowned. "*Earnest?* What is the *Earnest?*"

Hannah glanced at Chekhov. She'd almost forgotten he was there. Somewhat absentmindedly she said, "A spaceship. The *Earnest* is a spaceship."

In the corridor the boy shyly approached Dr. Strindberg. Hannah said, "Larry Chekhov, this is Luther Lufkin. Luther just turned ten last week." Chekhov noticed that the boy was small for his age, and if he wasn't mistaken, Luther seemed slightly immature. Hannah squeezed Luther's shoulder and said, "Luther knows all my secrets." Luther Lufkin grinned, and watched his hero walk down the corridor and disappear into her office.

FOUR

BLAZE

RICHARD HAD A polo tournament in Montecito, but "significant others" weren't invited. "It's another one of those guy things," he'd explained sheepishly. "Anyway, I couldn't concentrate on my game if you were watching."

A polo widow takes what she can get. Venus drove across town to Bella's home on Magnolia Bluff. Bella always proved entertaining, if intimidating company.

Burden, Lady Winsome-Diamond's house manager, answered the door wearing his perpetually sad expression. "Your mother has gone to dinner with the Spillbaums," he said. "She won't be home before midnight."

Inside the family home, she heard her voice echo familiarly in the foyer. "I'll just stay awhile," she said, and peeled off her coat. Burdon tried taking it from her. "Don't do that," she insisted "It makes me feel old."

"A gentleman always assists a lady with her coat," Burden countered.

"Well, I don't feel much like a lady right now," she said. "Right now, I feel like an abandoned alley cat."

Burden's lip twitched slightly, verging on a smile, or a sneer, she wasn't sure which. He said, "I am sorry to hear that, miss." He still called her *miss*.

The trip from the foyer to the kitchen covered forty-eight Venus-size steps. Bella's pad spanned more distance than most supermarkets. In the kitchen, Venus poked around in the refrigerator. Burden came up behind her and said, "The Thanksgiving turkey is kaput, I'm afraid. Even the frozen leftovers. We have some very nice fresh salmon."

"No thanks." Her voice came from inside the refrigerator as she explored its interior. "I've given up salmon."

Burden made a face she didn't see. "Given up salmon?"

She emerged from the cold box holding a container of milk. "They're going extinct," she explained. She went into the pantry and rummaged through cereal boxes, located the Cheerios and the Quaker Puffed Rice. Burden handed her a bowl. She poured a mountain of Cheerios, dusted it with puffed rice, carried this over to the breakfast table. She added two heaping teaspoonfuls of sugar, poured milk over the whole thing, and said, "Where's Timmy?"

Timmy was Venus's stepbrother, a small terror cloaked in charm and guile.

"Timothy has gone to bed, miss."

"But it's only nine o'clock. I thought small Tim stayed up until the wee hours."

Burden said, "I don't believe he is actually asleep. The young man informed me that he is reading a novel and doesn't wish to be disturbed."

"Hardy Boys?"

Burden pursed his lips. "I seriously doubt that," he murmured, and went away.

Venus turned on the television. The nine o'clock news had just started, and the image on the screen was terrifying. Flames and chaos. The news reporter intoned:

"On this bitter-cold December night, a terrible fire has destroyed Zanzibar's nightclub in downtown Seattle. Firefighters are desperately searching for possible survivors, but so far, it appears that all of the more-than-fifty people trapped inside the nightclub have died in the fire. The victims included a group of scientists who had reserved the club for a private party to celebrate the end of an international conference held here in Seattle.

"What we know now is that at about eight-fifteen this evening, a woman—as yet unidentified—was seen parking her Saab convertible in the lot at Zanzibar's. This was just a minute or two before the fire broke out. Witnesses say the woman stepped out of the vehicle, went around to the passenger side, opened the door, and removed a box that one eyewitness said resembled a pet crate. After locking up the Saab, she walked across the parking lot to Zanzibar's, carrying the crate by its handle. When she reached the Skagit totem pole that until just about an hour ago marked the nightclub's entrance, the eyewitness says, the woman paused, glanced over her shoulder, then went inside the nightclub. Seconds later, an explosion ripped through the club, setting it on fire.''

The reporter went on.

''Apparently, pandemonium overtook the trapped victims, and we can only imagine what went on inside the nightclub. It was just a terrible, horrific scene.

''Twelve minutes into the conflagration, the Seattle Fire Department arrived, and firefighters are still battling this blaze, trying to bring it under control. But even as it raged, Seattle's fire chief was calling the Zanzibar's fire the most malicious and heinous case of arson in the city's history.''

Venus turned up the volume, stared at the mesmerizing picture. The announcer continued his on-the-scene report.

''Now, this fire broke out at approximately eight-fifteen p.m., just fifty-two minutes ago. We've just learned that in spite of a state-of-the-art sprinkler system (it failed), fire-resistant building materials (they burned), and six conveniently-situated exit doors (they wouldn't open), somewhere around thirty-six partygoers, along with about ten club employees, five members of the funk band Flit, a uniformed security guard, and a reporter from the *Seattle Star,* were all trapped behind walls of fire.

''Seattle fire inspector Rusty Higgins says the club's six exit doors had been barricaded from the outside. And even as we report this horrible blaze that's still not completely extinguished, the governments of Sweden, Norway, Iceland, France, New Zealand, and Canada are already demanding to know who murdered their nations' best and brightest reproductive biologists, and why. Meanwhile, the owners of Zanzibar's wonder if a disgruntled employee set the fire, or if, as some are already speculating, it was set by the Mob in a dispute with the club's owners. Relatives and friends of the victims are rushing to Seattle to claim their loved ones' remains and to demand that justice be swift and harsh.''

Venus went outside onto the terrace. Bella's perfect view of Seattle's skyline was spoiled now by billowing clouds of acrid black smoke that poured across the night sky. This tragic, bitter-cold December night would be remembered for a very long time. She went back inside, stared at the televised conflagration, at the bowl of cold cereal. Her appetite had soured.

She went home and slept fitfully until Richard came in at two a.m. As he slid beneath the covers, she said, "Who won?"

"We did." He lay back and shut his eyes.

"There was this terrible fire..."

He put an arm around her, drew her close. "I heard about it."

"It was horrible, Richard. All those people burned to death."

He kissed her neck. "Shh. Go to sleep. There's nothing you can do."

She lay awake most of the night, wondering what evil had directed an arsonist's murderous hand.

SEATTLE DIDN'T NEED an international incident to put itself on the world's list of household names. Everyone who had ever heard of rain knew about Seattle, even if they couldn't actually locate it on a map. Somewhere up there in the left-hand corner of the United States. Near the salt water. No, actually *on* the salt water, a soggy town west of Microsoft, a place that spawned mossheads and Micro-millionaires. Too rich and wet and politically correct to be hospitable. A ''Keep Out'' sort of Emerald City, not keen on influxers at this stage of its gargantuan growth; not exactly a fuzzy-warm, open-arms kind of town. More like

Stonehenge: a cool place to visit, but foreboding—emotionally remote. The natives always liked it that way. Unfortunately, so did a few hundred thousand born-to-be-cool outsiders who had bought their way in, with hard cash the exact shade of green as Magnolia Bluff's madronas. Seattle, swollen with native wealth and non-native ambition, had at first welcomed the talented influxers who seemed to worship the very same gods of nature, fog, rain, and sardonic humor. Of course, most of the influxers had been faking it, and, once settled in Sogtown and accepted by the naive natives, unveiled their true colors.

They refused to learn the local vernacular. They tried to pretend Seattle was New York or San Francisco when all along any native could tell them that this was a unique spot on the globe that didn't imitate, that didn't need to. The influxers' arrogance seeped into the city's damp cracks, grew its own mold, and the mold spread around Puget Sound until the old Seattle, the peaceful *"Oz au naturel,"* was crushed beneath a glittering, gusty facade that shrieked superiority and, above all, exclusivity. Ironically, the influxers hated each other even more than they despised the native slugs. There were exceptions, and Hannah Strindberg was one of the rare influxers who had brought to the Pacific Northwest more than she demanded from it.

You'd think that a town blessed with constant drizzle would have the decency to rain on an arsonist's parade. But the rain didn't fall that cold December night, so fifty-three people burned to death, and all the *Seattle Star*'s bleeding-heart liberal editors could say the next morning was, mournfully, "God help the sick mind that set back the science of reproductive biology by fifty years."

The *Star* contained more details, more tragic images, more questions. Fifty-three victims—plus one survivor, a waiter, who was still in shock, with bad hand burns. Even if the arsonist, or arsonists, were caught, prosecuted, and punished, the Star editorialized, no reproach, no punishment, could ever restore the vast wealth of scientific knowledge lost in the Zanzibar's conflagration. And herein lay the most perplexing question of all: What scientific discoveries, what secrets that might have revolutionized life on Earth, had the scientists who burned in the Zanzibar's fire taken to their graves?

If you didn't count the nightclub staff, the five Flits, the security guard, and the one newspaper reporter who mysteriously showed up that night at Zanzibar's without assignment, the list of victims read like a who's who in the cloning world: Drs. Per Svenson and Martine Olaffson, from the University of Stockholm, had burned, and with them, the promise of a Nobel Prize for stellar achievements in reproductive endocrinology. The illustrious Professor Wen Lui from the University of Auckland burned along with his wife, leaving behind incomplete research on the effects of pollution on the reproductive organs of orangutans. Drs. Leslie Budnick, Don Cooper and Howard Loomis of MicroGenesis, Incorporated—the Palo Alto team that had developed the DNA protozoan catalyst technique—all burned in the fire, leaving incomplete notes and data. Professors Maurice Grossman and Pierre Chandler of the Sorbonne, developers of the latest synthetic cow uterus, also had died in the fire, their techniques and talent lost forever. Professor Arne Bjorgenson of Oslo University; Stella Zeiglar, Ph.D. from Columbia University School of Medicine; and Frank Lewis, Ph.D. of Hunt-Fordham Foods, Inc.; had once teamed up to develop an embryo-nutritive formula. They all burned in the fire, along with twenty-four colleagues and the Zanzibar's employees.

What the *Star* didn't say was why their cub reporter had been on the site, even though they hadn't assigned her to the event. The editors insisted they didn't know why the reporter had shown up, nor did her family, or anyone else in her (former) life. And what went unspoken, but stuck in everybody's craw, was the knowledge that each of the scientists burned to death in the Zanzibar's blaze had left behind a unique legacy, a scientific fingerprint. Each of those scientific fingerprints might present a clue to the identity of the arsonist. It didn't take a genius to figure that out.

VENUS AND RICHARD were lying in bed. It was eleven o'clock at night, twenty-six hours after the Zanzibar's fire. Richard, still full of victory from the polo match, wanted all her attention.

After they made love, Venus flicked on the television. She'd never done that before, but the Zanzibar's fire had everyone in Seattle—with the one possible exception of Richard Winters—mesmerized.

The eleven o'clock news reported that until moments ago, one victim of the Zanzibar's fire still remained unidentified. So charred were the corpses, that it didn't surprise arson investigators when they came across a pile of ashes in (what used to be) the club's corridor that could not immediately be identified. Speculation abounded, and then investigators found a woman's dinner ring. The simple platinum band held one rare gem, a 5.50-carat demantoid garnet, a stone that reputedly possessed a greater dispersion of light than even diamonds. Found beneath the pile of mystery ashes from the corridor, the ring was identified as belonging to Dr. Hannah Strindberg, the controversial scientist who ran the secretive Breedhaven project on Helix Island in the San Juan archipelago.

Venus sat up in bed. "Hannah Strindberg," she said. "She's Oly Olson's colleague. They were working together on a secret project. Olson would never let anyone else at Fish and Wildlife get involved. It was his pet. And he and Hannah Strindberg were close friends." Venus reached for the telephone, but Richard grabbed her wrist.

"Tomorrow," he said firmly.

"I have to call Olson," she insisted.

Richard shook his head. "You promised. No work for a year."

"This isn't about work," she insisted. "This is personal. Olson's got to be devastated."

Richard sighed irritably. "Don't get involved," he said. "You mustn't get involved."

She couldn't decide if he was asking or telling her. She punched in the office number. No one answered, just the voice mail, with Olson's voice. She left a message, saying she was sorry to hear about the fire, about Hannah. Then Richard took the phone from her, placed it in its charger, switched off the television and the bedside lamps. Electricity was slowly sabotaging the institution of marriage.

FIVE

DEVIL IN THE DETAILS

OLSON STARED OUT the window. From his eagle's-nest office on the thirty-eighth floor of the Bumbershoot Building, he could see most of Elliott Bay, most of downtown Seattle, Mount Rainier, the Olympics, and the faint outlines of several islands in Puget Sound. He could see the ships in port, the ferryboats plying the frigid whitecaps on the sound. When it wasn't raining. Just now it was raining, and Olson couldn't see anything but the weeping windows. And, in his mind's eye, Hannah.

Olson sat at his desk, his powerful arms crossed over his robust chest. A year ago, Olson's arms couldn't fold across his chest because the flab had interfered. Olson had taken it all off, replaced it with muscle, and now he looked twenty years younger than his sixty years, and felt it, too. Never mind the baldness. Olson had made peace with his hairlessness and some people—Hannah Strindberg included—actually found Olson's baldness attractive. Less than twenty-four hours before she had disappeared at Zanzibar's, Hannah had sat across a table at the Thirteen Coins and told Olson she thought his baldness made him sexy.

Last night Olson had dreamed he'd given birth to an infant—illegitimate—but he couldn't identify the infant's other parent. It might have all happened in a petri dish, but he couldn't recall. The dream baby gave Olson a raison d'être. Then he woke up. First he had felt horrified at the idea of giving birth, he had felt perplexed and yet sad that no baby existed. Not that he really wanted another child. A sixty-year-old male-chauvinist federal law-enforcement agent didn't exactly qualify as the ideal parent. The dream baby was a metaphor: His life had no goal, no central focus, and the dream baby represented a longing for one.

Death is as full of insults as life. Olson dropped Hannah Strindberg's mangled ring on his desk, picked up the phone, and punched in some numbers. On the other end, Venus's phone rang four times. Olson grimaced. Of course Venus didn't pick up. He'd been trying to call her for a week, but she kept her service on, didn't return his messages. He'd had that one sympathy phone call, a message left on the office voice mail a few nights earlier. That was all. *That's what happens,* Olson reflected, *when a couple of pampered thirty-somethings get hitched and cocoon.* How dare Venus languish in her privileged habitat when so much was wrong with the world? What perverted sense of entitlement granted her permission to ignore life's evil side? Olson left another curt message on her service, then hung up.

Hannah Strindberg had two living relatives—an orphaned grand-nephew and a distant cousin, who were traveling together outside the country, and were temporarily unreachable. No one else came forward to collect Hannah's remains, so Olson felt obligated. After all, the Fish and Wildlife Service had been Dr. Strindberg's partner at Breedhaven. And Olson was probably Hannah's best friend. Still, he was reluctant; not just because Olson felt he wasn't the appropriate person, but also because he wasn't convinced that the ashes were actually Hannah's.

To put it frankly, the conflagration had caused such pandemonium that as the victims stampeded toward the exits, many bodies had piled one atop the other into huge heaps that burned. Inevitably their ashes had mingled. Dental records, when available, confirmed identities, but in Hannah's case no dental material had been found among the ashes, and so identification had first been made solely and circumstantially upon the appearance of the distinctive ring. Hannah once had told Olson the ring was a family heirloom. The discovery of this ring, plus statements provided by several witnesses, including Olson himself, placed Hannah Strindberg at Zanzibar's on the night of the fatal event.

The event had been meant as a celebration for the directors of the World Congress on Reproductive Biology who, just that afternoon, had signed a global treaty banning the use of Prozigal, the controversial new cross-species reproduction medium. Op-

ponents of Prozigal touted the treaty's passage as a triumph of
human conscience over irresponsible scientific tinkering. The
Prozigal proponents, in the minority, claimed the treaty interfered with a scientist's freedom to experiment. But a party's a
party, and almost everyone had attended the celebration that
fateful night. Including, apparently, Hannah Strindberg.

Her black Saab convertible had been found in Zanzibar's
parking lot. Olson knew Hannah had taken the ferry to Anacortes and driven to Seattle for the conference. Olson had actually
spoken to Hannah a few hours before the fire. She had phoned
him from the Edgewater Inn, where she had taken a room for
the five days of meetings. Olson had asked Hannah if she'd like
to have dinner with him that night, but Hannah had declined,
saying she had this party to go to. She didn't invite him along,
which at the time had irritated him. But now, considering the
circumstances, Olson was relieved that Hannah had slighted
him. After all, he was still alive.

The most reliable eyewitness was a taxi driver. Olson had
gone over the cabby's statement a dozen times, looking for anything that might prove Hannah hadn't died in the Zanzibar's fire.
But each time he pored over the evidence, the dark reality
loomed and forbade him to hope—hope for a miracle, some
time-warp reversal of events. The cabby, who had dropped some
guests off at Zanzibar's on the evening of the fire, stated that
he recalled seeing a dark blue van parked across the street just
before the explosion. No, he didn't see the license plate. But
something else he recalled seeing was a woman matching Dr.
Strindberg's description, walking across the parking lot toward
the club's front entrance.

"Tall, slender. Lots of red hair. Had on a fawn beige suit.
Nice legs. A real babe, if you want my opinion."

Hannah.

The taxi driver continued, "I pay attention to people's looks.
You never know when a fare's gonna put a gun to your head,
so I like to remember the fine details, y'know? And she had a
big cage, some kind of pet cage. Like you'd keep a cat in."

What Olson hadn't learned until today, exactly one week after
the blaze, was that Hannah had apparently taken along the rare

Borneo Bay cat that night, and that the wildcat, the only Borneo
Bay in captivity, had apparently also burned to death in the fire.
What would possess Hannah to take the Bay cat to such an
event? Olson tried to elicit an answer to this puzzling question
from Hannah's assistants, but all they could do was shake their
heads in despair. They were as puzzled as Olson was, for the
little Bay cat had been the most prized creature at Breedhaven.
How could Hannah have been so careless?

Was it carelessness? Olson couldn't make up his mind. All
he knew now was that, unless Hannah's latest experiment succeeded—without her to supervise—the Borneo Bay cat, only the
second ever captured in jungles on the island of Borneo, would
be lost forever. Extinct.

This is going to be one hell of a dark Christmas, Olson told
himself, because no one else seemed willing to listen. Hell, Diamond wouldn't even answer her phone. If Venus was stubborn,
remote, and spoiled, Olson was irreconcilable and filled with
gloom.

When Special Agent Louie Song popped his head into Olson's office and saw Olson's deteriorating condition, he said,
"Anything I can do?"

Olson stared at Song's mirrored Revos, and at the visible
portion of Song's exotic Amerasian face. Song meant to help.
Olson said, "Yeah. Shut the door and leave me alone."

Song obeyed, because Olson was the boss.

Five minutes later, Olson heard a *shoosh*ing sound, and saw
a piece of paper slide under the door. He rose wearily, feeling
the vestigial weight of the world, went over, and retrieved the
note. It was Song's handwriting, a strange calligraphy. It said:
The devil is in the details.

Olson never thought of himself as a genius, but it would take
a very clever mind to sort through all the victims' experiments
and, from this complex material, tease out a theory that explained a motive for mass murder. He slipped Hannah's ring on
his pinky finger and held it up to the dim Seattle light. The
precious stone appeared dull, lackluster, uninspired. The opposite of Hannah.

OLSON SAT ON a log at Alki Point, his arms crossed as usual, protecting his rage.

Venus drove into the garage at precisely five o'clock, parked the Aston Martin, and walked around to the house's beachside entrance.

Olson snickered to himself, remembering that after fourteen months of marriage, Venus and Richard still referred to their palatial home as their honeymoon cottage. Everyone else called it Alki's twenty-first-century Taj Mahal.

Olson uncrossed his arms, got up off the log, and walked toward the palace.

Venus counted thirty-six steps from the driver's-side door, through the garage, along the narrow side garden, to the front of the house, where the front porch met Alki Point Beach. When she saw Olson, she frowned. An Olson apparition could only mean one thing. Sighing, she clutched her cashmere coat, her wifely security blanket. She waited for him to speak. Olson got right to the point. "It's your territory," he said, employing the same tired excuse he always used against her. "You know it better than any of us. And, too," he added, upping the ante, "it's Hannah."

Inside the Taj Mahal, she made tea and placed fresh scones on a plate. They sat in the enclosed sundeck overlooking the sound. The water was leaden, forbidding, reflecting the pall of clouds where a sky should be. Olson didn't pressure her, didn't cite righteousness and valor, which, he knew, would only irritate her.

If only he'd get moralistic, belligerent, she thought, I could just throw him out and be done with it.

Instead, Olson appealed to her sense of curiosity, her nose for trouble. "I can't believe Hannah is dead," he said. "And I'm convinced Breedhaven is what's behind the arson. It's a controversial project, with a lot of detractors."

She watched the evening's swarming of the purple swifts, the darkness engulfing Puget Sound and the beach. Finally, darkness reigned, and they sat in the soft light of a table lamp. She could hear a slight rattle in Olson's chest when he exhaled.

"You're catching that cold that's going around."

"Never mind." He waved her concern away.

She stood, walked to the window, stared in the near distance at her own reflection. Finally she said, "I promised Richard I wouldn't work for the first year."

"It's been fourteen months."

"But I worked for the first three. So we aren't counting those months. I have one month to go, to keep my promise."

"Aw, hell, Venus. Eleven months is close enough."

"Not in Richard's mind."

"What about your own mind? Or are you no longer capable of independent thinking?" he asked, irritated. When she didn't answer, except for the snide glance she tossed him, he said, "This is Hannah we're talking about, for chrissake. And it's the biggest case we've ever been involved in. Listen, three fire extinguishers, strategically placed throughout the club, were missing. The sprinkler system was recently installed and was inspected by the fire department that very afternoon. It failed only because it had been sabotaged. Particles of a remote-controlled incendiary bomb were recovered near the site where the cloakroom once stood. When it went off, its sparks ignited naphtha gel that had been sprayed throughout the club, on carpets and walls. This is terrorism, pure and simple. Now, six other countries are sending their best criminal investigators. This happened on American soil. I'll be damned if I'll sit back and let some foreign dick solve this case."

"Aha," she said. "So that's what it's all about."

Olson was angry now. "This isn't about anything except Hannah. Don't trivialize my motives."

She didn't bother arguing that point. Instead, she said, "Hannah was your colleague. Your friend. You were so covetous of her and her precious research that you never allowed me or anyone else on staff to get close to her. You never let me set foot on Breedhaven. Now you're asking me to feel sentimental about Hannah Strindberg. You're asking me to break a promise to my husband, and to myself, by the way. Anyway, this isn't our case. It belongs to the Seattle Fire Department."

Olson got up, walked over, and stood beside her at the window. In the reflection, she could see his hand come down gently on her shoulder. Hoarsely he said, "They're looking in all the wrong places, for all the wrong things. They're concentrating their investigation on the nightclub, and on the foreign victims. They want to believe this was done by the Mob, or by Arabs."

"Maybe it was."

He snorted. "Everything these days is done by Arabs. I don't buy it."

He turned her around to face him. Something had robbed her traffic-light green eyes of their usual verve. He felt as if he were staring into an empty house. He said, "What's happened to you?"

She pulled away from him, hugged herself. "I got married," she said softly. "And I quit my job to be a companion to my husband."

"Are you pregnant?"

She rolled her eyes.

"Well, then, what's wrong with you?"

She looked at him with those vacant eyes. She said, "We all change, Olson."

"Bull. You're depressed. That's what's wrong with you. And you're hiding behind this extended honeymoon facade. And now you're driving that Aston DB7, acting like some supercharged highway princess without a care for other people's troubles, as if there's no world out there except for your cosseted, handmade, three-hundred-horsepower, burled-wood nirvana. You put on a fine show, Diamond, but you don't convince me. I know you too well. You're depressed, and you need help."

She turned away, and he knew he'd struck a true note by the way she wrung her hands and fidgeted with her wedding ring. Olson considered himself a compassionate man. He didn't normally enjoy watching a friend suffer. But she wasn't just a friend; she was a colleague, one of the troops. One of his troops. She had no right to suffer, not on his watch, not when trouble knocked.

She said, "If I'm depressed, it's my concern, not yours."

"I'm your boss," he said. "It's my business, too."

"You aren't my boss now. Now I don't have a job, so how can I have a boss?"

He said, "You have a job."

"I'm on a leave of absence." She nodded at the teapot. He shook his head. She poured herself another cup, sipped delicately.

Olson said, "Which probably explains your depression."

"My leave?"

He nodded.

She smiled distantly. "Dr. Wong told me I suffer from 'spiritual suffocation.'"

"Who the hell is Dr. Wong?"

"So, who's right?" she asked, ignoring his question. "You, or Dr. Wong?"

Exasperated, he said, "The hell with it," and left her standing beside the teacart in her fairy-tale, futuristic Taj Mahal. He left by the front door, stepped into the cold night, pulling his collar against his neck. He walked half a block to his car, got in, turned on the ignition and the heater. He held his hands up to the heater, and when they had warmed, he held the warm palms to his bald head. Then, slowly, his hands dropped to cover his eyes, his body shook, and then the tears finally came. He cried her name.

"Hannah. Oh, my Hannah. Oh, Hannah."

He didn't hear the knock on the window until the second time she pounded on it with her chapped hand. He looked up from his tear-stained hands at the fogged-up window. He wiped clear a spot in the condensation and saw Venus's face. He opened the window.

She said, "You were in love with her."

Accusatory.

He rolled up the window, wiped his eyes, put the car in gear, and drove away.

Venus stood in the frigid night air and watched the car's taillights disappear around Alki Point.

THEY DINED LATE because Richard had meetings until seven and then a handball game at the Washington Athletic Club. He came into the sunroom at nine o'clock and found her sitting in the dim light, the dinner on the table cold.

"I had handball," he reminded her.

She microwaved the chicken and they drank a glass of wine in silence, both lost in private thoughts. When they sat down at the table in the sunroom, Richard said, "Remember that forestry official from Ivory Coast I introduced you to at the Banff conference?"

"The woman with the batting eyes?"

"That's his wife. The husband is the forestry official. Djekoule. The one in the serge suit."

"As I recall, they both wore serge suits."

"No. The wife wore a very sexy green-and-gold strapless silk sheath. And she wore a diamond tiara in her hair."

"How observant you are." Slightly caustic.

"Anyway, the husband. Djekoule telephoned me this afternoon. He's been made Minister of the Environment in the new government. They're having serious forest fires in the rain forests. They're out of control."

She shrugged. "So what's new? They're always having fires in rain forests. It's the swidden farmers who are forced to slash and burn in order to plant crops to feed their families. If the government would help them get other jobs, maybe the fires would stop before all the world's rain forests go up in flames."

"That's just it. Kadoudougou has lost nearly all of its old-growth stands. The new government has pledged to stop the swidden fires, and they've initiated a forest-rehabilitation program. Things looked promising. Until this fire. Djekoule believes it was started by arsonists."

"Kids, or what?"

Richard usually made eye contact when he spoke. Now his baby blues avoided her traffic-light greens. He watched the chicken on his plate as if it might get up and fly off if he didn't eyeball it. "Political saboteurs," he said. "Djekoule..."

"The guy in the serge."

"Djekoule says he has evidence the arsonists are members of the opposition guerrilla movement. Djekoule says they're trying to sabotage the new government's environmental program."

"Why?"

"To discredit the administration, make them appear ineffective."

"And destroy their own homeland in the process?"

Richard shrugged.

She sipped her wine and worked at sounding more than mildly interested. Any other time, she would have been fascinated by the intrigue. Just now, she couldn't shake the vision of Olson weeping at the wheel of his car.

Richard said, "I need to ask you something."

She glanced at him, but as soon as their eyes met, he dropped his gaze again.

"What is it, Richard?"

"Djekoule needs someone to help him douse the political flames. A government consultant who can present a strong image of international environmentalism, an authority on forest rehabilitation."

"A Richard Winters."

He said, "Djekoule asked me to take it on."

She stared. "Ivory Coast's government wants to hire you?"

"As a consultant. They would contract with my foundation, bring me over as an expert. A temporary arrangement."

"Kadoudougou is a far cry from the rain forests of the Olympic Peninsula."

Richard grinned. "Still, I've had some experience in other countries, and—well, it's not a permanent sort of arrangement. Djekoule wanted me to come for a minimum of six months. I negotiated a three-month trial project, to see how we're accepted—that is, how *I* am accepted."

She didn't say anything. She waited for him to explain. Beneath the suave veneer, he was an anxious boy trying to wrench permission out of his parent.

He said, "I think the job can be done in three months. Maybe four. Of course, it will be high pressure, night and day in the field. The smoke from the fires is pretty bad. And there's guerrilla warfare and intertribal warfare, too. It's not the safest or healthiest place. I wouldn't want you caught up in it."

Something about the way he said it struck a sour chord and she instinctively bristled against his protectiveness. She waved a hand.

"Hey, remember me? Venus Diamond? The federal anti-poaching agent who's tracked poachers in the Chiang Mai, who stared down a crazed bull elephant in Johor? Not to mention my domestic adventures. Who's the real daredevil in this marriage anyway?''

He laughed. ''That's just it, babe. If you came along, I wouldn't be able to keep you out of trouble.''

''So?''

He couldn't think of a response.

She said, ''Let's see if I understand what you're so bravely trying to say. You want to spend three months, give or take a stray weekend, in Ivory Coast rain forests, without me, working on forest rehabilitation. You are reluctant to include me in this arrangement because you feel it might expose me to danger— or rather, that I might get into trouble. Therefore, you are proposing that for the good of Ivory Coast's forests and all the endangered species dwelling within, and for my own safety, you and I will be separated for the greater part of—at the very least—three solid months.''

''We'd have romantic interludes twice a month.''

She said, ''Now we have them at least twice a day. So what's the sales pitch here?''

''I'd fly you over to Kadoudougou for a few days each month. And I'd fly back here once a month, to check on things at the office, and so we can spend a few days together. That would give us at least a week out of each month just for each other. The time will go fast. And I promise you, when this is over, we'll meet in some exotic destination—''

''Singapore?''

Richard raised an eyebrow. ''You're agreeing, then?''

She said, ''I only brought up Singapore because it has romantic connotations related to our brief but Byronic courtship period.''

''I remember.''

They moved from the table to the couch where a few hours ago she'd sat with Olson and turned down his plea to return to work. For the sake of her marriage. She sat a little distance from Richard and said, ''Tell me again why this is so important.''

''It's probably the last chance we have of saving Ivory

Coast's rain forests. I can help the government get its environmental act together, and they trust me, so we just might succeed. It's now or never." He leaned into her, nuzzled her neck. "That was nice in the Aston this afternoon."

"A little cramped." She stared out the window. There was nothing to see but raindrops on the windowpane. As she stared, they formed an image of Olson weeping, then they rearranged into Hannah Strindberg aflame in a trapped building with other burning bodies; then the raindrops rearranged again, this time into Dr. Wong's gentle, serene countenance.

Dr. Wong says, "If I am going to treat you, you must move out of your husband's home."

She says, "What if he takes a powder for, say, three months?"

Dr. Wong smiles and nods approvingly.

"What did you just say?" Richard said.

She said, "That I think you should go to Kadoudougou and save Ivory Coast's rain forests."

He studied her expression. She seemed serious enough. He said, "You mean that?"

She looked him in the eye. "I do," she said firmly. To herself, she added, *Indeed I do.*

SIX

CAT'S TEETH

THEY HADN'T BEEN LOVERS, though Olson would have welcomed that intimate aspect to their relationship. But they'd all but consummated their mutual devotion, and then both had hesitated, for different reasons. Then she had to die. When fate swindles constantly and brutally, a man has a right to cry.

Two years earlier, when Hannah Strindberg had marched unannounced into his office, determined to sell him on the Breedhaven project, Olson had been astounded by her boldness, her audacity in barging in without an appointment. But Hannah's plainspoken, unaffected personality had captivated him instantly, as had her futuristic vision. In two rapid-fire hours, Hannah convinced Olson that the Earth's endangered species, which were fast losing their native habitats to human encroachment, could be saved from extinction by reproducing them in petri dishes and, well, the rest of her plan had to be whispered. It was too audacious, too radical to be revealed publicly.

When she turned and walked out of his office, Olson nearly died from desire at the sight of Hannah's long, slender legs and—oh my God—the rest of her. The palms of his hands ached to touch her, to caress certain strategic points of her anatomy. They had, eventually; practically overnight, their relationship developed into more than a professional partnership. He felt the chemistry was strong and Hannah had responded appreciatively, though she stopped him cold the one time he'd suggested (by innuendo, not words) that they throw all caution to the winds, to hell with emotional damage. They'd come pretty damn close more than once, but she dreaded the emotional consequences, and he didn't push her, out of his own fear. Not of performance ability—God knows, Olson possessed a bull's stamina—but he feared peeling away the layers of psychic retread encasing his own soul.

He had spent hours alone in his office trying to figure out what bothered him, then gradually the realization dawned: Hannah preferred the company of women. Emotionally and intellectually, if not physically. How did Olson know this for a fact? He didn't. He could only guess, and go on his keen intuition. Olson had nothing against gays, he just didn't want Hannah to be "one of them." Whether or not his observation proved correct—Olson might never know—he had never entirely abandoned the desire to make love to Hannah. Eventually he had convinced himself that, more than the desire to penetrate her body, he wanted to enter her vision, to participate in Hannah Strindberg's dream of saving Earth's endangered species with her quixotic, secret mission. What kind of mind would conceive this vision? Naturally, at first, he was skeptical.

"How the hell do you expect cheetahs or leopards or white rhinos to survive your bold experiment?" Olson had asked Hannah.

Her reply was matter-of-fact: "If humans can, then so can rhinos. In embryonic form at first, of course. And the big cats. And the chimps. The frogs and birds. All of them can live wherever humans can build a habitat."

Olson had laughed and said, "Humans are the galaxy's worst predators. You put humans near these creatures and they'll kill them off, one by one. To hell with humans."

To Olson's surprise, when he said this, Hannah had blushed deeply, as if he had just told an offensive, off-color joke. But she didn't criticize him for his cynical take on humankind, or for anything else, for that matter. Hannah never criticized, only blushed, or smiled demurely, and changed the subject. He never understood how she could be so intellectually gifted, so professionally aggressive, and yet possess the social skills of a schoolgirl. Not that she was immature—not by a long shot. Hannah had the most finely honed sense of humor he'd ever encountered, and she was articulate and self-confident. Except with him. And that was the rub. With him.

Olson had embraced Hannah's vision, and together they had

convinced the Secretary of the Department of the Interior that the federal government should invest in the Breedhaven Endangered Species Habitat and in Hannah's bold vision. Now, two years into the project, Hannah was gone and Olson was left, the illogical but legal heir to Hannah's rare collection of frozen DNA and endangered-species embryos, the collection Olson had dubbed Hannah's ark.

He missed Hannah more than was appropriate. Or maybe it was appropriate, considering their intense professional and personal involvement. Emotions aside, Olson had been responsible for convincing DOI to sink multimillions of dollars into Breedhaven and into Hannah's secret project, and—together with Hannah, like a couple of overattentive parents—they had nurtured the project from its infancy to where it was now, about to be tested and proven. But now that Hannah was gone, he had no intention of trying to carry on their work. How could he? How could anyone, for that matter, duplicate Hannah's scientific work, her unique vision? Her assistants at Breedhaven never fully supported her, and she never told them about the secret vision she and Olson shared. Only he, Olson, had given Hannah unconditional support and encouragement. No one could replace Hannah, and now Olson was faced with the grim reality that without Hannah, the secret project, too, would die. He'd have to call Wexler, tell him. The Secretary would croak.

Hannah. Oh, God, Hannah.

Olson felt tears coming again. Before Hannah's death, he hadn't cried in years, not since the day his wife and his only child, a pretty teenage daughter, had died in a gruesome head-on collision on the I-5 reversible lane near the Bellevue exit. Since losing them, Olson had switched off his heart, had learned to live without love, to feel fondness but never affection for friends and colleagues. Affection was too risky. Then he'd turned soft over Hannah, and just look what happened.

He was wiping tears from his cheek, weeping like the rain-splashed windows, cursing, when a familiar voice said, "Okay, I'm back."

He glanced up. The soft cashmere was gone, replaced by the familiar black leather. Her blond hair was cut short again, punked back with pomade, in that androgynous style that bothered him. She stepped into his office, leaned over his desk.

"What's wrong, Chief?"

He waved a hand, its fingers still damp with tears. "What the hell are you doing here?"

Venus said, "Reporting to work."

He recovered in record time, before she had a chance to change her mind. He said acidly, "It's almost Christmas."

She smiled. "I've worked holidays before."

Olson looked at his watch and said—as if she'd never taken a leave of absence—"Damn. I promised to meet Rusty Higgins ten minutes ago. He's got the latest DNA results from the fire. God, I hate to go through that again...."

Venus said, "I'll go see Rusty now."

Olson stood up, put a hand on her arm, squeezed. "Thanks," he whispered.

"Don't thank me," she said breezily as they walked toward the elevator. "Thank Dr. Wong."

He started to ask her again who Dr. Wong was, then the elevator arrived. She stepped inside, joining a raucous lunchtime crowd. The door shut and the cold steel chatterbox descended. Olson went back to his office, and the perpetually weeping windows.

THE TROUBLE WITH using "local celebrities" in print advertising is they become local icons for a while, and even after the celebrity wears off, they still think they're famous. Rusty Higgins, Chief Forensics Inspector for the Seattle Fire Department, had fallen victim to this syndrome when Nordstrom's "local personalities" ad campaign hit the Seattle newspaper. A full-page color photo of redheaded Rusty Higgins appeared one Sunday in the *Seattle Star*'s Lifestyles section and suddenly Rusty's social life sprang into being. Something about red-haired men and Seattle women. Now, wherever Rusty appeared in public, drooling fans would swarm around him to ogle and coo over the fire inspector's famous flame-colored mop. Since the Nordie's ad, meeting Rusty in a public place was like trying to have a private coffee with Brad Pitt at Starbucks.

Venus met Higgins at the Oasis Lounge in Belltown. Once the commotion over Rusty's red corkscrew curls had waned, she sat down at Rusty's table. When the waitress had stopped pawing Rusty, Venus got her attention and ordered a Beck's near-beer.

"It was her," Higgins said. "I ran the tests personally. It was her DNA in those ashes. It was definitely Hannah Strindberg. That makes it a wrap."

"All the bodies definitely identified?"

The waitress came back with the Beck's, and Higgins's usual Oly. Higgins swallowed a mouthful of beer and nodded.

"No room for error?"

"Not that I can see." Higgins checked to see if the fan club was still alert and attentive, then added, "DNA doesn't lie."

Venus picked up the medical examiner's report. "Let's review the evidence. All missing persons accounted for. Fifty-three corpses. All indisputably identified through dental records, or, in Hannah Strindberg's case, through DNA analysis. All died from smoke inhalation."

"Correction. Forty-three succumbed to the smoke. The other ten weren't so lucky."

"Why's that?" Venus pulled on the Beck's. It went down cool and straight, and it didn't fuzz her brain.

"They suffered more. Eight victims caught fire before losing consciousness. A ninth had heart failure—which was probably a blessing, actually—and the tenth croaked under the stampede of people trying to escape. She was literally stomped to death. Somebody stepped on her head with a spike-heel shoe. Punctured the skin at her temporal lobe. We found little shoe nails inside her skull."

"Who was that?"

"That victim?" Higgins ran a finger down the autopsy list. "Here she is. Martine Olaffson."

"The Swedish biologist."

Higgins shrugged. "One of those Scandie countries, anyway."

Venus said, "What's the margin of error in these results?"

"Like I said, next to zero. DNA doesn't err."

"So this list of victims is accurate and complete?"

"Totally." Higgins swigged and sloe-eyed the fan club.

Venus said, "Your fire inspectors were at Zanzibar's that same afternoon, correct?"

Higgins said, "That's what the club's day manager tells us."

"What about your own inspectors? Have you checked with them to be sure they went to the club that day?"

Higgins seemed preoccupied, maybe with the brunette in a miniskirt walking past the table on her way to the bar. His eyes followed her path, and her curves. He said, "Yeah, sure."

"Did the club manager mention any other visits that day? Like delivery people, or maintenance workers?"

"Just the exterminators. Their quarterly pest-control treatment."

"That checked out, too?"

The brunette was en route back from the bar, Rusty's eyeballs locked on. He said, "Uh-huh. Yeah."

Venus said, "What about the autopsies? Any interesting or curious aspects to the autopsies? Besides the spike-heel factor?"

Higgins peeled his eyes off the brunette and made a face. He couldn't think of any. Except maybe one. "The victims from New Zealand both wore dentures. Full sets. I found that interesting. Being that they're scientists and all."

Venus said, "Anything else?"

Higgins shook his head and showed his empty palms.

Venus persisted. "Think hard. Anything else weird?"

Higgins shrugged. "Not unless you consider transsexuality weird. I don't."

She said, "One of the victims?"

"Three, actually. All waiters. Maybe the club's owner liked to hire them. I don't know why they would be any different than straights, or just plain gays. As waiters, I mean. Three of the waiters were in the midst of sex-change procedures. Two were males who had gotten as far as growing breasts. The third was a former male who had completed the surgery and was female when he/she died. A waitress named Carla."

"Could this have been a hate crime? Some bigot who hated transsexuals?"

Higgins said, "That's my theory."

Venus finished her Beck's, raised a hand for the waiter. On the second Beck's, she said, "There's got to be something else."

Higgins laughed. "Why? Isn't it interesting enough as it stands now? I mean, a conflagration that wipes out fifty-three people in twelve minutes, including thirty of the world's greatest scientists and three transsexuals, isn't interesting enough for you? What do you want, a survivor maybe?"

She said, "That would be nice."

"Well, you're in luck. There's one surviving victim, a waiter who arrived for work late. He witnessed the blaze from the club's entrance. But he's in no condition to talk to anyone, according to his physician, anyway. Maybe in a few days."

"Was he injured?"

"A moderate hand burn from when he tried to douse some flames. It's PTS. Post-traumatic stress disorder. Maybe in a day or two we can talk to him."

"Where is he?"

"At home, but under strict orders to rest. I spoke to his physician this afternoon. She says he's still too fragile. Says we have to wait until she releases him from medical observation. We can't overrule her."

"What about the foreign investigators? Have they shed any light on a motive?"

"Naw. They all think they're Hercule Poirot, and none of them speaks very good English. They're wasting their time, and ours. They're pains in the ass, just getting in my way. We couldn't work with them snooping around everywhere, so we finally assigned a public-relations team to hold them at bay. Like I said, nobody's come up with a truly solid lead."

"So what's your take, Rusty?"

"Probably the bigot theory. Probably a hate crime. Transsexuals make a great target for a bigoted psycho."

"You don't think the scientists were the target?"

"Naw." Rusty sucked his teeth, made little squeaking noises through them. "Looks to me like this was aimed at Zanzibar's, at the owners of the club. Because they hired sexual deviants. I mean, what the arsonist considered sexual deviants. Like I said, I don't consider transsexuals all that unusual.''

He stopped then, and seemed to consider something else. ''Of course, then there were the cat's teeth. Now, there's a sexy angle, if you stretch the definition of 'sexy,' and it sounds like you want to do that.''

''Tell me about the cat's teeth.''

''In the foyer of the club, near the remains of one of the American scientists, we found three teeth, a couple canines and a molar. Our coroner says they're cat's teeth. Must have been a stray, because we asked the club's owner, and he insists he didn't own a cat, and he said he never allowed animals inside the club.''

''The scientist whose remains you found in the foyer, wasn't that Dr. Hannah Strindberg?''

''Right.'' Rusty slapped his knee, and said, ''Hey, you're good.''

''The news reports said a cab driver witnessed the explosion, and that he saw a woman resembling Hannah Strindberg go inside the club just before the explosion. The cab driver said the woman was carrying a pet crate. Maybe she had a cat in there. Maybe that's where the teeth came from.''

Higgins yawned. ''Could be. I don't see why it matters.''

''Where are the teeth?''

''At the morgue. Why? You want 'em?''

''Can I have them?'' Surprised.

Higgins said, ''Sure. Why not? They don't mean anything, far as I can tell. But if you folks discover something interesting, let me know.'' He slugged back a swallow of Oly. ''Come over and pick 'em up any old time.''

Venus read her Swatch. ''Let's go right now.''

''I haven't finished my beer.''

''Come on,'' she said. ''I'm in a hurry.''

On the way out into the rain, Higgins said, ''I didn't mean to call them sexual deviants. It just slipped out.''

Venus said, ''Sure. Now, let's go fetch those cat's teeth.''

THE TEETH WERE small, sharp, yellow, plaque-coated, but free of cavities. She sent them to Oregon by helicopter, to the forensics lab at Ashland, with a note to expedite the lab analyses. At six o'clock, the phone rang. It was Claudia Paganelli, USF&W's forensics chief, calling from Ashland. Claudia said one word: "Wild."

"You're sure?"

"Positive. Domestic cats' teeth aren't this healthy. These specimens are cavity-free. It was male, an adult male."

"You can tell that from the condition of teeth?"

"I can tell lots of things from teeth," said Norwegian-born, matter-of-fact Claudia. "What else would you like to know?"

"You're sure it wasn't a domestic cat?"

"Whether it was wild or domestic, the cat suffered. Like the human victims, it burned to death."

Venus said, "What else can you tell from the teeth?"

Claudia sighed. "Just what else do you want to know?"

"I need to know where that cat came from."

"What do you mean, where it came from?"

"I mean, its land of origin. I need to identify the species."

Claudia sniffed. "Well, that's one thing I can't tell you from these particular cat's teeth."

Venus said, "I can't believe she had that Bay cat with her. I need something to go on. Anything. Find a distinguishing trait. Cat's teeth must have distinctive traits."

"Some do," Claudia replied coolly. "Most do not."

OLSON ANSWERED on the first ring. Venus told him about Claudia's test results.

Olson said, "I don't want to hear about it."

"You have to hear this. They found the cat's teeth near Hannah's ashes. Apparently, she had a wild cat with her. This seems to prove it."

Silence; then Olson said, "Why the hell would Hannah take a rare species to a nightclub? She was smarter than that. I just don't buy it."

"Then where's the Borneo?"

Olson growled, "I don't want to discuss it right now. Come into my office. I've got something more substantial than cat's teeth."

When she arrived, he handed her a floppy disk.

Back at her computer, when she opened the disk, she saw an alphabetical list of the dead scientists. Beside each scientist's name was a list of his or her publications and research projects. She spent two hours scrolling through this information, and when she broke for dinner, she felt no closer to inspiration. She called the Seattle Fire Department, asked for Rusty Higgins. He wasn't working late. She left a message on his service, detailing what Claudia's tests indicated about the cat's teeth. If Venus were a betting person, she'd bet that Rusty Higgins was lounging in the Oasis right now, tossing his corkscrew tendrils at some petulant brunette. Feline plaque was the last thing on Rusty's preoccupied mind.

SEVEN

EARNEST

ANOTHER BRISK MORNING dawned, dark and freakishly frigid, catapulting Olson to the brink of despair. Snow threatened, and already black ice coated the pavement. Olson and Venus navigated the slick downtown sidewalks to the law firm of Tapp, Tapp and O'Toole, where Dr. Hannah Strindberg's attorney prepared to read Hannah's last will and testament. They were the first to arrive at the postmodern suites on the forty-second floor of the Seneca Building. Venus would have preferred to follow up on the cat's teeth angle, but Olson had commanded her to accompany him. She went along, out of compassion for Olson, not morbid curiosity about Hannah Strindberg.

The tall, leggy strawberry blonde who was Hannah's attorney bore a striking resemblance to her deceased client. Olson tried not to stare, but his eyes kept finding hers, and each time their glances locked, a knife pierced his heart. Lawyers shouldn't resemble their clients. Olson grew surly, crossed his nice arms over his muscular chest and averted his gaze, leaving Venus to chitchat with the Hannah look-alike.

The attorney, Kristen Johannson, was Hannah's second cousin once removed, daughter of an immigrant Swede boatbuilder, another Ballard native—ya sure, you betcha—for most of her childhood. Graduated from Lutheran Middle School, then Ballard High. Olson piped up, saying he had lived in Ballard all his life, that he still lived in Ballard, and he didn't remember seeing Kristen Johannson around the neighborhood. Johannson allowed, somewhat acerbically, that that must be because she'd cut out of Scanville at a tender age, and never returned except to visit her aging father, until he died last year of Alzheimer's. Olson didn't want to know so much about Kristen Johannson, but he listened intently, hanging on every word in hopes he'd hear Hannah's name mentioned, and each time Johannson mentioned Hannah's name, Olson suffered-savored the bittersweet sound. *Christ,* he thought to himself, *her voice even sounds like Hannah's.*

Johannson passed them off to a male legal assistant who showed them into a sedate conference room where rows of folding teak chairs were arranged facing a sleek table and a bank of floor-to-ceiling windows that overlooked the Pike Place Market and Puget Sound. Venus peered out and saw Elliott Bay's shivering wintry surface reflecting springlike cumulus clouds, and saw how the bay's silvery mirror shattered in the wakes of seagoing vessels. Lately, the weather didn't make any sense. When a Pacific gull swept past the windows, Venus blinked. The bird had Dr. Wong's cold blue eye. Olson came to the window, stood beside Venus and looked out. It was easier than focusing on Hannah's look-alike cousin who had returned with a tray of coffee things.

Kristen Johannson set porcelain cups and saucers beside a large silver coffee urn on a side buffet, told them to help themselves to coffee, then left the room. Venus went over, poured two cups of coffee. The sugar bowl and the creamer were Uncle Remus and Aunt Jemima figures with exaggerated lips and nostrils, caricatures in blackface, bad ceramic jokes. Venus poured one cup of coffee, black, steaming, and set it aside. She poured another, and into it, poured politically incorrect half-and-half from the politically incorrect Aunt Jemima's kerchiefed head. She carried the black coffee over to Olson. He accepted it without looking at her, without even a grunt of acknowledgement, his usual form of thanks. He kept staring out the window at the sound's reflective surface, but his focus was clearly fathoms deeper than the visible plane. She left him standing by the window, took her own enriched coffee, and sat down on one of the teak chairs in the last row at the back of the room. From here she could see everyone who entered, and she could watch them during the reading of Hannah Strindberg's last will and testament. You never know who will show up for the reading of a murder victim's will. Maybe a murderer. Or murderers.

A great bustle announced the arrival of four Breedhaven trustees, ushered into the room by the legal assistant. Bustle always accompanied the arrivals of Ardith Pierce the widowed commodities heiress, Stan Rowe the fish man, Frances Fanny Faber, God's gift to society pages, and aromatherapy guru Tina Medina, younger and more attractive than Ardith and Fanny, but not as effusive and therefore less ubiquitous in the press.

The legal assistant, whose name was Bradford, peeled off the new arrivals' various wraps. A faux sable fur coat fell from Mrs. Pierce's environmentally-responsible shoulders, a camel's-hair topcoat and Stetson hat from the flashy fish man, a flamboyant quilted gold artifact from Fanny Faber's fastidious form, and finally, stacked so high on top of the growing pile of outerwear you couldn't see Bradford's nose, Tina Medina's inflammatory sealskin coat. The four trustees sat stiffly in the front row while Bradford, fresh from the coat closet, poured coffee. Venus watched Bradford draw sugar from Uncle Remus's gray hair, half-and-half from Jemima's kerchief.

Next to arrive were Breedhaven's five laboratory assistants, doctoral students on loan from various universities. Only one of the five seemed remotely interested in being there: the cool brunette who wore an Ungaro suit from the latest collection. Women in Ungaro stand out in a crowd. In this case, the youngish brunette also stood out against the blandness of the other four. Olson came over, sat down on Venus's right. "Rosemary Poole is the overdressed one," he said in an audible whisper. "She's Elmer Poole's granddaughter. Very bright, very sexy. She's working at the habitat as Ted Vigil's assistant."

"Who's Ted Vigil?"

"Oh, that's right. You don't know any of these Breedhaven folks. Ted Vigil is Breedhaven's geneticist. He's a very bright fellow. He was Hannah's associate. Hannah wasn't fond of him."

She looked at Olson. She said, "Are you just saying that because you were jealous of his relationship to Hannah?"

Olson shook his head.

She said, "I don't mean to be impertinent, or to give you a hard time. I'm just trying to work out the relationships."

"Like I said, Hannah wasn't fond of Vigil. He's very competitive. Always wanted to be named second author on her papers when he had no role in the research."

"Lazy?"

"Not lazy. Ambitious. He publishes volumes of his own research."

"Then why?"

Olson said, "He's an opportunist. He'll use anyone and everyone to forward his own career. He plans to be famous."

The lab assistants didn't merit Bradford's fawning attentions. They hung up their own coats, poured their own coffee. Venus watched them crowd around the coffee table, heard them commenting on the sugar and creamer. One of the younger scientists whispered, "Is this supposed to be Bill Cosby or Eddie Murphy?"

An adolescent boy entered the room, pale and thin, appearing slightly ill-at-ease. Bradford rushed over to the newcomer, took his overcoat, rubbed the young man's shoulder, and murmured something in his pale ear. The young man nodded and sat down tentatively beside the knockout Rosemary Poole. Poole tilted her head slightly, honored him with a once-over, then turned away. He wasn't old enough or handsome enough for her tastes. Olson whispered, "That's the grand nephew from Lake Louise, Bjorn Pedersen. I've met him. A very lonely boy. Lost his parents when he was a baby. I believe Ms. Johannson raised him. They just returned from an African safari."

"He looks young."

"Hannah left him the ring."

"The demantoid garnet?"

Olson grunted. That meant, *"Right."* Then he said, "Now pay attention. Here comes Ted Vigil. And right behind him, the chap with the diamond stud in his ear? That's Breedhaven's most colorful trustee, Larry Chekhov."

Venus watched the two men settle in, observed how Chekhov greeted the other trustees with grand theatrical gestures and air kisses. Vigil had more of a Volvo personality, bland yuppie mannerisms, and he wore those chic little eyeglasses. He reminded Venus of a badger she'd met once during a butterfly safari on the banks of the Thames. Only the badger, she reflected, had more personality. She leaned over and mentioned this to Olson.

Olson said, "An obsequious, scheming acolyte is how I would describe him. Hannah hired Vigil for his research skills, not for his personality."

Rosemary Poole abandoned her seat among the lowly doctoral candidates and joined Vigil and Chekhov near the front, seating herself between the two men, leaning into Vigil, permitting her hips to brush provocatively against Chekhov's.

Olson leaned over and whispered to Venus, "You realize she was the crucial link."

Venus looked at him inquiringly. Olson said, "Rosemary Poole is a doctoral candidate. She was working under Hannah's supervision. She studied with Hannah down at Palo Alto. It was Rosemary who introduced Hannah to her grandfather, Elmer Poole. That's how Breedhaven was created."

"Whose idea was it originally?"

"Hannah's, of course. Down at Stanford, she had described her vision of Breedhaven to Rosemary. Then Rosemary got the brainstorm to introduce Hannah to her grandfather. Rosemary realized that old Elmer wouldn't be around forever, and that his acreage might be up for grabs. Rosemary brought Hannah and her grandfather together, then Hannah planted the idea for Breedhaven in Elmer's mind just as he was revising his will."

"He was tricked into donating the land?"

Olson leaned in closer to avoid being overheard by the others. "Not tricked. Convinced. You might say 'converted.' He had originally planned to donate his property to the Helix Island Preservation Land Trust. But he was pissed off at someone, one of the islanders connected to the trust, as I recall, and so Hannah, with impeccable timing, suggested he leave the property to the Breedhaven project. Elmer was easily convinced to change his will. Hannah told me all this. I never met Elmer Poole, but I gather he was quite a strong-willed old geezer, not in the least gullible."

Right now, Rosemary Poole seemed anything but strong-willed, clinging like a wounded moth to Vigil's tweedy arm, her shoulders slumped, her expression forlorn. Maybe grieving. Yes, that must be it. Rosemary was mourning Hannah, her mentor. Maybe more than a mentor.

Vigil didn't drink coffee, but he went over to pour Rosemary's, and while he was gone, Venus saw Rosemary place her hand ever so seductively on Chekhov's knee. When Vigil came back and handed Rosemary her coffee, her hand sprang off Chekhov's knee and through veiled lashes, she made goo-goo eyes at Vigil.

"Help me out here," Venus whispered to Olson. "Which one of those guys is her main squeeze?"

Olson said, "Both"; then Kristen Johannson swept in and announced that, due to incompatible schedules, one of Breedhaven's trustees wouldn't be attending the reading. Venus counted heads. Fourteen, not including the attorney and Bradford. Kristen Johannson checked her wristwatch, nodded at Bradford, who went away. Johannson opened the proceedings with a terse introduction.

"Ladies and gentlemen, I apologize for asking you to come here so close to the Christmas holidays, but unfortunately, this legal business must be wrapped up before the year's end. It is my somber duty today, as Dr. Strindberg's executor, to inform all of you of her last will and testament. But unfortunately, one person who must be present in order for these proceedings to continue is not... Ah, here he is now."

All heads turned to face the door, as a man of African ancestry crossed the threshold, nodded to Johannson, and walked confidently into the room. He had an athletic build, a healthy glow. He wore a meticulous dark poplin suit, inadequate for the freakish winter cold, a tropical-weight shirt, and a bolo tie. He had on snakeskin cowboy boots. He wasn't from here, Venus noted, and she knew from the relieved expression on Johannson's face that whoever he was, wherever he came from, this man played a key role in the proceedings.

Johannson said, "I would like to introduce Captain Dave Dillon, from NASA's Houston Flight Center." Dillon waved a hand casually. Tics and murmurs erupted, but Johannson obviously wasn't ready to satiate the collective curiosity. Instead she added, "In due time, you will come to understand why Captain Dillon has joined us for these proceedings."

Venus watched Dillon walk to the side table, pour a cup of coffee, pick up the Aunt Jemima creamer, stare at it. It wasn't the fatty half-and-half that bothered him. He walked to the last row of chairs and sat down on the opposite end from Venus and Olson. Olson leaned across Venus and nodded at Dillon. Dillon nodded back. Like they knew each other. Then Dillon nodded at Venus and smiled, and she felt a thrill engulf her, like he'd just handed her the map to a hidden treasure, or a winning lottery ticket. She smiled back, her dazzling best know-it-all, faux confident visage, but Dillon wasn't transfixed. His attention had turned to Johannson.

The reading of the will proceeded. Hannah Strindberg's personal effects included a comfortable 401k savings stash, a hefty IRA account, and a few personal possessions, all of which she had willed to her closest living relative, her nephew Bjorn Pedersen, the pale adolescent Rosemary Poole had found so humdrum. Hannah also left young Bjorn the demantoid garnet-and-platinum ring, and this, along with a thick envelope of paperwork, was handed to him.

As her executor, Kristen Johannson received a generous cash payment, which had been deducted from Hannah's savings before it was turned over to young Bjorn. When the material possessions had been doled out, Johannson cleared her throat and said, "Now we arrive at the critical stage of this proceeding. Hannah left strict instructions as to the disposition of her scientific work—that is, her intellectual property."

Ardith Pierce, the most vociferous Breedhaven trustee, piped up, "That all belongs to the trustees."

Johannson smiled patiently. Olson frowned at Mrs. Pierce's backside. Venus felt a wave of tension ripple through the room. Johannson said, "As all of you know, the scientific work Hannah was conducting was a joint project of Breedhaven Endangered Species Habitat and the United States Department of the Interior, under the auspices of the Fish and Wildlife Service. Because of the joint nature of ownership of these scientific projects, and because one experiment in particular was unfinished,

Hannah's work will continue under the same joint auspices, but will now be supervised directly by the regional director of the United States Fish and Wildlife Service, Special Agent Oly Olson.''

Vigil jumped up. "I am in charge of Hannah's work now. Not anyone else.''

Johannson raised a hand. "Please sit down, Dr. Vigil. If you please.''

More muttering undercurrents, squirming in chairs, creaking teak, general fussing. Fanny whispered in Chekhov's ear.

Johannson went on: "Breedhaven, and the Fish and Wildlife Service, will continue their joint efforts on the habitat premises. Dr. Vigil will, of course, be in charge of all experiments until a suitable replacement can be found for Dr. Strindberg. Dr. Vigil will report directly to Agent Olson, who is ultimately in charge of all activity at Breedhaven. The chain of command is quite straightforward and in line with the agreement originally negotiated between Breedhaven's trustees and the United States Department of the Interior. If anyone takes issue with this arrangement, I suggest you contact the Secretary of the Interior Department.''

Vigil and Rosemary exchanged glances. Venus thought she saw Vigil blanch around the gills, and Rosemary opened her mouth as if to speak but nothing escaped. Olson and Dillon both folded their arms across their chests. Venus sipped her coffee, felt the half-and-half coat her tongue, savored its sweetness.

"Well, that ark belongs to us,'' Ardith Pierce piped up. "We trustees financed the creation of the ark.'' A groundswell of applause erupted from the trustees, and Venus felt a strange sense of *mal de mer*.

The tics and murmurs grew strident, more staccato. Trustees bent their heads together and exchanged battle plans. This could mean war. Johannson held up her tired hand. "Hannah's ark is the property of the United States Department of the Interior. Legally speaking, these genetic materials were, as I have said, Hannah's personal intellectual property.''

"We'll see about that,'' said Larry Chekhov to the obvious approval of his fellow trustees.

Johannson said, "May I remind all of you that Breedhaven's trustees have no fiscal interest nor rights of possession in the property and experiments conducted at the habitat? Breedhaven's trustees financed reclamation of the habitat and the costs of constructing the lodge, the scientists' private cottages, and the animal hospital. The research laboratory and all its contents, including DNA and other biological organisms, were financed by the United States Government, and Hannah's ark, which represents the work of federal officials in concert with Dr. Strindberg, is now the legal property of the federal government."

"The hell it is," barked Chekhov. "We'll see you in court."

Tina Medina, the aroma doyenne, stood and squared her shoulders. "Perhaps, Miss Johannson," she purred menacingly, "you haven't been so well informed. The federal government provided funding for the research—that much is true. But as the trustees of Breedhaven have personally contributed a not-insignificant sum toward the operations and upkeep of the habitat, we also have an interest in the ark. I am with Mr. Chekhov on this point. I believe we trustees have a legal right to at least partial ownership of those embryos."

"She means the ark," added Stan Rowe acidly. "And I agree with her."

More applause from the trustee gallery. Bradford rushed forward with a plate of shortbread and chocolates, as if bonbons would appease this astringent group. Venus glanced at Olson. His arms were still crossed over his chest. He wasn't obviously salivating; maybe he had finally lost his sweet tooth. Maybe Olson was one of those rare individuals for whom diets actually worked. Maybe Olson had succeeded in permanently altering his dietary habits. Tiredly, Johannson said, "Captain Dillon, would you kindly come forward and address the ladies and gentlemen?"

This invitation silenced the room. The tanned, balding man with the trim moustache set his coffee cup down neatly beneath his folding chair, stood and walked to the front of the room. So still was the roomful of people now, that Venus could hear Dillon's boots padding across the Berber carpet. When he arrived at the front of the room and turned to face the group, Dillon projected an aura of supreme confidence. *He's an astronaut,* Venus thought hopefully. *I want him to be an astronaut. He's got that astronautish look, that cachet.*

Dillon's voice was strong, his manner articulate. "Dr. Strindberg," he began, "with the aid and support of the Fish and Wildlife Service, put together a priceless collection of genetic materials, DNA, of several hundred highly endangered species. Dr. Strindberg's first and foremost concern was always protection of these rare materials. She wanted to be absolutely certain that, should anything ever happen to her, the collection would not fall into the wrong hands, would not be exploited for financial gain, or the resulting species used in research experiments. So Dr. Strindberg developed a plan, which she proposed to NASA, and which we wholeheartedly embraced. This joint project between Dr. Strindberg, the Fish and Wildlife Service, and NASA was scheduled to culminate just six months from today, when the new space shuttle *Earnest* departs Cape Canaveral for a rendezvous with the international space station."

He made it sound like a routine shuttle between Washington and New York. Maybe space travel now seemed that routine to the Cape Canaveral crowd.

"As everyone in this room knows," Dillon continued, "Hannah's ark represents several million dollars' worth of federal research funds. You may also remember that Dr. Strindberg had taken a leave of absence last summer. What Dr. Strindberg did not tell anyone at Breedhaven was that she spent last summer in astronaut training school. Dr. Strindberg and her specimen collection were to fly on the *Earnest*'s maiden voyage. Until today, the NASA project has been largely kept secret. Hannah's ultimate vision is similar to NASA's, that is, while NASA searches for planets or moons that humans might populate, Hannah envisioned more endangered species living eventually in new worlds. Meanwhile, Hannah stipulated that the ark is to be stored for safekeeping in the international space station, for a period of no less than fifty years, and not to exceed one hundred years. Hannah also devised a code to protect the materials. The decode materials will be stored along with the ark in a time-sensitive capsule."

"Where did Hannah write down her permission to do this?"
Vigil barked.

Johannson broke in: "In documents that Hannah kept here
with me, on file in this office, for security purposes. The actual
ark was, of course, kept at Breedhaven. At Hannah's request,
one Breedhaven trustee whom she trusted took the decoding
materials from Hannah for safekeeping elsewhere. That trustee
is to remain anonymous."

Olson frowned. Venus leaned over and whispered, "What's
wrong?"

"She talks too much."

So Olson and Hannah Strindberg had had more cooking than
just a tight friendship. Maybe this space trip had been planned
from the beginning. Maybe when Hannah Strindberg had approached Olson, she had already planned the space voyage, already had NASA lined up, already had her space reserved on
the *Earnest*. Then Hannah Strindberg had convinced Olson to
persuade USF&W to support her mission, and he had been so
enthralled that he had done just that, securing the federal funds
to support Hannah's work.

Olson was watching Venus again. Like he could read her
mind. When she caught his eye, he nodded slightly, as if veri-
fying that the details she was turning over in her mind were
correct. So Hannah Strindberg had been more than Olson's love
interest. Olson had made a critical investment in Hannah; now
his professional reputation was at stake. But, with Hannah
gone...

"We plan to carry out Dr. Strindberg's vision, to store her
rare collection in space," Dillon was saying.

Vigil squirmed in his chair. Rosemary elbowed him in the
ribs. Vigil shot her a nasty look, but settled down, quit squirming. In the front row, Ardith Pierce, apparently bored, was ap-
plying lipstick. Stan Rowe was playing with the brim of his hat,
twirling it, catching it, twirling it. Venus noticed almost everyone else in the room now sat still and silent, arms folded across
chests. Protecting their private thoughts.

Ted Vigil finally broke the silence. "I don't see what right
you have to the embryos. Hannah's ark belongs to Breedhaven.

We can take care of the embryos ourselves. What's this business about shooting it off into space? Who needs that? You shouldn't even be here. What are you doing here, anyway?"

"Yes," Larry Chekhov joined in. "We demand an explanation."

Tina Medina spoke up next, addressing Kristen Johannson. "We aren't sheep, Ms. Johansson," purred Medina hostilely. "Don't try pulling the wool over our eyes."

"Oh, come now, come now," put in Fanny Faber. "Let's hear Miss Johannson's explanation."

Kristen Johannson spoke up. "Captain Dillon came here today at Dr. Strindberg's request. In anticipation of the space flight, Hannah had requested that I prepare certain legal documents, including her last will and testament, in the event that something should go wrong. Then, just after Thanksgiving, Hannah came to my office and informed me that she had an uneasy feeling she was in danger. She honestly feared for her life, though she couldn't say why, beyond her own intuitive feelings. She told me, though, that on two separate occasions at Breedhaven, over Thanksgiving weekend, she had been preparing to go to bed and discovered that her bedroom window had been unlocked. On both occasions, she specifically remembered locking the window, but someone else had apparently unlocked it. Also, Hannah told me that during the same long weekend, while she was walking on the preserve, someone fired a gun in her direction. The bullet struck and killed a male cat—I believe it was one of the two rare servals Hannah was raising on the preserve."

Vigil said, "That bullet was meant for Hannah." He cleared his throat and added, "That's my opinion."

Rosemary Poole's elbow struck out again, nudging Vigil's ribs. Vigil ignored the jab and added, "And it wasn't the serval. It was a domestic cat. A research animal."

Ardith Pierce said, "Why would anyone want to destroy a research animal, Ted?"

Vigil said, "I have my own opinion, but no one listens to me."

"Well, you can tell us, dear," purred Mrs. Pierce.

Kristen Johannson said, "Please, first let's finish this proceeding. Captain Dillon, kindly finish your presentation."

Dillon stepped forward. "If all goes as planned, the ark will fly on board the *Earnest* next June. Dr. Strindberg, along with officials of the Fish and Wildlife Service, chose an alternate candidate to accompany the ark, in the event that something happened to Dr. Strindberg. That individual is here with us today, and it is my duty to inform all of you of NASA's choice to succeed Dr. Strindberg on the space shuttle *Earnest*."

Olson was staring beyond Captain Dillon's broad shoulders, out the window, as if absenting himself from the proceedings. Rosemary Poole was warming the edge of her chair. Vigil leapt to his feet and cried, "Just what are you saying?"

"That when Dr. Strindberg began fearing for her life, she naturally became concerned about her work, about the security of the ark. Besides encoding the material in the ark, she came to see her attorney, and then she contacted me by telephone at first, then by fax, requesting a successor be named to accompany the ark on the space shuttle *Earnest*. Of course, the candidate had to be approved by the Department of the Interior, and by NASA." Dillon drew a deep breath and said, "The individual we agreed upon to serve as Dr. Strindberg's successor was in fact already an applicant for astronaut training, although this individual had originally applied to do research on butterfly reproduction in space.

Vigil blanched. "I am not a lepidopterist," he snapped. "I am a geneticist."

Dillon said, "The candidate selected to accompany Dr. Strindberg's work on the space shuttle *Earnest*'s maiden voyage is Fish and Wildlife Special Agent Venus Diamond."

Her chair fell backward, hit the buffet, and the sugar and creamer rocked over onto the floor. Jemima fell on top of Remus and both shattered into ceramic shards.

Captain Dillon grinned and said, "But first she'll need some antigravity training."

EIGHT

RHODODENDRONS

MOTHER-DAUGHTER relationships are rarely pretty. Venus heard Bella's Ferragamos clicking along the foyer tiles, heading for the dining room, felt her own heart pound, and felt a light sweat break across her brow. Near the picture window, Bella's sharpei, lolling in thin sunlight, raised her thick corrugated face to the air and sniffed. The clicks sounded closer and closer, then the diva herself appeared at the dining-room entrance, all-powerful, all-lovely. Venus felt a shiver along her spine. The sight of perfection chills a flawed soul, inspiring awe and trepidation.

Bella Winsome-Diamond arched the world's most perfect eyebrow and chimed, "Venus, what in the world are you doing at my breakfast table?"

"Eating a crumpet, Mother."

"You have your own breakfast table now." Bella slipped into the place of honor, drew a damask napkin from its silver ring, and smoothed it across her narrow lap. "And you have a husband, even if he doesn't respect crumpets. Pass the sugar, if you please, dear."

Passing the sugar bowl, Venus's croc paws made accidental contact with Bella's elegantly manicured digits. The improbable parental unit frowned disapprovingly at her daughter's chapped, neglected hands.

Venus said, "Richard's gone to Kadoudougou."

"Kadoudougou?" murmured Bella, sweetening her beverage. "Why Kadoudougou?"

"Forest fires."

"It's those poor swidden farmers, hacking and burning the primeval growth, trying to feed their families." Bella buttered her toast. "But I don't understand what Richard has to do with Ivory Coast forest fires."

"The government in Kadoudougou hired Richard's forest-conservation foundation to consult on ways to reeducate the swidden farmers, to stop the slash-and-burn farming and rehabilitate the forests."

"Sounds entirely political, if you ask me."

"How astute you are, Mother." A bit too saccharine, pandering.

Bella scoffed. "Any fool could work that out in his feeble brain. Now, given that Richard has traipsed off to Ivory Coast, it is perhaps understandable that you may have felt lonely at your breakfast table this morning, and thus have joined mine. But you haven't touched that crumpet, dear, and so I am obliged to suspect that your visitation involves more than a mere yen for maternal companionship and crumpets. Stephen," she sang out in the direction of the kitchen, "bring me the telephone, if you please—that's a darling."

Stephen was Bella's personal assistant.

"Mother, before you commence your morning telephoning, I have a question to ask you."

"Put it right out on the table, then."

"What would you think about my becoming an astronaut?"

"Stephen, also bring me my little digital telephone book, will you please? Now, Venus, you certainly have a most vivid imagination. You remind me of your great-aunt Flo. And you know how she ended up."

"Actually, no, I don't. How did Aunt Flo end up?" Part genuine interest, part pandering.

"It's isn't pretty."

"I love a good, juicy ancestral tale." More lickspittle.

"Some other time. Aunt Flo's demise isn't appropriate subject matter for the breakfast table. Now, I detect a slight tremor in your body. What is that all about?"

Venus lied. "My husband of fourteen months has deserted me in favor of some Ivory Coast conflagration where guerrilla warfare includes machete torture. That's enough to make anyone sweat bullets."

Bella scoffed. "Don't exaggerate. More likely you're irked because Richard deserted you this time, instead of the other way around. Need I remind you who deserted whom in the very earliest stages of your nuptial contract?"

"Fair enough. But I have other reasons for feeling dread."

Stephen swept in, brandishing the telephone and the digital directory. He placed these at Bella's perfect fingertips. He was on the way back to the kitchen when the shar-pei loped across the dining room and nuzzled the diva's magnificent leg. Bella purred, "Stephen, will you kindly put Pansy outdoors? She is obviously in need of fresh air. Now, what were you saying, Venus?"

"It's a long story, but, to begin at the beginning—I've been assigned to the Zanzibar's nightclub arson case."

"You're being absurd again. You are not a fire inspector, so how can you investigate a fire?"

"One of the victims was Dr. Hannah Strindberg, an embryologist who was working with our agency on a sensitive research project involving the reproduction of endangered species. My chief, Oly Olson, was managing Dr. Strindberg's research. Olson thinks the fire investigators are way off base, looking for the arsonists in all the wrong places."

"How do you mean, 'arsonists,' plural? Might it not have been just one arsonist?"

"The evidence clearly indicates more than one arsonist. It's unlikely that one individual would have the time to go around and blockade all those exit doors, sabotage the sprinkler system, plant the incendiary device, and, by the way, steal three fire extinguishers from the hallway. At least two individuals were involved. Possibly more."

"Dear, you refer to an incendiary device. Why don't you just say 'Molotov cocktail' or 'bomb' and be done with it?"

"This wasn't a bomb or a Molotov cocktail. This was a naphtha cocktail."

"Whatever. I don't see how this arson business connects to your apparent physical discomfort. Something is making you jittery."

The crumpet had grown cold, its holes clogged with congealed butterfat. Venus stared down at it and wondered if this was what clogged arteries looked like. The problem with Bella was that she was one of those sterling human specimens whose offspring never could have lived up to her standards—unless, of course, they had been cloned. Maybe there was a place in the world for petri dishes, after all.

Sighing disconsolately, Bella smoothed gooseberry preserves across her toast and said, "I don't understand how all five of my children developed into such extraordinary eccentrics. Dagne, after three divorces, eloping with that oversexed steeplechase jockey was bad enough. Then Rex, such a gifted young man with so much potential, had to go and divorce that second wife, and now is frittering his life away living on a sailboat running drugs. And you, Venus, without a shred of femininity to soften your flinty edges—you really should do something about that hair, dear. Ever since you had malaria, your hair has resembled a badger's...."

A sibling's first duty is defending one another from parental censure. "I thought you liked the steeplechase jockey," Venus said.

Bella sniffed. "That was before I realized he is such a prolific baby machine."

"But, you're against Dag using the pill...."

"Of course. A Catholic does not approve of artificial measures."

"So, then, if Dag shouldn't use birth control products..."

Bella waved her hand.

Venus said, "What? You think they shouldn't have sex?"

"I will not have that subject raised at my breakfast table."

"Yes, Mother. But what's wrong with Rex's living on his sailboat?"

"It is not so much the sailboat as it is the drug running. That is what fries my sensibilities."

"Mother, Rex isn't doing anything illegal. He sells spirulina."

"An unregulated food substance. These so-called health foods ought to be better regulated. The world is poisoning itself with these herbal medicines."

Stephen swept into the dining room, poured more coffee, set the pot down on the table, and swept out. Bella waited until he was out of hearing range, then murmured, "People who live on sailboats are gypsies. I won't have a gypsy for a son."

So far, they'd covered the two older siblings. Venus, the middle child, had a built-in excuse for coming up short of Bella's expectations. At thirty-one, she still resembled an androgynous fairy, a wispy, five-foot-tall waif who had stopped growing at age twelve, who in her most psychologically formative years heard Bella refer to her in public as, "my third child, the Dickensonian anomaly." She'd never cut the mustard in Bella's genetically superior milieu. Unlike the other four siblings, Venus hadn't inherited Bella's greyhound physique and razor-sharp wit. Skipping over herself, Venus said, "What about the twins? The twins haven't disappointed you yet, have they?"

"You must be joking," sniffed Bella. "Ever since Echo had her navel pierced, I haven't been able to communicate with her. It's as if her brain was located down there where they perforated. And now Bliss has changed his name to Carlos and joined the International Workers of the World. Do you have any idea what it feels like to have given life to five oddballs?"

Venus started to answer, but Bella cut her off.

"Just look at Woofy Denson's six children. All happily married, successful family people. Not one divorce among the lot. Nothing sinister or peculiar. And no abnormals."

"Abnormals, or anomalies?"

"You heard me. Stephen, is Pansy still out sniffing the shrubs?"

"She refuses to come in," Stephen called from the foyer. "Something near the rhododendrons is attracting her."

Bella sighed. "Pansy needs a companion. You ought to consider acquiring a pet, Venus. That would settle you down."

"More coffee, Mother?"

"Thank you, dear. Why don't we go shopping for your Christmas gift this afternoon? A new Christian Lacroix might thaw your persona."

"Mother, remember the Madge Leroux crisis down in Ozone Beach?"

"Certainly. Madge was a friend. When friends are murdered, one remembers."

"Remember that I had just returned from Singapore with a horrible case of malaria?"

"How could I forget? In case you have forgotten, Venus, it was I who dashed to Oceana and rescued you from that nasty hospital ward."

"I haven't forgotten, Mother." Venus hesitated, then threw caution to the wind. "Do you recall that just before I went down to Ozone Beach to work on the Leroux case, I sent a letter off to NASA? And you and I...discussed it."

"I don't have amnesia, Venus."

"Mother, what if I told you that after three years on the waiting list, and in spite of the malaria history, I'm finally being accepted into astronaut training?"

"Stephen, the toast is cold, my love. Has the mail carrier arrived yet?"

Stephen, still lurking in the foyer, said, "Just arrived. But Pansy is holding her at bay again. Burden is out there running interference."

Bella said, "Oh dear. I better go out myself and retrieve Pansy."

"That won't be necessary," said Stephen. "Burden is coming this way now. I can see him down by the rhododendrons. He is carrying Pansy in his arms and the mail between his teeth. So we have avoided disaster."

Bella smiled. "Another close call. Bring me the mail, please, Stephen. Goodness, look at all those catalogs. And tell Burden to put Pansy in the pantry for time out. I don't understand her. Shar-peis aren't supposed to attack postal carriers. Now, what were you saying, Venus?"

"Oh, nothing important. Just that I'm going to put on a space suit and fly into outer space on the new shuttle, *Earnest*, where I will prepare for storage a virtual Noah's ark of embryonic life forms. All this is dependent, of course, on my passing muster at astronaut training school."

"Look, dear, the Chekhovs' Christmas card is panoramic this year."

"Did you say Chekhov?"

"Larry Chekhov, his wife Ilona, and their three youngsters. My, how they resemble their father. How unfortunate for them." Bella sorted through a stack of holiday greeting cards. Stephen stood beside Bella's chair, collecting the detritus.

Venus said, "You know Larry Chekhov, Mother?"

"Marginally. We served together on one or two charity boards—"

"Mother, are you by any stretch one of the Breedhaven trustees?"

"Not since last year when I cut down on my commitments. And I do not care to discuss that chapter of my life, so kindly change the subject."

"Did you know Hannah Strindberg?"

"Hardly at all. Now, I have made it clear that the subject of Breedhaven is off limits."

"So...Chekhov's married?"

"I certainly hope so. He and that darling Ilona have those children, after all. Larry claims to be the great-great-grandnephew of the writer, but I say that's rubbish. Now, who is that odd person lurking down in the rhododendrons?"

"That would be Mr. Oki," offered Stephen.

"Mr. Oki is not pink," said Bella. "This individual is pink. And Mr. Oki does not employ a handgun to trim the shrubbery."

"Mother, watch out. That man sees us."

"Of course he sees us. We are sitting in front of the window. It is getting harder and harder to enjoy one's privacy."

"Duck, Mother."

"Oh, *please,* Venus, stop all this silly paranoia...."

"I'm shoving you to the floor, Mother."

"Venus! I won't have you mauling me. Stephen, stop making that appalling noise."

"That was gunfire, madam. Are you all right?"

"Other than being thrown to the carpet by my own flesh-and-blood, yes, I am quite all right. What happened?"

"Someone shot through the window, Mother. The window-pane shattered."

"Honestly, Venus. Whenever you join me at breakfast, some-

one shoots out my picture window. And always from the rhododendrons. I find that very queer. If you are going to be chased
by gunmen all the time, don't come to my breakfast table. Now
I suppose my toast is coated with glass shards. Has he gone
away?''

Stephen, emerging from under the far end of the table, said,
"I believe the coast is clear, ma'am. May I help you out from
underneath the table?"

"Fine, Stephen. And call the police, will you?—that's a darling. Venus, where do you think you are going now?"

"To chase the man who shot at us."

"Nonsense. You'll do no such thing. That man might murder
you."

"I have my gun, Mother."

"Venus! Come back here this instant."

"I am afraid she has gone," Stephen said, and picked glass
splinters off his coat sleeve.

"Well, that's the last time I allow Venus at my breakfast
table. Do you realize that my daughter had a gun underneath all
that horrid black leather? You can't even trust your own offspring nowadays. Hand me that napkin, Stephen, darling. I believe I have taken a glass shard in the shin.''

The man with the gun had escaped through the rhododendrons, leaving no more evidence than faint footprints in the sod-
den ground, a shattered picture window, and a .44-magnum bullet plied out of the dining-table leg. Fortunately, Lloyd's of
London insured Bella's legs. She wouldn't suffer much—it was
only a nick—but the incident would set back her filming schedule by three days while Bella's priceless gam rested upon a silk
cushion, the faithful Pansy at her lithesome side. Meanwhile, the
sharded-window incident was reported to the Seattle Police Department, and an officer came out to investigate.

"When you find him," snapped Bella from her invalid's
perch, "you tell him the next time, my daughter will shoot him.
My daughter carries a gun and she knows how to fire it."

"Is that right?" said the police officer, and then he left.

NINE

ETHICS

ONE OF Olson's neighbors had loaned him a book on grieving, written by an obscure Lutheran minister. Although Olson had Lutheran roots, he was not at all religious, and hardly considered himself a spiritual person. He would be mortified if anyone caught him reading this how-to-grieve manual. So when Venus barged in, he dropped the book in his lap and looked up, annoyed. He said, "What now?"

Venus pulled a chair up close to his desk, straddled it backward, and said, "You want to open this proceeding, or should I?"

Olson closed the book on his lap and sighed. "Go."

"First of all," she said, not cheerfully, "this NASA appointment must be some sort of joke. I don't appreciate jokes about my career goals."

Olson looked surprised. "It's no joke. It's real."

She studied his face. He seemed serious. She said, "If it's a genuine appointment, then when do I start astronaut training?"

"That's between you and Captain Dillon. Dave's in charge of astronaut training. He trained Hannah; he'll train you. Talk to Dillon."

"Dillon went back to Houston yesterday, right after the reading of the will. He left before I had a chance to speak to him."

"Oh, yes, I remember. You were picking yourself up off the floor after so gracefully falling on top of Aunt Jemima and breaking her."

"And Uncle Remus. Don't forget Remus."

Olson said, "So give Dillon a ring. He's the man you need to interrogate."

Next she told Olson about the shot fired through Bella's dining-room window.

When she had finished, Olson said, "I feel sorry for Bella, I really do."

"What about me? Don't you ever feel sorry for me?"

Olson said, "I mean, I feel sorry for Bella because she has you for a daughter. Now, stop whining. The last thing you need is pity."

"Oh yeah? I can't manage to contact my husband; somebody shot at me through my mother's window; now you've got me tangled up in some ethically questionable genetics-engineering experiments—and I don't deserve even a smidgen of pity?"

"Your husband is fine. You showed me the fax from Ivory Coast, from the prime minister's office. Richard is incommunicado, somewhere in the jungle, but he's fine, the prime minister said. Stop worrying about Richard. God knows, he doesn't worry about you."

She ignored that and said, "The fax says he's okay, but I haven't heard his voice since I put him on the plane to Kadoudougou. Unless I hear his voice, how can I know he's okay?"

"Will you stop whining? It drives me up a wall. In regard to the shooting at Bella's, that might have been someone shooting at crows for all we know."

"With a .44-Magnum snub-nose?"

"Okay, it's suspicious. What do you want me to do? Assign you a bodyguard?"

"I'd like someone to watch my mother's house. Maybe I'm being paranoid, but since Bella was once a trustee at Breedhaven, I just want take every precaution."

Olson stared. "If the gunman was after you, why watch Bella's house? What about your own house?"

"That, too. I'd like agents posted at both places. Just for a few days."

Olson laughed harshly. "Sure, and how will we pay these security guards?"

Venus sighed. "I don't need a guard. Bella has a full-time security guard. But I want one of our agents watching her house, just in case the gunman goes back there. I want to catch him, and I can't depend on Bella's security guard to do our work."

"All right, but just for a day or two. I could put Louie on that watch. But I don't have two agents to spare. It's either your place or Bella's. You choose."

"Bella's," she said. "And thanks."

Olson said, "And, for your information, there's nothing ethically questionable about Hannah's work."

"Playing God with the genetic materials that create life isn't open to ethical probing?"

Olson waved a hand. "Probe all you want. Only a right-wing fundamentalist extremist would object to what Hannah was doing—work that we're going to continue, in the name of saving some very endangered species."

"Lots of people who aren't right-wing fanatics object to genetic tinkering."

"We aren't tinkering. Anyway, Dolly's been done—so have dozens of mice and God-knows-what-else. Cloning is a reality, and the technology suggests some important improvements for humankind. Genetic flaws can be corrected, for example, or entirely eliminated. Certain diseases might be completely eliminated, in fact."

"What about the inherent sanctity of life?"

"If life is inherently sacred, cloning will make life inherently disease-free."

"Maybe disease is part of nature's grand plan."

"Maybe. But you can't stop the wheels of human progress."

She stood up and leaned over his desk. "Look, I don't want to argue over this. I have some serious philosophical and ethical questions about genetic engineering, and I haven't begun to work them out in my mind—okay, and in my heart. I need to know more about these experiments at Breedhaven before I can agree to go any farther on this case."

He looked up at her. "The case is simple: Arson is murder. Fifty-three people, some thirty of whom happened to be the world's leading reproductive experts, were set on fire and burned to death by cold-blooded murderers. Where's the ethical problem?"

She held up a hand. "Okay. Right. No argument there. But when it comes to the next step, the NASA stuff, I refuse to go forward with it until I know what the ark actually contains."

"And if you object to the contents of Hannah's ark, on philosophical or ethical grounds, you would turn down the opportunity to fly on the *Earnest?*"

"I would."

Olson whistled. "I'm impressed." He put a hand on his desk, patted a stack of papers. "Here it is," he said. "The contents of Hannah's ark are listed here. Including the encoded materials but excluding the decoding formula, which is in the hands of a Breedhaven trustee."

"When do we get the decode materials?"

"We don't. The trustee has been instructed to deliver Hannah's decode materials to NASA directly. For security reasons, she didn't divulge that information to anyone else."

She scanned a sheet of paper on Olson's desk, picked it up, and began reading. "What is this, a journal of some kind?"

"Hannah's journal. She kept it at her attorney's office for safekeeping. It's a record of her experiments, including the complete list of the genetic materials she stored in the ark, the histories of all her embryological work, going back to her early captive breeding projects, and a detailed description of her latest surgical procedure."

"Which was?"

"The Borneo Bay cat. We were trying to reproduce it using a new method Hannah developed, a method that could revolutionize surrogate breeding programs."

"So there's still hope for the species? Why didn't you tell me this before?"

Olson shrugged. "It's been on my mind, but so have a million other things."

"But this means we might save the species from extinction."

Olson nodded. "If one of the four cats Hannah artificially impregnated delivers a litter, it will be purebred Borneo Bay. Yes, that would save the species. But it won't bring Hannah back." He slipped the book on grieving into a desk drawer, but she saw it, saw the title.

She wanted to shake him. "Olson, don't you see how important this is? Tell me about the cat."

Olson sighed. "It's an interesting animal, a small, elusive felid. It's considered a subspecies of Temmink's golden cat, the smaller island version. It lives—or lived—in Borneo's jungle highlands. It has been captured only twice that we know of: Once in 1992—that was a female; and then this male we just lost. Before that, the species had been described only from limited sightings and a few animal skins in museum collections. It can be ferocious."

"What did it look like? The male Borneo?"

"Very distinctive. Its coat was golden red with faint dark spots on the underside and on the limbs. It had a white stripe across its forehead and cheeks, and it had these black hairs in its ears. The underside of the tail was white, and it had a black spot on the tip, like it had been dipped in an inkwell."

"What about the other captured cat?"

"The single female Bay cat captured in 1992 died within a week of her capture. But before she died, Hannah managed to extract ova from it. She froze the material, in hopes of eventually finding a male of the species to fertilize the ova. Just after Hannah approached me with her Breedhaven proposal, she acquired the male cat. It had to be kept quiet, because it was the only known member of its species in existence."

Venus said, "You say 'acquired.' How did Hannah acquire it?"

"She bought it from a Bornean native who bought it from a hunter who had captured it. The hunter had no idea of its value, and was actually selling it for meat. The buyer recognized it as a rare species, although he certainly didn't realize how rare, and tried selling it on the black market to endangered-species collectors. Hannah got word of the cat, and rushed to Borneo. She made a deal with the owner just in time. She paid a fortune for the cat—or rather, we did."

"We financed a black-market deal?"

"We had to, otherwise we risked losing the species altogether," Olson said. "Hannah got into a bidding war with some sultan who apparently collects endangered cats. Hannah won out, and the sultan wasn't pleased. Then Hannah brought the cat back here and we kept it on the preserve."

"Where was the sultan from?"

Olson squinted. "Hell, I don't know. Some island called Lumbai or something weird like that. It doesn't matter."

"So she brought the Bay cat to Breedhaven. Toward what end?"

Olson said, "Theoretically, the female ova that Hannah had harvested and stored would be mixed with this male cat's sperm—in the lab, of course—and the resulting embryo's implanted into several female domestic cats, at least one of which would successfully deliver a litter of Borneo Bay kittens. Further reproduction efforts would include cloning experiments with genetic materials from the offspring. Should this fortunate set of circumstances prevail, the species would be saved; otherwise, the Bay cat species will be lost forever."

"Now what?" Venus asked.

"Several weeks ago, Hannah did impregnate four domestic female cats with Borneo Bay embryos she had shepherded through a petri dish. She used frozen ova from the female Borneo, and she used sperm from the male cat at Breedhaven to fertilize the ova. Hannah told me she got twelve healthy embryos, a jackpot. She impregnated the four domestic cats, and they're due to deliver anytime."

"Where are the cats now?"

Olson said, "I presume at the habitat, at Breedhaven. Hannah used four cats belonging to islanders on Helix. The owners knew about the experiments and agreed to cooperate."

"Why would she do that? Why not use laboratory cats?"

"Hannah had learned from many years of trial and error that domesticated laboratory animals often don't have the stamina to survive the complex surgical procedures or the unusual hormonal changes that we have to induce so that they can carry a different species. In order to surrogate these wild species, the domestic cats have to be hormonally altered. It's too complex to explain."

"Keep going. You're doing just fine."

"Hannah realized that many of the so-called domestic cats

living on Helix Island spend a lot of time outdoors, that in fact they are semi-wild creatures. They aren't exactly owned by people, but they've been sort of adopted, fed and cared-for. Hannah located several of these semi-domesticated cats and asked permission of the people who cared for them to recruit the cats as surrogates. She told them exactly what she was doing—that is, impregnating them with the Borneo Bay embryos and using them as surrogate...well, wombs."

"Go on. Don't stop there."

"The kittens would be nursed by the surrogates, then weaned and turned over to Breedhaven. These would, of course, be purebred Borneo Bay kittens. With any luck, most of them would survive, and we would have saved a cat species that many experts believe is already extinct. Hannah has performed this sort of surrogate reproduction with the endangered African bongo, implanting bongo embryos into elands, another, more prolific African antelope species. Those procedures actually saved the bongo from extinction. Even before she accomplished that, her surrogate program with chimpanzee embryos saved a rare subspecies. Hannah's years of diligent research offers us one last chance to save these rare animals. This is Hannah's legacy. We're going to keep it alive."

"You're wandering. Who's monitoring the pregnant cats?"

Olson sighed. "For chrissake, Hannah's assistants, of course."

"You remember yesterday at the attorney's office, Vigil mentioned that a research cat was shot and killed in a supposed attempt on Hannah's life?"

Olson nodded.

"I wonder if that was one of the four impregnated cats." she said.

Olson shook his head. "Vigil assured me it wasn't."

Venus said, "The Earnest trip, what does that involve?"

"Don't worry. We're not planning to send endangered species of any order into space. Not just yet. It's still too early. The reproductive materials we're planning to store in space are frozen DNA and embryos. We're not taking any live creatures into space."

"An embryo bank in space?"

"If you say so."

"How do we know the embryos won't suffer harm? Or the newborns?"

"Calm down."

"How can I calm down? I don't have enough information. All I know about is butterflies. My training as a biologist didn't include embryology." She was pacing now. If she kept moving that way across the rug, she'd wear a path in it.

Olson got up, went over and placed a hand on her arm. "Sit down," he ordered. "Sit." When she had settled back into her chair, Olson said, "Anyway, before you go tearing off to astronaut training school, we have to solve this arson case."

"Louie could take over the arson investigation."

"Oh, so now you're all eager and ready to go?"

"I've always wanted to be an astronaut."

Olson said, "May I remind you how you secured this NASA appointment? Without Hannah's paving the way, you'd never have been selected for the space program. Your proposed experiment on Mariposa hatching and storing the eggs in space was, if I may use Dave Dillon's description, flimsy. Granted, you and Hannah both had a vision of safekeeping animal reproductive materials in secure, gravity-free environments. But you got no further than the vision. Hannah, on the other hand, worked for twenty-five years, came up with convincing data, and earned a seat on the spaceship *Earnest*. You'll be sitting in for Hannah. You owe it to Hannah to find her killers."

She stared at Olson.

He handed her a floppy disk and said, "So, go find them."

On the way out, Venus turned to Olson and said, "By the way, I don't like how Rusty Higgins is handling this case."

"What's your beef with Higgins?"

"He's got his mind made up that this was a hate crime. He's sloppy and easily distracted. And, too, he's lazy. I don't trust his work. Other than that, nothing."

The floppy disk contained the list of genetic materials in Hannah's ark. Venus scrolled down the list:

Pentalagus furnessi (Amami Rabbit), 6 embryos.
Daubentonia madagascagiensis (Aye-Aye), 18 embryos.
Bonobo, Pan paniscus (Dwarf Chimpanzee), 4 embryos.
Neofelis nebulosa (Clouded Leopard), 4 embryos.
Felis badii (Borneo Bay Cat), 12 embryos—Note: Implanted.
Hapalemur aureus (Golden Bamboo Lemur), 4 embryos.
Hylobate shoolock (Hoolock Gibbon), 12 embryos.
Ceratotherium simun (White Rhinoceros), 0 embryos. Ova.
Kara-Tau aragali (Central Asian Sheep), 3 embryos.
Ciconia boyciana (Oriental Stork), 24 fertilized eggs.
Arctocephalus philippi (Juan Fernandez Fur Seal), 2 embryos.

The list went on. She stared at the screen until her vision blurred, then she broke for lunch.

TEN

EDNA

HELIX ISLAND IS a far cry from New Orleans, and no one knew that better than Edna Furbank. God, how she missed the sights and sounds of the Big Easy, the smell and taste of Lucky Dogs, the cloying humidity that made her feel sexually alert, the French Quarter banquettes where she had met so many interesting conventioneers from all parts of the world. Life was sweet back in New Orleans, whereas here on this godforsaken rock in the soggy hinterlands of civilization, all Edna Furbank ever felt was frigid. How had she come to this?

If Sleeper Sexton had never traveled to New Orleans for that volunteer firefighters' convention, he never would have run into Edna at the Carousel Lounge in the Monteleone Hotel, where she was riding the bar. He never would have bought Edna all those Sazeracs and then got into her capris. He would never have convinced Edna to abandon New Orleans' sultry miasmic sweetness. It wasn't love that had inspired Edna to accompany Sleeper Sexton back to the Pacific Northwest. It was desperation.

A plain girl like Edna Furbank had to make her hay while the sun shined, but Edna had let all those sunny days of youth pass by without so much as a fleeting thought to her future well-being and security. When you live in the French Quarter, with instant access to all the whiskey and drugs and bed partners you ever dreamed of, and live off the few little dollars you earn bagging groceries at Schweggman's, and wake up of a morning just as the local beat captain peels you off the banquette, well, you don't tend toward thinking too far ahead. It gives headaches.

So Edna had lost her youth and her chance at snaring an upright man who might bring home the bacon instead of other chicks. One morning, Edna woke up, looked in the mirror, and

screamed. Youth had fled, leaving Edna with no options whatsoever, unless she was willing to hitch up her hind end a time
or two more at the Carousel Bar over at the Monteleone, and
maybe—just maybe—strike a home run. Whoa, buddy, did Edna
ever strike a homer with Sleeper Sexton. Talk about luck, and
in the nick of time, too, just before the law caught up with her.

Edna Furbank stood on the stern of the *Klikitat,* waving di-
rections at vehicles boarding the ferry. This December morning,
the usual passengers loaded for the trip from Friday Harbor to
Victoria, British Columbia, with stops at Shaw, Lopez, and Helix Islands. The nine a.m. ferry had already picked up passengers
on the mainland, and a few others had boarded at Shaw and
Lopez. By the time the *Klikitat* had docked at Helix at eight-
forty a.m., twenty-three vehicles had come aboard, carrying—
according to tickets sold—thirty-eight passengers. The walk-ons
totaled five, for a total of forty-three passengers. Now at Helix
dock, Edna counted eight additional vehicles with one passenger
each and no foot traffic, for a grand total of thirty-one vehicles
and fifty-one passengers. An average winter-morning count.
Edna was unraveling the rope from the pier in preparation for
sailing when a dark blue Ford van appeared on the crest of the
hill, heading fast for the ferry dock.

Edna fumed. Laggards threw off the schedule, sometimes by
a crucial five minutes. More than once Edna had heard com-
plaints from islanders about some tourist's vehicle holding up a
boat departure, causing everyone else on board to have to wait.
Not that islanders cared so much about four or five minutes of
real time; it was the interruption of life's accustomed rhythms
that annoyed the islanders. A late ferryboat was like a hiccup in
the tides; not tragic, yet it throws off the whole rhythm.

Edna's wristwatch said 8:59:30, so technically speaking, the
blue van wasn't late if it reached the dock within thirty seconds—which it would if it kept up the pace as it flew down the
hill. Edna muttered crossly and signaled to the ferry's pilot to
wait. As the van approached, Edna noticed it had California
license plates, which didn't surprise her, honestly. Leave it to a
Californicator to hold up everyone else. Sheer arrogance.

The van slowed as it reached the boat ramp; Edna saw an

arm reach out the driver's-side window, a hand pass money to the ticket-booth operator. The exchange made, the van rolled onto the ramp. Edna waved her right arm, directing the van to the left-hand side of the boat's lower deck, directly behind Betty Thurston's VW Jetta and beside Dan Ferguson's Jeep Grand Cherokee, the laughingstock of the islands. Jeep Grand Cherokees are what the weekenders drive. A true islander, a year-round islander, wouldn't think of owning a Grand Cherokee. Talk about suburban.

Edna scooted wood tire-stays under the Ford van's two rear tires, went back to the dock, unraveled the rope again, tossed it to a fellow ferryworker and jumped back on board just as the *Klikitat* pulled away from the dock. By the time the *Klikitat*'s throaty horn signaled its entrance into the treacherous strait between Helix and Dot Islands, Edna was two decks above, in the cafeteria's coffee line. As she waited her turn at the latte machine, Edna stared out the window at the marvelous view. Even a dedicated sourpuss like Edna Furbank had to admit that this passage was a breathtaking sight in any season. That is, when the fog didn't obscure the view; but then, when the fog was too thick to see, the ferry didn't run. Today was a clear, cold winter morning. But Edna had a goose nose, and she sensed precipitation in the air. Maybe it would finally rain, and end the long drought.

Edna felt a presence, and when she turned around, she realized a man had come up behind her so silently that she hadn't noticed. He was medium height, stocky, with pale skin, thick black eyebrows, a five o'clock beard, and steely-gray eyes. He looked faintly familiar, but Edna couldn't place him right away. He wore a black watch cap pulled down over his ears, but Edna noticed a small diamond stud in one earlobe. When he saw Edna checking him out, he grinned, and if Edna had felt any sense of danger from the man, it dissolved instantly. But Edna wasn't friendly anymore, and she didn't appreciate total strangers smiling at her. Still, the man's superficial grin somehow neutralized his effect, and later Edna would wonder if that was what he had intended—to neutralize his existence in her mind, in her memory. The man reached into his pocket, maybe for his wallet. A slip of paper fell to the floor. Edna wasn't the helpful type, so she didn't lean down to pick it up for him. But she looked down at the paper, and she had twenty-twenty vision. The paper was a business card. It said, *Pro-Gen, Limited.* And something underneath, in small print she couldn't make out. He leaned over, snatched up the card and frowned at her. Edna huffed and tossed her head. His kind didn't deserve the time of day.

Edna carried her steaming latte to a table by a window, scooted onto the bench, and sipped, her back facing the aisle. God help any friend, acquaintance, or stranger who dared invade Edna's private space. Most islanders knew better; most islanders coveted their privacy as much as Edna coveted hers. But a few ignoramuses had the gall to inject cheery babble into the sacred privacy an islander needs most of the time. It happened a lot on ferry rides, which some misguided individuals considered social occasions. Far from it; ferry rides were to the islanders just like anyone else's daily commute. How would the mainlanders like it if Edna Furbank invaded their cars as they drove to work during morning rush hour along the I-5? Same difference. Ferry rides are extremely personal, a private ritual.

The stranger in the black cap bought coffee and a butterhorn, and Edna watched him disappear down the iron stairs leading to the lower decks. Probably returning to his van to eat and drink in privacy. That need for privacy didn't fit the usual profile of a Californicator up here in Paradise, thought Edna, but maybe he was different. The *Klikitat* had reached open waters in the Haro Strait. Edna leaned back and closed her eyes.

She had a bad headache and her eyes hurt. She'd been up half the night waiting for Sleeper to come home and then they'd had an awful argument. Not a lovers' quarrel—Edna and Sleeper hadn't had sex in ten months, so she wondered if they actually qualified as lovers at this point, and anyway, they'd never argued over that aspect of their relationship. They argued politics. Last night's argument had been a doozy. No wonder her temples throbbed and her head ached.

Sleeper had come home late again, the scent of merlot on his breath and his clothing reeking of fancy food and somebody's Chanel Coco. Claimed he'd been over at Breedhaven Endangered Species Habitat, commiserating with some of those snooty (Edna's opinion, not Sleeper's) trustees about that nightclub fire that had killed Dr. Hannah Strindberg. Some people deserved to burn, in Edna's opinion.

Edna didn't mind the Chanel, what bothered her was the wine breath, the food scents. How dare Sleeper eat and drink with the enemy? Edna had demanded an explanation, but all Sleeper would say was, "Never mind, Edna," and he walked away, leaving her standing there by herself.

"'Never mind, Edna'?" she had retorted. "Need I remind you that Breedhaven is at odds with everything this island stands for?"

Sleeper went into the bathroom and shut the door. Both Edna and Sleeper scrupulously honored each other's toilet privacy. Edna had no interest in seeing Sleeper on the john. But Edna seriously doubted Sleeper was tending to any real business in there; more likely avoiding her. She sat in the armchair by the kitchen door, where she had a perfect view of the hallway, and summoned all the negative energy she could muster, aimed it at the bathroom door, and waited.

Half an hour later, Sleeper came out, wrapped in a bath towel, his clothing draped smartly over one arm. He padded down the hallway to the bedroom without so much as glancing at her, and gently but firmly closed the door. Edna could take one door shut in her face, but two in a row was just too much. She sprang from her chair, hurtled down the hall, and shoved open the bedroom door. At least he hadn't locked it.

"I demand an explanation," Edna shouted at Sleeper, who by now was tucked up under the bed quilt, a copy of Walt Whitman's *Leaves of Grass* spread across his lap.

Sleeper had vowed to read all the classics before he turned sixty next year. He was through the Greeks, the Romans, Shakespeare and Marlowe, Dickens (no small accomplishment), Voltaire, Tolstoy, and Dostoevsky. He might meet his deadline.

Sleeper glanced up from *Leaves*. In a quiet, measured voice, he said, "Don't push me, Edna."

"Push you? Push you?" Edna screamed. "You mean, like this?" Edna shoved Sleeper right off the edge of the bed. In some lovers, this sort of physical contact might serve to quickly diffuse the anger and transform it into playful romping. Not so with Edna and Sleeper. Unfolding from the floor, Sleeper stood up and smoothed out his striped flannel pajamas.

"Now, cut it out, Edna," he said, and he crawled back into bed.

"You tell me what happened tonight at Breedhaven," Edna demanded.

Sleeper sighed, seeing the folly in trying to calm Edna down. Once Edna lost her temper, nothing but getting her own way would diffuse her vitriol. Still, Sleeper was a stubborn man. The argument escalated and lasted into the wee hours. Edna screamed until she was hoarse. Sleeper grew calmer and more subdued in direct proportion to Edna's escalating fury. Finally, predictably, Edna brought closure to the event by flinging the alarm clock across the bedroom. She was smart enough not to aim at Sleeper. She aimed for the window.

Bull's-eye.

Sleeper had slept in a draft until six a.m., when he got up and found Edna curled up on the living-room couch, the afghan and her winter overcoat for cover, a scowl distorting her face. He thought she was asleep, but really, Edna was awake and peeping at him through her thin eyelashes.

Sleeper had left the house without so much as an apology for his behavior. Then Edna found the note he'd left her on the kitchen table: *Edna, I won't be home for dinner.*

Recalling the bitter night, Edna fumed. Maybe there was another woman. More likely, Sleeper was embroiled in some political intrigue at Breedhaven—Edna had noticed a certain amount of comings and goings and general hubbub around Breedhaven. Maybe Sleeper knew something and he wasn't willing to share the excitement with Edna. How selfish. Edna smiled bitterly. She had one trump card, and maybe the time had come to play it. As the *Klikitat* sailed into Victoria Harbour, Edna went down to the boat's main deck and prepared to direct the unloading procedure. When the blue Ford van drove off the ferry, Edna tried to catch a glimpse of the driver through the tinted windows, but the tint was too dark and she could only make out a vague silhouette. At this point, two thoughts came simultaneously to Edna:

1) The driver of the blue van was transporting contraband.
2) The time had come to play her trump card against Sleeper Sexton.

Canadian Immigration was often slow and tedious. Accustomed to the tiresome process, the ferry crew waited patiently as the passengers debarked and new passengers cleared Canadian Customs, then rolled aboard. Directing the vehicles to their parking spots, Edna blinked rapidly when she noticed the same dark blue Ford van reboard the ferry. The guy had just debarked, for crying out loud. Why was he turning around and coming back aboard?

Edna sniffed. Some people are just plain crazy. She directed the blue van to its parking spot on the portside middeck. It was the first vehicle in that row, which meant that when the boat docked at Friday Harbor, the van would be the first to debark, the first to go through U.S. Immigration and Customs.

The other vehicles poured aboard, and Edna forgot about the van. During the long sail back to Friday Harbor, she didn't see the man in the black watch cap. He might have stayed in his vehicle. When the *Klikitat* sailed into Friday Harbor, Edna went forward to direct the debarking vehicles. The blue van rolled off the ferry, then the other vehicles, one by one passing through U.S. Immigration and Customs. When all the vehicles were off, Edna turned over her job to another ferry employee and went ashore to lunch at Friday Harbor.

She had planned to meet her friend Shannon at Hiroko's sushi bar. Edna hated sushi, but Shannon was addicted to hot ginger and wasabi, and it was Shannon's turn to choose a lunch spot. The trouble with good friends is, you have to accommodate them. Edna passed Immigration and was walking up the steep hill that led into town when the familiar blue van suddenly appeared out of nowhere and jerked to a stop beside her. The passenger door opened and someone reached out, grabbed Edna and before she could scream or protest, pulled her up inside. Edna felt something pressed against her face, then she lost consciousness.

ELEVEN

GOD'S WATCHERS
(NUNS IN SPEEDBOATS)

WHEN SLEEPER SEXTON arrived home on Thursday evening, and
noticed Edna's Saturn wasn't parked in the old barn, he naturally
assumed that Edna had gone up to the Mercy on the Rock Cloister for her weekly pinochle game. The last time he'd seen Edna
was on Wednesday morning, when she'd left for work. Edna
hadn't come home Wednesday night, and Sleeper had assumed
Edna was punishing him, and had stayed overnight with her
friend Shannon who lived on San Juan Island, at Friday Harbor.
But Edna never missed a Thursday-night pinochle game at
Mercy on the Rock, so Sleeper guessed that's where she was
now, and he guessed that she'd be home any minute.

Edna belonged to that exclusive group of islanders invited to
join Thursday-night pinochle at the cloister. Only two other islanders were ever invited to the convent, for pinochle or anything else. Morris and Teensy Fluke were the other two the nuns
deemed worthy to enter the controversial cloister.

Sleeper could care less about being invited to the nunnery.
He never had trusted Mother Beatifica. Every islander recalled
when two nicely dressed women first had visited Helix, posing
as retired widows on a real-estate hunting mission. They had
paid hard cash to the Morgan widow for her fifty-six acres ad-
joining the ferry landing on the northeast tip of Helix Island. At
the time, Sleeper had been suspicious of the two strangers and
had said so to Edna and to Morris Fluke, but Edna and Morris
had derided his suspicions, so Sleeper dropped the subject and
just kept his growing dread to himself. A month later, the
women returned swathed in religious garb, with twenty-five nuns
in tow. Mercy on the Rock Cloister was established, and the

"widows"—now known as Sister Pontifica and Mother Beatifica—immediately founded "God's Watchers."

God's Watchers—nuns in speedboats—functioned as self-appointed environmental police. Whenever God's Watchers spotted a cruise boat dumping trash overboard into the strait's pristine waters, or a tourist littering one of the island's shoreline picnic spots, or a pleasure boat dumping its sewage, the black-robed renegades would fire water cannons at the perpetrators and howl through electronic bullhorns, "Polluters to Purgatory!" Their war chant.

God's Watchers spread their message via their Internet Web site, on which they peddled environmentally correct recycled paper-pulp undergarments that the nuns manufactured at the convent. Sleeper had heard the underwear sold like hotcakes because God's Watcher's unisex "Feelgoods" not only were flushable, they came with a newsletter describing the Watchers' environmentally correct sea battles. Sleeper had seen pictures of the underwear on the Internet, but had never been curious enough to order a pair. But then Edna started wearing God's Watchers drawers, which was at about the same time they stopped having sex.

Like Sleeper, most of the islanders weren't fooled by the nuns' pious facade. They had more than prayers up their wide sleeves, and sooner or later, Sleeper fervently hoped, their true colors would show. But the sisters were clever and they eventually had won over two council members: Morris Fluke and Edna Furbank. It was just a matter of time, Sleeper believed, before the other islanders succumbed to the nuns' tactics and Beatifica and her penguins ruled Helix Island, unless Sleeper and Jean Teaweather and a few other islanders remained alert and watchful.

Sleeper ate supper alone, glad for the second quiet evening in a row without Edna barking in his face. God, life was peaceful with Edna out of the house. One good thing he could say about the nuns: They took Edna out of the house one night a week.

Sleeper built a fire with cedar logs and kindling and settled back with *Leaves of Grass*. Time passed quickly when Sleeper read the classics, and before he knew it, the fire had burned down to embers and the clock on the mantel said ten thirty-five. Edna still hadn't come home. *Pinochle must be hot tonight. Thank God for small favors.* Sleeper took a hot bath, soaking for a long time—until the heat relaxed his muscles, until he felt pleasantly drowsy, ready for bed.

Edna still hadn't come home. Sleeper reached across the bed for the telephone, paused, then decided against calling the Flukes. If Edna wanted to stay up all night playing cards with a bunch of pseudo-religious fanatics, that was Edna's business. Sleeper doused the light and fell into dreamland.

WHEN SLEEPER AWOKE Friday morning at five a.m. and turned on the light, he was annoyed to discover Edna's side of the bed was empty. Edna might have stayed overnight with Shannon a few times, but she had never before gone so far as to stay overnight at Mercy on the Rock. This was a new development. The first idea to cross Sleeper's sleep-fogged mind was that perhaps Edna had upped and joined the sisters of Mercy on the Rock.

Wishful thinking?

Next, Sleeper imagined Edna's Saturn rolled onto its side on that hairpin curve alongside Libb Lufkin's orchard. Edna, dead at the wheel. God forgive him, Sleeper actually experienced a pleasant thrill at the thought of a dead Edna.

Now Sleeper visualized Edna in the Pine Fresh Motel over on the Olympic Peninsula, in one of those dingy rooms, locked in the arms of a besotted burly stranger. Sleeper didn't admonish himself for painting this vivid tableau. After all, he'd met Edna and bedded her all within one hour at a New Orleans hotel. Edna had that capability, that looseness to her character, and Sleeper supposed some people's characters never changed.

Sleeper lay in bed and thought back to when he was a naive kid growing up on Helix Island. Back then, no more than nine or ten families lived on the rock, and Sleeper had attended the one-room schoolhouse with just three other kids. There was Sleeper, and the Dorlup boy, Jimmy, who later died in Vietnam, and the Poole boy, old Elmer's only son, Jasper. And there was Jean Teaweather. Back then Sleeper had seen a darkness in Jean's character, and he was surprised that she seemed to have matured out of it. Nowadays, Jean was such a bright, optimistic person. Come to think of it, Jean Teaweather and Edna had similarities in their characters. God help him, maybe Edna would grow out of her own darkness.

Both Sleeper and Jimmy Dorlup had volunteered for Vietnam, but Jasper Poole had fled to Canada. After Jimmy died in action, Sleeper had returned home to the sneering and derision of his own generation, the ones who didn't serve, the ones who stayed home, far from the foxholes and machine-gun fire, the death and cruelty, safe in their marijuana stupor. At the University of Washington, where Sleeper studied architecture on the G.I. Bill, he was older than the other students. After graduation, he had come back to the home he inherited from his parents on Helix Island, got a job on the mainland, and within six months, was married to Sally.

Why do good memories always fade sooner than the bad ones? Lately Sleeper had been looking back on his life, trying to put his present circumstances into perspective, and now, lying in bed alone, without Edna to distract him, he wondered if all this retrospection was a sign of growing old. Does every fifty-nine year-old think more about the past than about the future?

What future? Sleeper sighed. Not much to look forward to. More years with Edna. Then what? How had his life managed to just peter out, day by boring day, until he was left with little more than an inconsequential existence with Edna Furbank?

Just to sate his curiosity, Sleeper picked up the telephone and called Shannon in Friday Harbor. Like Edna, Shannon was an early riser. When she answered the phone, Sleeper asked Shannon about Edna.

"Why, no, Sleeper," Shannon said. "I haven't seen Edna since last week. And I'm pretty ticked-off, too. She stood me up for sushi at Hiroko's on Wednesday."

"She hasn't been staying with you?" Sleeper sat up and flicked on a light. At this time of year, darkness lingered long past daybreak. It was day, but looked like night.

Shannon said, "No, Sleeper. But I know that she's pissed off at you, so I'm not surprised she hasn't come home. Have you called down to her brother, Clyde, in New Orleans?"

"No, Shannon. No, I haven't. I'll try Clyde Furbank now."

Clyde Furbank's telephone had been disconnected. No forwarding telephone number. Sleeper tried Directory Assistance, but the operator couldn't find a Clyde Furbank anywhere near New Orleans. Probably back in prison, Sleeper reflected, for dealing drugs again.

She's at the convent, Sleeper told himself. *I just know she's at the convent.* He lay back and daydreamed some more, this time about Sally.

Sleeper and Sally had met at the Safeway in Anacortes the day he had graduated from architecture school. He'd pushed her grocery cart out to her pickup, helped her load the bags, and they'd got to talking and pretty soon Sleeper had invited Sally out to dinner. They went to the Crab Broiler in Anacortes, had clam chowder and crab legs, then saw a movie, but Sally had been struck with food poisoning halfway through the film, and Sleeper had rushed her to the emergency room where they pumped all the tainted chowder out of her. When she opened her eyes, Sleeper proposed.

They married the following week, honeymooned in Banff, then settled down on the old Sexton property on Helix, where Sally made a home and sewed quilts for a pastime, and Sleeper commuted daily to the mainland, where he worked as an architect for the town of Bellingham. They had no children, because Sally couldn't conceive, and they had decided against adopting. Still, life was sweet. Sleeper bought Sally a long-haired red dachshund they named MacGruff, and on Sleeper's fiftieth birthday, Sally had given Sleeper a beautiful handmade .38-caliber silver pistol that actually worked. Sleeper set up a target range out back of the house and practiced shooting until he got pretty good. But Sally was always a better shot, hitting the bull's-eye just about every time. And she'd had the gun with her the day she died, nine years ago last summer, but the gun never had been found.

Sally became active in island affairs, volunteered at the Helix Island Lending Library, and was secretary of the Helix Island Preservation Land Trust. Once, when old Elmer Poole had gotten a notion to turn his land into a tourist resort, it was Sally

Sexton who had talked him out of it, saving the island from the ruination of tourism. The islanders loved Sally Sexton's gentle manner, her sweet disposition, and her wry wit, and Sleeper had been immensely proud of his wife. But it had ended with the terrible freak boating accident nine years ago, just offshore of Elmer Poole's estate: Sally's little skiff had apparently capsized and Sally, a crack swimmer, had drowned.

No islander would ever forget that evening when, in a pouring rain, Elmer Poole had stood down at the ferry landing waiting for the *Nisqually* to dock. When Sleeper drove off the ferry, Elmer had motioned him over to the side of the road and told him about Sally. Sleeper had dropped to his knees on the rain-soaked ground, and it took both Elmer and Morris Fluke to get him up off the ground and out of the rain.

Sleeper became active in community affairs in Sally's memory, trained and became a firefighter, organized the island's volunteer fire department, and eventually was elected president of the island's governing council. Sleeper soon earned the respect of every islander, and was universally revered as a level-headed leader, a wise man whose word was trusted.

Then came Edna.

Sleeper looked at the clock. Six forty-five. Maybe she had finally had enough of their increasingly frequent quarrels. Since the day they met, they had quarreled. Sleeper thought it might be something in Edna's genes, a quarreling gene that caused her almost daily eruptions. Sleeper rarely raised his voice at her, but Edna screamed at the slightest provocation, and she cursed worse than a sailor. Whenever Edna let loose with her cursing, which was often nowadays, Sleeper could feel his blood pressure rise and his heart beat hard against his chest. A time or two, Sleeper had wanted to put a sock in Edna's mouth, to shut her up for good. Instead he'd taken to walking out. It was safer than staying in the presence of shrew Edna. Once or twice, Edna had lost her temper during island council meetings, and Sleeper had had to calm her down in public, a source of deep embarrassment for him. Nothing embarrassed Edna.

Sleeper remembered how brash Edna had been the night they met, at the Carousel Bar in the lobby of the Monteleone Hotel

in New Orleans' French Quarter. It had been just a year since
Sally's death, and he was attending a volunteer firefighters' sem-
inar. He was sitting at a table with three other volunteer firefighters—three fellows from Maine—and was enjoying their
company immensely when he noticed a woman staring at him
from the revolving carousel bar. Sleeper looked away, and when
next he looked up, she had disappeared. Then she came around
again, and again. Each time she appeared, she stared at Sleeper.
When their eyes met, she winked seductively, then slowly disappeared again. The fifth time she came around on the carousel,
Sleeper tried hard not to look at her because he didn't find her
at all appealing, but something compelled him to look, and when
their eyes met this time, the woman stepped off the revolving
carousel bar and walked toward the hotel lobby, turning her back
to Sleeper. One glance at her backside was all it took. Sleeper
stood up, excused himself from the table of firefighters, and
followed the woman into the hotel lobby, and that was how
Sleeper and Edna Furbank first connected.

That was—what?—eight years ago, and still Edna could do
that thing with her backside that thrilled Sleeper. Unfortunately,
Edna did little else to thrill Sleeper, though he had to admit, she
had her good qualities. Edna was kind to the elderly islanders,
she always volunteered for community service, she was a responsible if inflammatory member of the island council, she held
a good job with the Washington State Ferry System, and she
could cook. Certainly no one could ever replace Sally in
Sleeper's heart, and after Sally Sexton the other islanders had
trouble accepting Edna Furbank. It took three solid years of
proving herself before the islanders had finally accepted Edna,
and even then, some folks didn't like her.

God, those early years with Edna had been hell, Sleeper recalled, squirming in his bed at the prickly memories. "This
whole damn island is against me!" Edna would scream. "Even
you, Sleeper Sexton! All of you's against me because I wasn't
born here—because I'm smarter than all of you islanders put
together." And off she'd go.

The worst day in Sleeper's life—not counting the day Sally
drowned—was the day Edna had bought ten acres up on the

northern end of the island and then promptly sold the back five to the Sisters of Mercy for one dollar. Edna had been bragging around the island about saving up and buying the piece of land, and to win friends among the islanders she had frequently made promises of donating the land to the Helix Island Preservation Land Trust. But when the islanders didn't warm up to her, Edna turned to the sisters over at the convent. The sisters were real nice to Edna, even gave Edna free honey from their beehives and fresh cream from their dairy cow. So when Edna had saved up enough to buy the parcel of land, she bought it and sold that back five-acre lot to the Sisters of Mercy for a song. The islanders were livid. Old Elmer Poole had never forgiven Edna for selling to the nuns.

How Sleeper had endured those early years with Edna, he'd never know. Gradually, the islanders (except for Sleeper) had grown accustomed to Edna's vengeful character, and in truth Edna seemed to have softened over the years. Eventually they had accepted Edna for who she was, or at least, for who they thought she was. Sometimes Sleeper honestly wondered if he really knew the true Edna, or if Edna was hiding some aspect of herself from him. The thought came to him now, and Sleeper felt a chill on his neck as he glanced at the clock again. Seven-fifteen.

Still no Edna.

TWELVE

THE CHARTREUSE SANDAL

OLSON TURNED to face the window. Christmas Eve morning had delivered a gray pall that matched his mood, as mornings so often did lately. Hannah used to say that the gray winter days energized her, and Olson could never understand that. Hannah loved the moody Pacific Northwest weather, the dreary, drizzly afternoons when going outdoors seemed to Olson a dull, unpleasant duty. Hannah had taught him to appreciate the weather. When it rained, she'd make him put on tall rubber boots and take him for walks on the habitat, and she would show him little miracles of nature. Mushrooms growing before their eyes. Pitcher plants opening their throats to drink. Giant ferns coiling like snakes. The sighing earth beneath their feet. The way a cedar frond releases its perfume into the rain. And when he kissed her, he felt the rain on her warm lips and he would never forget how it tasted. When he closed his eyes, he could still feel the touch of Hannah's lips against his own, and the strength of her embrace. He could feel her gentle hand touching his face, and, yes, he could still recall her response to his mouth on hers.

Olson didn't hear the phone ring. Mike Maguire, the agent on phone duty, poked his head into Olson's office. Mike was a forensics rookie, wet behind the ears. "I thought you were here," Mike said. "Why aren't you answering your phone?"

Olson abandoned his reverie, mumbled, and picked up the receiver. A familiar echo made him think of deep-sea diving. He recognized the long-distance connection from Helix Island to the mainland, via a cable laid on the floor of the Strait of Juan de Fuca—a call from Breedhaven. But it wouldn't be Hannah. Gruffly he said, "Olson here."

"It's Ted Vigil, sir." Vigil sounded like he was gargling. "I'm afraid I have some very bad news."

Olson hadn't spoken to Hannah's assistant researcher since the reading of Hannah's will. "What is it?" Suddenly Olson felt tired.

"The ark..." Vigil began, then fumbled for words.

"What about it?" Impatiently.

"It's gone missing."

Olson squinted. Vigil's feigned British accent, his supercilious phrasing, and tone of voice combined to deliver this most distressing message in a disturbingly bland vehicle.

"What do you mean 'gone missing'? Speak American, for chrissake. I can't understand you."

"It has disappeared," Vigil said patiently. "When I came into the lab this morning, I found the door to the specimen storage area forced open. The freezer unit was unlocked—that is, the padlock had been sawed right through. The contents of the unit were undisturbed, except for the container holding all the specimens...."

"The ark?"

"Yes, sir. Hannah's ark. The entire ark, it's gone—" He started to repeat "gone missing," but caught himself just in time.

Olson rubbed his face. "Have you checked with the staff?"

"Yes, of course. Nobody was in here overnight except for the caretaker. He tells me nothing seemed amiss during the night. When the junior researchers came in this morning—they were ahead of me by just half an hour—they didn't come into the laboratory, but were holding a meeting in the library. They didn't notice anything unusual, but then, the junior researchers aren't allowed in the laboratories without myself or—before she died that is—Dr. Strindberg."

Vigil sounded so damned composed. Olson said, "How long ago was this?"

"I entered the lab a bit less than half an hour ago. I only just arrived, you see, because I missed the first ferry from Victoria. My home is on the Canadian side, you see. I was a good half hour behind my usual schedule. But it has been less than thirty minutes since I discovered the ark missing. I've already spoken to everyone here at Breedhaven. No one has been in the laboratory building since I locked it up last night. No one saw anything, nothing strange, nothing out of place. We haven't had any visitors, of course, since Hannah's death. Except for some islanders who came to pay their respects, but they're all quite harmless. Surely the ark didn't just disappear. Someone has broken in, sir, and stolen the ark.''

Olson rubbed his eyes. ''The material—what about the genetic material?''

''That's what worries me,'' said Vigil. ''Unless the thieves know how to care for the material, it will deteriorate rapidly. Some of these specimens are the only existing genetic material for several species. If they deteriorate, we lose the species.'' Vigil added, ''Maybe that's what they intend—to destroy our research.''

''Why the hell would anyone want to do that?'' Olson stood up, walked to the window. The window was dirty. A light rain drizzled down, streaking the dirt-filmed windowpane. He couldn't see anything beyond that.

''We do have our competitors,'' Vigil said. ''In the scientific community.''

''Maybe it was vandals. Island kids.''

Vigil said, ''Ought I to notify the sheriff, or some authority?''

''Hell no. Stay put. I'm on my way up right now.''

''All right. Meanwhile I'll have the caretaker look over the grounds again.''

''When did the last ferry leave the island?'' Olson asked.

Vigil thought a minute, then said, ''Let's see. There was the six a.m. boat to Anacortes. Then another boat arrived thirty minutes later. That was the ferry I came over on from Victoria. It left almost immediately, without taking on any passengers. There's another boat docking soon. It will board passengers and depart within half an hour.''

''You better have the sheriff check every passenger loading from Helix,'' Olson said.

''That's impossible, sir. The sheriff's office is at Friday

Harbor. The boat has already left Friday Harbor. It's too late to put a deputy aboard.''

Damn ferries. Olson said, "Then go yourself, Vigil. Watch every vehicle that goes aboard. Take license-plate numbers, vehicle descriptions.''

"Good idea." Vigil's manner brightened. "I'm on my way.''

"Vigil?''

"Yes, sir?''

"Up there.... Is it raining yet?''

"No. I'm afraid we still haven't got that rain. God knows we need it.''

Olson told Mike to pack a forensics bag. He found Venus in her cubicle, studying a book about exotic cats. When he said her name, she looked up, startled. "Gad," she said, "you shouldn't sneak up on people.''

"The ark," Olson said.

"What about it?''

"Stolen.''

Venus stared. "The embryos?''

"All of it. Without temperature controls, none of the materials will survive more than a few hours. The samples could decompose. We can't just re-create rare genetic material. We can't replicate this stuff. We've got to locate the ark.''

She stood up. "Then let's go.''

OLSON SET the Bell Jet Ranger down in a pasture behind Mercy on the Rock Cloister. In a barn on the edge of the pasture, a black-robed sister sat on a three-legged stool, milking the nunnery's cow. The noise from the chopper's whirring blades startled the cow, who kicked her rear leg, knocking over the milk bucket. Sister said, "Shit.''

When the blades wound down, Olson took off his earphones and said to Venus, "Now I'm going to show you something.''

As they trudged across the meadow, Venus noticed they were being chased by a nun wielding a stick, who was being chased by a black-and-white heifer that thought it was a bull. Venus thought the nun was cursing but that might have been her imagination. Then the cow caught up to the nun and they tussled in the pasture and forgot about the interlopers. All this activity barely registered in Venus's brain because other, more pressing concerns demanded her attention. She spotted Ted Vigil, Hannah Strindberg's associate, standing on the roadside, opposite the convent, watching the three DOI agents approach. Vigil waved, a stiff, short-lived gesture.

Vigil's Volvo sped south on the island's main road. Venus sat beside him in the passenger seat, Mike Maguire and Olson in the rear seat. Olson leaned forward to hear what Vigil was saying in his tight, stingy voice. Recounting his discovery, Vigil explained that he'd missed the morning ferryboat from Victoria (where he lived) because he'd forgotten something back home, and halfway to the ferry, he remembered it and turned around and drove back home. What he'd forgotten was a silly bureaucratic document, nothing of great importance, but he'd gone back for it anyway. Now he wished he'd just continued on to the ferry. Maybe if he had caught that first boat to Helix Island he could have prevented the theft. He was certain the theft had occurred shortly before he arrived at the lab at Breedhaven, he said, because the lab's freezer door, the one that had been broken into, had a timer on it that started counting whenever the door was opened, and it had ticked off twenty-six minutes when he made the discovery. If Vigil hadn't missed the first ferry, he'd have arrived at Breedhaven a full hour earlier, and thus could have prevented the theft.

Venus watched the island scenery roll by, dense sylvan landscapes interspersed with neat little pastures, meticulously maintained farmhouses, and the occasional million-dollar estate, and these, too, were tidy. Even the shoreline was spick-and-span, too steep to form beaches that accumulate the ocean's detritus. Everything was in its proper place, so unlike nature's usual chaos; here was Nature at its most obsessive.

At the entrance to Breedhaven, Vigil got out and did something to the gate. Venus counted Vigil taking ten steps to the gate, eleven steps back to the car. Olson, oblivious to her counting, leaned forward and said, ''You are now on the threshold of Paradise.''

Paradise spanned four hundred acres of softly rolling meadows, thick evergreen forests, tranquil wetlands, and steep salt-water shoreline. As they drove through the verdant landscape, Vigil, too calm for Venus's tastes, pointed out salient features. "Over here," he said, gesturing toward the left side of the Volvo, "are the wetlands. That shrubby hardhack is a native plant, perfect for nesting yellowthroats. We've completely restored the marsh and have stocked it with endangered marine and avian species. There in the red alder? That's a pileated woodpecker. Natives call it the Rain Bird."

"How are the domestic cats doing, Vigil?" Olson asked.

Vigil seemed to miss Olson's question. He said, "These pastures over here are planted in African field grass. We want our white rhino and our big African antelope to feel right at home. We also keep a pair of bongos, and over there in the forest"— he pointed across Venus—"some Japanese deer. They don't seem in the mood for company just now, but maybe you'll get lucky and spy them on the way out. Now, the smaller cats, you'll never see them. They're very shy, elusive creatures."

Olson, in the backseat, repeated his question. "The four surrogate cats, the ones carrying the Borneo litters, Vigil—how are they faring?"

Vigil coughed lightly. "That's the one other bit of bad news I have to report. It seems that the caretaker accidentally took them off the habitat and released them."

Venus and Olson exchanged a glance before Olson erupted.

"What!" Olson shouted. "What are you talking about? Why would he do that?"

Vigil said quietly, "We used local island cats for the procedure. Gordon, our caretaker, didn't realize they were carrying special litters. He recognized them as just some island felines. So he drove them off the habitat and let them loose. He was only trying to do his job. We try to keep the exotic species and research animals separated from domestics, as you know. We searched everywhere, but couldn't find them. We contacted their owners, but so far nobody has seen the cats."

Olson groaned, "This can't be true."

"I'm afraid it is. And, of course, we all realize the consequences of this careless act. If we don't find them, and the litters are lost, we've lost the Bay cat species." Vigil clucked his tongue. "If only Hannah hadn't taken that male Bay cat to the club with her."

"But why did she do that?" Olson almost screamed.

"As you knew, certainly," said Vigil, "Hannah frequently brought the servals along with her to public events. She thought it helped to educate people about these exotic species. But lately the servals have matured too much to allow them to interact with strangers. Hannah told me that she planned to take the Bay to the event, instead of the servals, to show it off. You see, several of the scientists attending the congress were, you might say, fans of Hannah's work, and offered her a great deal of collegial support. The Borneo Bay was of particular interest to them, as it was so rare. Naturally Hannah thought the gathering would be a nice opportunity to reward her colleagues for their faith in her work."

Venus said, "You're certain she took the Bay cat to the club that night? Maybe she took it somewhere else. Maybe the cage was empty."

Vigil shook his head. "She told me explicitly that she planned to take the Borneo Bay to that event."

Olson buried his head in his hands. "I don't believe this is happening."

But apparently it was, and now Olson knew that, in spite of Hannah's futuristic vision, in spite of his agency's support, in spite of their joint dedication and painstaking research, somehow things had gone very wrong.

Vigil said, "The worst of it is that Hannah used up our supply of Borneo Bay ova in this last procedure, so that was our last chance to replicate purebred Bays. It was extremely irresponsible on Dr. Strindberg's part, taking that rare cat out in public."

FURIOUS, DISCONSOLATE, Olson remained in the lodge, unwilling, or too emotionally crippled, to help search the grounds. While Maguire went to work collecting fingerprints and other potential evidence, Breedhaven's careless caretaker, Gordon Mantle, showed Venus around. As Gordon unlocked the front door to Hannah's cottage, an orange tabby met them inside. The tabby was obviously pregnant.

"This wasn't one of the four cats?" Venus asked.

"Oh, no," Gordon said. "This was Dr. Strindberg's own pet. No, she would never use Purim for an experiment."

"But she's obviously expecting a litter."

Gordon nodded. "It was a domestic male. I saw them."

Gordon said that Purim had been left in his care whenever Dr. Strindberg had traveled. Now he had adopted Purim, he said, though he allowed the cat to stay in Hannah's cottage.

"If you don't mind," said Venus, "I'd like to take Purim back with us."

Gordon stared. "Why would you want Dr. Strindberg's cat?"

"I'd like to keep her under observation until she drops her litter."

"Well, I don't know," Gordon said, and hesitated. "I suppose if you think it's okay to move her ..."

"Don't worry about Purim. I promise we'll take good care of her."

"But what about the kittens?"

Venus smiled. "We'll take good care of them, too. Very good care."

The air inside the cottage felt cold and damp. "She always turned the heat down when she traveled," Gordon said. "And she put the cats over at the main lodge."

"Cats? Her own? You mean there's more than this one tabby?"

"The two servals. Exotic cats Dr. Strindberg's trying to breed. They aren't old enough yet to be let out on the preserve. Dr. Vigil, he tried to care for the servals after Dr. Strindberg died. But Homer—that's the male serval—he doesn't like Dr. Vigil and so I have to feed them, because otherwise Homer attacks Dr. Vigil. And, too," Gordon said, "she kept the little Bay cat indoors, until...well, until..."

"The servals—where are they now?"

"In Dr. Strindberg's office. She kept them with her when she worked. Now I let them stay there; it's like home for them. She used to bring the servals and that Bay cat back home to the cottage at night. But I couldn't bring the servals back here, with Purim in here expecting a litter.''

The cottage was clean, airy, everything neatly in its place. Venus said, "Did Dr. Strindberg employ a housekeeper?"

Gordon shook his head. "She cleaned her own house. She told me one time that she liked doing housework. Said she got her best ideas dusting."

"How about visitors?"

"She didn't have many visitors," Gordon answered. "Kind of a recluse. She spent most of her time over in the lab facility, or out on the grounds with the species."

" 'The species'?"

"That's what I call 'em," Gordon said. "The wildlife out here. I can't remember all their names. Mostly wildcats, and deer species, but we've got a white rhino from Africa, and a couple of what's called bongos. Some pretty rare exotic birds, too. And a type of goose." Gordon shook his head. "This cold dry spell can't be good for them. Dr. Strindberg had special heaters installed in the outbuildings, so the species can go to their feed shelters and have a warm spot. But them that's roaming out on the preserve, I don't know what they do in this cold. I put out fresh water every two hours. Otherwise the poor critters would dehydrate."

Hannah's bedroom closet contained shelves neatly stacked with heavy sweaters and outdoor gear. On simple wire hangers hung several lab coats, a few sensible skirts and pairs of trousers, shirts, and a couple jackets. The single nod to femininity was a midnight blue lace evening dress, floor-length, carefully hung on a satin hanger. Her shoes, mostly plain Aerosole flats, size nine, were neatly lined up on a shelf. On the closet floor were two shoeboxes. Inside one was a pair of black satin ballet slippers, size nine. Inside the second box was one chartreuse patent-leather sandal, barely worn, maybe from another lifetime. Size nine and a half. Venus studied it, then held it up to Gordon.

"Ever see her wear this?"

Gordon shook his head. "Not around here. Not suited to the terrain, let alone the culture."

"You don't have any idea where the other sandal is, do you?"

Gordon blushed; what a question to ask a man. "Naw."

Venus pulled a plastic bag from her pocket, opened it, and dropped in the chartreuse sandal. She didn't tell Gordon that on the inside of the sandal a name and address had been carefully inscribed in permanent ink, and it wasn't Hannah Strindberg's. The name was Martine Olaffson's. The address was Stockholm, Sweden.

A cedar chest of drawers held socks and lingerie; all cotton and wool, nondescript. Hannah hadn't been a seductress. Still, Olson had been attracted to her, and maybe some other men, too. Had Vigil been sexually attracted to Hannah Strindberg? As if reading her mind, Gordon said, "She was a handsome woman, and she was smart, too. The men all liked her. I could see why."

Gordon put Purim in the kitchen, gave her food and fresh water, and locked up the cottage. They walked back toward the main lodge and the parking lot, where a black Humvee was parked in a spot marked, "Caretaker."

"What about Vigil?" Venus asked. "Was he romantically interested in Hannah?"

Gordon's eyes flickered. "I guess he would have jumped at the chance to have something going with her. But Dr. Strindberg didn't care much for Dr. Vigil. She didn't take her meals with him, and in the year that I've worked here, I never saw Dr. Strindberg invite Dr. Vigil to her cottage. That says a lot to me. They weren't fast friends, that's for sure. Not like her and that Mr. Chekhov; now, they were pals."

"Larry Chekhov?"

Gordon scratched his head. "'Way I understand, Mr. Chekhov's one of the habitat's trustees. He's a Russki, but he lives here in America. He and Dr. Strindberg got along real nice. I've seen him put an arm around her a time or two, not meaning to spy, but just noticing. And, too, Mr. Chekhov visited Dr. Strindberg here at her cottage. Came for dinner once or twice. Then there was the Lufkin boy. Luther Lufkin. That's Libb Lufkin's son. They live down the road not far from here. Luther idolized Dr. Strindberg. He wants to be an animal breeder like her when he grows up. Luther came and went around here pretty regular-like. He's just a boy."

Combing the habitat, Gordon at the wheel of the Humvee and Venus beside him, they stopped on the eastern side, in hilly grass country. Gordon gave Venus a pair of binoculars, and she held them up to her eyes and scanned the grasslands. Where the edge of the meadows met woodlands, she saw the pair of bongos and three impalas—two adults and one fawn.

"Look there," Gordon said, and pointed to the top of a hill.

Venus looked through the binoculars and saw the white rhino standing on the hilltop, silhouetted against the blue sky. The rhino was a bull adult, gray in color, and had one very large horn. It was grazing, using its wide lip to gather grass.

Gordon said, "Dr. Strindberg told me that it's called a white rhino even though it's gray."

The species *Ceratotherium simum,* the northern white rhinoceros, was named after the Dutch word for wide, describing the rhino's wide, square-shaped grazing lip. The word eventually was anglicized, to *white. Rhinoceros* literally means, "hornnosed." The African white rhino grows up to six feet tall, and can weigh as much as eight thousand pounds. Rhinos are nearsighted, and can see clearly only up to about thirty feet. Because of the set-back placement of their eyes, rhinos turn their heads from side to side in order to see straight ahead. Their acute hearing and sense of smell compensate for their poor eyesight. A rhino can pinpoint the exact origin of a sound, charge, and hit its target dead-on.

Rhinos are solitary herbivores. They love mud-wallowing, which helps clean the ticks off. Poachers kill rhinos for their horns, which are used in Asian black-market medicines. Powdered rhino horn was the original Viagra. In the Middle East, a dagger with a rhino-horn handle is as macho as the American gun rack.

Gordon drove south of the meadow to a deep marshland. "The rhino comes here to wallow," he said. "And those birds?" He pointed into the marshes. "Helmeted hornbills— from Borneo. Hornbills are prized for the 'casque' on their beaks," said Gordon, proud of his wildlife knowledge. "That casque is carved like ivory, and it brings more than twice what ivory's worth on the Asian black market. That's what Dr. Strindberg told me.''

The west side of the habitat was all forest. As they followed a narrow path through the ancient firs, Gordon said, "Don't worry about those cats, miss."

She looked at him. "The ones carrying the Bay litters?"

Gordon nodded. "I'm pretty sure we'll find them. I've already notified their owners to watch out in case they return home,''

"That's good, Gordon.''

"Don't you worry about a thing," he repeated.

The forest ended abruptly at a rocky bluff. Gordon stopped the Humvee. They got out and walked onto the rock ledge. Directly below them, about thirty feet, was the saltwater strait and a narrow wood dock. A small outboard cruiser was tied up to the dock. "This was Elmer Poole's dock," Gordon explained. "He used to go fishing off this dock. And when he wanted to boat over to the other islands, he'd go from here. That's his old cruiser, too. He left it to Breedhaven. Not much of a boat, though. I'd be afraid to ride in it—afraid it'd sink.''

She said, "Is this where Elmer Poole found the skeleton of San Juan Man?''

Gordon grinned. "You got that right.''

AFTER AN HOUR of scouting, Gordon said, "We can't cover it all today. You come back here another time, I'll show you around the rest.''

"Is there any place to hide out here?''

Gordon looked at her. "What do you mean by 'hide'?''

Venus said, "Could someone hide out on the habitat, without being discovered?''

"You mean, like a hermit or a homeless person, something like that?''

She said yes, that's what she meant.

Gordon shrugged. "Well, I suppose so, if he wanted to. There are a couple old cabins on the western side, in the forest. And there are the outbuildings where we provide shelter for the species. So, yeah, I guess if you really wanted to escape from the world, this would be an excellent spot.''

"Gordon?"

"Yes, miss?"

"Why did you let the cats go?"

Gordon hung his head. "I'm awfully sorry about that. It was an accident. See, they kept the four of them in a pen behind the lab building. I went back there and saw them in the pen, and I thought since they were domestic-like cats, that they had sneaked onto the habitat through the woods. We don't want to take chances mixing species, so I rounded them up, put them in the Humvee, and drove them up the main road to the center of the island. See, I didn't know which cat belonged to which owner, but I figured they'd all find their way home. Cats are smart."

"But none of the owners have found their cats?"

Gordon shrugged. "It was just this morning that I let them go."

"You'll keep checking with the owners, won't you?" More a command than a question.

Gordon nodded. "Like I said, we'll find 'em."

After Gordon parked the Humvee, Venus went to the laboratory building and poked her head inside the front door, which led to a wide hallway. The building was huge, with several rooms opening into this central corridor. If she hadn't known where she was, she would have thought it was a hospital for humans. Through a window in a corridor, she saw Vigil inside a laboratory, apparently tending to an experiment in progress. A little farther down the hall, in a small office just off the entrance hall, she found Rosemary Poole. Rosemary was very curt, very cool. While Venus looked around, Rosemary followed close behind, narrating like a tour guide.

"Here is where we gather and test DNA material.... This room is where we perform artificial-insemination procedures.... This next operating room is for birthing when there is a problem with one of the larger pregnant animals.... This next room," she said, leading Venus into a small, refrigerated space, "is where we kept Hannah's ark. That's what everyone around here called it. This is the room that was broken into, as you can see."

The door had been forced open. Inside the small space were

several small freezer and refrigerator units. Only one freezer's lock had been tampered with, and Rosemary said, "That was where we kept the ark. No one had keys to the lock except Hannah—Dr. Strindberg—and Gordon, the caretaker, in case of an emergency. Of course. Gordon is entirely trustworthy."

There was nothing else to see, so Venus moved on to the other rooms. There were three holding pens with restraining devices, where sick animals were kept. In one holding pen, an ailing tapir lay on its side, its eyes rheumy, its mood laconic. Rosemary said the tapir had a bacterial infection but was expected to recover.

There were two classrooms for instructing doctoral candidates, as well as administrative offices, small laboratories jammed with computer systems and other scientific equipment, and the scientists' offices. A small room adjacent to Dr. Strindberg's private office held various medical instruments and laboratory vials. Venus held up a vial and said, "What are these scratch marks?"

"Hannah's very primitive security system. She marked every vial each time it was used."

"Mind if I borrow a few of these empty vials? For evidence?"

"Whatever." As Venus gathered up vials, Rosemary added, "A shame about that male Borneo Bay, isn't it?"

"You're sure she had it with her at the nightclub?"

"Absolutely." Rosemary brushed hair out of her face. "I saw Hannah load the cat into her car out here in the parking lot when she left for the conference. Yes, she definitely took it with her."

"You couldn't possibly be mistaken? Could Dr. Strindberg have loaded another cat into her car? Maybe a domestic cat?"

Rosemary considered. "I suppose so. But I'm almost positive she took the Borneo Bay male with her. I didn't exactly get a close-up look, but I saw her put a cat into a crate, and it looked to me like the Bay cat."

"How far away from her were you when you saw this?"

"Hannah was in the parking lot, right outside here, loading up her car. I happened to see her loading the crate when I looked out this window. Just twenty or thirty feet, maybe a little more."

Rosemary seemed to defrost slightly when they entered Hannah's private office, a sleek, mahogany-paneled room with a wall of glass doors facing a tranquil forest scene. She said, "Often while Hannah was working in here, she would keep the Bay cat and the two serval kittens in here with her. The Bay had to be kept in a cage, of course, but the servals were raised by Hannah, and quite tame. They love to play on this wool carpet, and when one of the red deer wanders up to the window to peek in, the servals scream at it."

"Where are they now?"

"The servals?" said Rosemary. "Oh, I have to keep them in the bathroom when I can't babysit them. Do you want to see them?"

They were the size of large housecats, their short glossy fur the color of tigereyes, spotted black. They were rambunctious, very affectionate and playful. Venus held the male, Homer. When she stroked his head, Homer purred. Rosemary scooped up the female and nuzzled her.

"This is Ardith," she said. "We named her after one of the habitat's trustees."

Venus said, "The four domestic cats carrying the Borneo Bay litters—where did you keep them before the caretaker accidentally let them loose?"

Rosemary took a brief mental holiday, her eyes scanning the middle horizon. She set the female, Ardith, on the carpet. She scampered to join her sibling. Rosemary said, "Didn't... Didn't Ted tell you?"

Venus set Homer down; the serval scampered over to Hannah's desk and climbed into her chair. Venus said, "No."

Rosemary put a hand to her mouth. "Then maybe you'd better ask him. I'm not sure if I'm supposed to talk about it."

"The litters belong to our agency," Venus said. "You can tell me where you were keeping the cats."

Rosemary smiled weakly. "We had them locked up in a pen just outside this window, right out here. And the pen was clearly marked that they were research animals."

"You're kidding."

Rosemary said, "I wish I were. It's very embarrassing, actually. I shouldn't be telling you this. Dr. Vigil should be the one to tell you.''

''How could the caretaker have made such a serious mistake?''

''Maybe he just got distracted. You see, we have so much to track these days, with Hannah gone... I really hate to get anyone in trouble.'' Rosemary bowed her head. ''Poor Gordon. He didn't understand that those cats were part of an experiment. He thought they were just local strays, when actually we had borrowed the cats from people here on the island. Oh, God, I shouldn't be telling you this, it's so mortifying.''

Venus said, ''I want a list of the cats' owners before we leave here today. I want you to contact these owners every hour and ask if the cats have returned. I want you to find those cats. Do you understand?''

''Oh, we have been looking for them.'' Defensive.

''I want you to *find* them.''

Rosemary said, ''I'll tell Ted—Dr. Vigil. We'll find the cats. It's just that we've been so busy. I mean, since Hannah's death.... We've all been so distracted.''

They had finished touring the laboratory building and were walking to the lodge when Gordon approached them. ''Purim's got away,'' he said, ''She ran into the habitat, and I can't find her.''

Rosemary stared at Gordon. ''You let her out? How could you let her out?''

''I didn't let her out,'' Gordon shouted. ''She must have slipped out when I was locking up the cottage. Don't worry, she'll come back. She does this all the time.''

Rosemary hurried off toward Hannah's cottage. Gordon started to follow her, but before he got away, Venus stopped him.

''When you find Purim,'' she said, ''you'll let us know, won't you?''

''Oh, yes ma'am.'' Gordon loped off.

Mike Maguire came out of the main lodge. ''This crime scene is pristine,'' he said. ''Whoever stole the ark pulled off a clean job. There's not a shred of evidence to be found.''

"We'll see," said Venus.

Rosemary Poole delivered the list of names of the four cats' owners: Sleeper Sexton, Luther Lufkin, Mr. and Mrs. Morris Fluke, Jean Teaweather. Venus borrowed the Humvee, and Rosemary, and went to call on the neighbors.

Sleeper Sexton wasn't home. The Sexton house was silent, no signs of humans or cats.

Rosemary said, "Mr. Sexton works on the mainland. He usually comes home on the six-thirty ferry. Maybe we should leave him a note. His was the marmalade cat. He named her Dundee."

Venus wrote Sexton a note, left it on the door.

Morris and Teensy Fluke were having a late lunch and watching a game show on television. They offered Venus and Rosemary a cup of tea, and while they sipped the tea, Teensy said, "Our little Pearl hasn't come home. Since Gordon called a little while ago, Morris has driven all over the island looking for her, but so far we haven't seen her."

Morris added, "She'll come home. Pearl knows who her family is. She'll come home. Siamese are very bright." Venus left her phone number, and the Flukes promised to call as soon as Pearl showed up.

The Lufkins' house fronted on the north-south island road. Set down in a valley, the property had been carved out of the forest, leaving most of the older trees standing. One huge cedar stump remained where a logger had abruptly ended its two-hundred-year-old life. On top of the cedar stump, an old rowboat lay upside down, dry-docked. The Lufkins weren't home, and there were no signs of a cat near their house. Venus left a note.

At the little post office/grocery store just next to the ferry dock, Jean Teaweather was selling some stamps to an elderly couple when Venus and Rosemary walked in. Jean looked up, recognized Rosemary, and said, "She hasn't come home yet. I sure hope you folks haven't lost my Abby." Abby was Jean Teaweather's Abyssinian. Mrs. Teaweather promised to call Venus as soon as Abby came home.

Still with no sign of Purim, Gordon drove Olson, Mike, and Venus to the helicopter. When they arrived at the grassy field behind the Mercy on the Rock cloister, a nun came out of the barn and shook a pitchfork at them. A gaggle of geese circled the nun, honking.

When the helicopter lifted off, the nun screamed, "Polluters to Purgatory!" But nobody heard her in the din of chopper blades.

THIRTEEN

DNA

VENUS FOUND the former Zanzibar's waiter resting in bed in a dingy apartment complex in West Seattle. The waiter, a slightly built Hispanic recently renamed Gina, was halfway through a sex-change process, still struggling with her identity.

Gina had come late to work; she had come upon the blaze and tried to beat out the flames on the Skagit totem pole at the club's entrance. Suffering from residual nightmares and a painful hand burn, Gina nevertheless thought she could now talk about the fire without breaking down. But she remembered little beyond the sound of the victims' screams.

"Try to recall your surroundings," Venus urged Gina. "Can you remember what was going on around you when you encountered the blaze?"

"Nothing," said Gina, struggling with her memory. "Except the burning totem. I'll never forget that sight."

Venus said, "Call me if you remember anything. Anything at all."

Tearfully Gina promised to do so.

RUSTY HIGGINS HAD left his office on the early side, so Venus walked to the rear of the Seattle Fire Department and knocked on a door marked, *Assistant Forensics Inspector.*

Venus heard a woman's voice say, "Come in."

The assistant forensics inspector was Mary Lou Mullins. Venus asked Mullins about the Zanzibar's inspection. Mullins peered over the top of her drugstore reading glasses and said, "What inspection?"

"The one your department conducted on the day of the fire. To check out the club's new sprinkler system."

Mullins smiled. "I don't think I understand you, Agent Diamond. What makes you think we inspected that new system the day of the fire?"

Venus recounted her several conversations with Rusty Higgins, and his corroboration of a news report that inspectors had visited Zanzibar's to certify the club's new sprinkler system on the same day the fire broke out.

Mullins listened, shaking her head the whole time. When Venus had finished, she said, "That news report was erroneous. I have asked Rusty to correct that in the press, but apparently he has been too busy. The point is, our department never conducted an inspection of the club's new sprinkler system. I wish Rusty would be more careful about details."

"You're sure?"

"Absolutely." Mullins removed the reading glasses. "Look, Agent Diamond, if this department had conducted an inspection of that nightclub, I would have been there. So I guess I'd know about it."

"In your experience, what sort of group would use this particular method to commit arson?" Venus asked.

Mullins tilted her head and said, "You know, I've been going over and over my files, looking for a similar case, anything involving the use of naphtha and remote-control detonators. I haven't found anything even vaguely like this—that is, in our country."

Venus nodded grimly.

Mullins said, "But if pressed for a comparison, I could suggest one rather far-fetched possibility—I mean, very far-fetched."

"Go ahead, please."

"At the risk of sounding extremely foolish," said Mullins, "I found several similarities between the methods used by the Zanzibar's arsonists and...well—the Russian Mob."

"Is that so?" Venus leaned forward, fascinated. "What similarities?"

"You aren't laughing at me?" Mullins said. "You don't think I'm nuts?"

"Not at all. Please, what did you find?"

"The detonation device was manufactured in Eastern Europe, back in the days of the Soviet Bloc. That's the first similarity."

"What else?"

"The use of naphtha. This is a little-used but well-known tactic of the Russian Mob. I can show you the files, if you like."

Venus said, "I'd like that, Inspector Mullins. But just now, I'll take your word. Anything else?"

"The naphtha had apparently been applied to the carpet and walls; sprayed on at the corners and along the baseboards—that's another Eastern European mob tactic. That's it. That's all I have to offer. Thanks for not laughing at me."

Venus left in a hurry, and when she had gone, Inspector Mullins shut her eyes and seethed. Out loud, she said, "Damn Rusty Higgins."

ACROSS TOWN, at Ace Extermination Company, Venus found the manager and asked to see the company's files. A thorough inspection revealed there had been no visit to Zanzibar's on the day of the fire. "Can you be absolutely certain," Venus asked the company manager, "that none of your technicians visited Zanzibar's that day?"

Ace's manager nodded gravely. "Yes indeed. Absolutely certain."

AXEL GORNALL, the honorary Swedish consul, had lost his patience with the Seattle Fire Department, the Seattle Police Department, the FBI, and everybody else. He was shouting into the telephone at Rusty Higgins. The Swedish consulate's windows afforded a pleasant view of Lake Washington's eastern shores, and if Axel craned his neck, he could see north across the lake as far as Bill Gates's compound. Just now, the consul wasn't interested in craning his flushed neck for anyone. He was listening to Rusty Higgins's monotonous apologies and useless excuses, and the consul was fuming mad.

"We are doing our very best, Consul Gornall," Higgins was saying for the umpteenth time. "Don't worry, we will find them and we'll arrest them."

"Do you know what I think, Higgins?" Gornall's face was

now as flushed as his neck. "I think that you and your colleagues are a bunch of nincompoops."

"But, Consul, this is a very complex case, and as you know, we have a limited staff and budget—"

"It's a clear-cut case of international terrorism," Gornall shouted into the phone. "I don't want to hear any more about your limited budgets and limited staff. I am tired of reminding you, Mr. Higgins, that this is more than a case of arson. This is *murder* we are concerned with here. Sweden has lost two of its most brilliant scientists, and I am interested not in excuses, but in discovering who committed this heinous act of terrorism."

"But, sir—"

"Don't 'but, sir' me, Mr. Higgins. I won't have it. I want to know who murdered my Swedish scientists. You had better have an answer for me very soon, or else I will bring in my own investigators, and I don't care what your government says about it. Do you understand me, Mr. Higgins?"

"As I was saying, sir—"

"Oh, shut up." Gornall slammed the phone receiver down and made fists with his hands. His blood pressure had risen, and he could feel his breathing coming faster and his heart beating too rapidly for a man of seventy eight. He reached into his coat pocket and fished out a little vial of nitroglycerine tablets, popped two tablets under his tongue, and tried to calm down. Someone knocked on the door; Gornall glanced up and yelled, "Go away. I can't be bothered now."

Gornall's secretary, a meek young man who was quite accustomed to the consul's mercurial behavior, tactfully opened the door an inch, and in a soft voice said, "You have a visitor, Consul. An American federal agent."

"I don't want to meet anybody," snapped Gornall. "Least of all, an American federal agent. Tell him to go away."

"It's a she, sir. And she is rather adamant."

"Did you hear me, Fuss?" Gornall shouted. "I can't be bothered now."

"Yes sir," said Fuss, and the door shut quietly.

Fuss turned to Venus and said, "I am afraid the consul is not up to company this morning. It's this arson business, you understand. We have lost our country's two greatest geneticists. And on his watch." Fuss bowed his head sadly.

Venus was carrying an opaque plastic bag. She tucked it under her arm and said, "That's what I want to see the consul about." She explained the connection between her agency and Breedhaven. "Breedhaven's director, Dr. Hannah Strindberg, was one of the Zanzibar's victims. My agency suspects one of your scientists may also have been the arsonists' target."

Fuss looked dubious. "I see. But I simply cannot bother Consul Gornall while he's in one of his tempers. He has a heart condition, you understand. Perhaps you could come back later?"

Venus said, "I'm not leaving."

Fuss frowned. "Pardon?"

"Tell the consul that I'm waiting out here to see him, and that I won't leave until he agrees to see me."

"Oh, but that would excite him, you see. And his heart can't take any more excitement just now."

She went over to a blond leather couch, sat, folded her arms, and smiled at Fuss.

Fuss stammered, "I am very sorry, but..."

Venus glanced at her Swatch. High noon. She'd give the consul ten minutes, and then she'd barge in on him.

Fuss pleaded with her, but soon realized she was as stubborn as Consul Gornall. He approached the consul's office door, hesitated, then knocked lightly.

From inside came a low voice. "What is it now?"

"Excuse me, sir, but the agent insists on seeing you." Anticipating, Fuss covered his ears.

Gornall exploded. A stream of Swedish expletives poured into the reception room.

Venus stood up, went over to the door, jerked a thumb at Fuss. Fuss stepped aside and she walked into Gornall's office.

Gornall's eyes bulged. "How dare you invade my office?"

When she showed him her badge, he swept it aside. "I don't care about badges and agencies and all that. Now go away."

"If you'll give me five minutes," she said, "I promise to go away after that."

Weary, ill, and too tired to argue anymore, Gornall groaned,

"Oh, all right. Just get on with it, then." He buried his head in his hands and moaned softly.

"Do you have any reason to believe that your scientists, Per Svenson and Martine Olaffson, might have been targets of the arsonists?" Venus asked.

Gornall's pulse gradually slowed. His blood pressure had gone down and he felt a little better. He said, "They were all potential targets. All the scientists could have been targets— individually, or as a group."

"What is your opinion, Consul?"

Gornall frowned. "That terrorists did this."

"The fire inspector's case centers around a different theory."

Gornall flicked his hand. "I know, I know. They want to believe that this was a Mafia job, or that, in any case, it was somehow related to the ownership of the nightclub. But I do not accept that theory."

"If terrorists were involved, where did they come from?"

Gornall said, "Arabs. Frankly, I think it was Arabs."

"And the motive?"

"Obvious," Gornall said. "To set back the advances of the international scientific community. And they succeeded, too."

Venus said, "I could understand your theory if the victims had been nuclear scientists. But why would Arab terrorists want to murder a group of reproductive biologists and cloning experts?"

Gornall shook his head. "That is a question I cannot answer. Why do crazy people do crazy things?" Rhetorically.

"I have been to see the consulates of all the victims who died in the fire," Venus said. "You might be interested in hearing what I've learned so far."

"Not particularly," muttered Gornall.

"The New Zealand consulate," continued Venus, ignoring Gornall's rudeness, "has already sent in an investigator who is taking the same position as the Seattle Fire Department. Norway's and France's investigators are conducting separate independent investigations, both aimed at the international-terrorist theory. As for the American victims, their corporate employers have jointly hired a private investigation firm that is pursuing the terrorist angle. That makes one official investigation, and four unofficial ones. But the several dozen private eyes running around looking for answers are all expected to cooperate with the Seattle Fire Department. Then there's my agency. We have official permission to investigate the arson, but even in our case the Seattle Fire Department is ultimately in charge of the overall investigation, and we're required to answer to them.''

"Rusty Higgins," Gornall uttered scornfully. "Incompetent ass.''

"Higgins is the official in charge, whether we like it or not. Now, I need to know two things, Consul. The first is whether or not Sweden plans to send in its own investigators.''

Gornall glanced up. His eyes were bloodshot. He said, "We're going in with Norway. I've just spoken with Consul Thornquist. Norway and Sweden are cooperating in an investigation. What is your second question?''

Venus said, "Had Svenson or Olaffson been threatened?''

Gornall shook his head. "We haven't heard of any threats against Svenson or Olaffson, although Olaffson was controversial in her personal life. But I doubt that had anything to do with it.''

"How was Dr. Olaffson's personal life controversial?''

Gornall pressed his lips together. Grimly, he said, "Dr. Olaffson had a son who last year was convicted of murder.''

"And that reflected badly on Dr. Olaffson?''

Gornall said, "Huh, you bet—because Petre Olaffson murdered a member of Swedish Parliament. You bet it reflected badly on his mother.''

"Why did he do that?''

Gornall shrugged tiredly. "Petre Olaffson is a common thug. It was a simple robbery. Nothing political.''

Venus thought that over, then said, "Were Martine Olaffson and Per Svenson working on anything particularly controversial?''

Gornall laughed. "If you consider cloning human beings controversial; it certainly seems to enrage some people. The idea of creating exact copies of humans in a little dish has its detractors, yes.''

"So Svenson and Olaffson were involved in experiments with human DNA?"

Gornall nodded.

"That's very interesting."

"Why is it interesting? Most of the victims of the fire were working with human DNA."

"Actually," said Venus, "they all were, with one exception. The American scientist, Dr. Strindberg, was working with animal DNA. Her experiments were primarily with apes and exotic antelopes. And cats."

Gornall made a face. "A zoologist? Then why was she at that conference in the first place?"

"Dr. Strindberg wasn't a zoologist. She was a renowned embryologist. Dr. Strindberg held a medical degree in gynecology, a Ph.D. in embryology, and was nearing completion of a major experiment. Dr. Strindberg worked with animals because of a dedication to preserving endangered species."

Gornall said, "Well, now, there's someone with some brains. We sure don't need any more humans."

"My boss at Fish and Wildlife, Oly Olson, was working closely with Dr. Strindberg in this research," Venus said. "From what little Agent Olson has told me about her experiments, it appears that Dr. Strindberg had developed radical procedures for implanting exotic-species embryos into surrogate mothers. An experiment of this nature had entered a crucial stage when Dr. Strindberg died in the fire at Zanzibar's."

Gornall said, "Your five minutes are nearly up. Please get to the point."

"Yesterday, less than two weeks after the fire, Dr. Strindberg's collection of endangered species DNA and embryos was stolen from her laboratory at Breedhaven Habitat, up in the San Juan Islands. The collection still hasn't been recovered. The collection is known in embryology circles as 'Hannah's ark.' The ark contained frozen embryos and DNA samples from several hundred endangered species that Dr. Strindberg hoped eventually to save from extinction. My agency suspects that the theft of Dr. Strindberg's ark may be related to the arson fire."

Now Gornall seemed mildly interested. "Give me a reason to believe you," he said.

"The ark contained the most valuable collection of endangered-species DNA in existence. Some of the species are already listed as extinct, but Dr. Strindberg had managed to collect and freeze DNA from these species before they completely disappeared. The collection is priceless. Apparently some of her admirers also wanted to get their hands on her research materials. Their motives could be professional jealousy, or material profit."

Gornall squinted. "What in God's name does this have to do with my Swedish scientists' dying in a nightclub fire?" he whispered.

Venus scratched her forehead. Her Third Eye itched. "While going through Dr. Strindberg's personal belongings," she said, "I found a green—actually, chartreuse—sandal."

Venus opened the plastic bag and produced the sandal. Gornall stared at it.

Venus said, "If you'll look closely, Consul, you will see a name and address written with a marker pen on the inside of the sandal." She handed the sandal to Gornall.

Gornall held the sandal up to the window light, peered over his eyeglasses, and read out loud, "'Martine Olaffson, Narvavagen 23, 116 22 Stockholm.'"

Gornall looked at Venus. "Yes," he said, "this is her address."

Venus fished another object out of the bag, a small, round glass vial with a white label, and handed it to Gornall. Gornall held this also up to the light and squinted at the label.

"'Number 225. Galapagos, 1999. M. Olaffson.'"

Gornall gently set the vial on his desk, folded his hands, and became lost in thought. After a while, he peered over his eyeglasses and said, "Anything else in that bag?"

Venus removed the last object from the bag, another vial, slightly larger than the first, labeled in blue. She handed it to Gornall.

"Number 356. Kenya, 1998. M. Olaffson. Pro-Gen, Ltd."

Gornall set this vial beside the other on his desk. "What is 'Pro-Gen'?"

"I was hoping you could tell me."

Gornall looked at his desk and said, "These vials are empty."

"Now they are."

"But not always?" Gornall asked.

"They used to contain DNA samples from endangered species, before Dr. Strindberg used the samples in her research. These vials, along with dozens more, were stored in Dr. Strindberg's laboratory. They have been cleaned and sterilized, but each vial has a number on it, and the number corresponds to a record Dr. Strindberg kept on a disk file. Number 356 contained bongo sperm; number 225 contained Galapagos red-spotted frog sperm; and so forth."

Gornall held his head as if it were about to explode.

Venus said, "According to my boss, Agent Olson, these samples were obtained by Martine Olaffson for Dr. Strindberg while Olaffson was on research trips. The effort to reproduce endangered species is, of course, of great scientific interest to all embryologists, whether they are trying to clone humans or animals. Apparently, Dr. Strindberg's research had attracted the attention and cooperation of her colleagues around the world, scientists from several countries who—informally, at least—cooperated with her research by contributing specimens whenever they could—including Dr. Olaffson. I went through the records of empty vials in Dr. Strindberg's lab. There were dozens, as I said before, and Dr. Strindberg herself collected most of them. But at least a dozen vials came to Dr. Strindberg from Martine Olaffson. Maybe it's just coincidence that both scientists died in the fire, but I think not. I think they were both targets."

"What makes you think this isn't just coincidence?"

Venus said, "The theft of the ark."

Gornall's eyes brightened. "Ah, yes, the theft of this 'Hannah's ark.'"

Venus waited for him to say something else. Gornall chewed on his cheek and stared at the chartreuse sandal and the two glass vials on his desk. Then he carefully handed them back to

Venus. She placed them back in the bag. Gornall pointed at the door.

She said, "I'd like permission to examine Dr. Olaffson's research materials."

"Why?" Gornall stood up, ushered her to the door, opened it.

Venus said, "I think the arsonists who set the nightclub fire were somehow connected to Martine Olaffson. I think Martine Olaffson possessed some valuable information that they didn't want her to reveal."

"Like what?" Gornall held the door open. Venus stood her ground.

"Maybe some exciting new research findings. Or, maybe she caught someone doing something unethical."

Gornall goosed her over the threshold. "Get out," he said, seething. "You are as crazy as the rest of them." Gornall slammed the door, locked it.

Venus found Fuss at a computer screen. She asked, "Have you heard of an outfit called Pro-Gen?"

Fuss turned to look at her. "Pro-Gen?"

She nodded.

He thought it over. Finally he said, "No. Never heard of it. What do they make?"

She said, "I don't know. Maybe cats"—and left.

Back at the Bumbershoot Building, she rode the elevator up to her office. She went into her little cubicle, turned on the computer, logged on to the Internet. She spent two hours chasing after Pro-Gen leads and came up with nothing more titillating than a vitamin supplement for aging boomers. She tried calling Richard, but the international operator said the line to Kadoudougou was busy. Someone else was on the phone. Bummer. She counted thirty-eight steps from her cubicle to the coffee cart.

AT FIVE O'CLOCK she was sitting at her cubicle in the Bumbershoot, reading an Internet site devoted to genetics-engineering corporations, when Gina, the waiter, called.

"I've thought of something, Agent Diamond. But it might just be my imagination."

"Go ahead."

"That night, when I parked my car in the lot outside the club," Gina said, "there was a woman entering the building. She was carrying a crate—like the kind they keep pets in? From my car, I saw her enter the building. She went in just ahead of me."

"What else? Can you recall anything else?"

"Yes." Tentatively. "But I'm not sure if this is a false memory."

"What is it?"

"There was a van parked across the street from the club—I don't remember what make or anything, but I seem to recall it was black, or dark blue."

Disappointed, Venus said, "We took that information from another eyewitness immediately after the fire."

"Oh. I didn't know. Well, I guess that's all."

"You know how to reach me if you think of anything else," Venus said.

She was about to hang up when Gina said, "If this seems paranoid, stop me—I think someone's trying to kill me."

"How so?" Venus thought Gina sounded paranoid.

"I know this sounds totally like my own insecurity, but I've been noticing some strange men hanging around the apartment complex. Rough-looking guys. Just since the fire. This morning, my neighbor discovered a little bonfire on my front porch. She put it out. It wasn't very big, but someone had put a pile of sticks and crumpled paper there and lit a match. I think it might be these same men."

"When did you last see them?"

"They're out there now. Usually I have someone here with me and I don't feel so insecure. But tonight I'm alone, and, well, I just have the feeling they're watching my place. See, they drive a dark blue van. That's what reminded me of the van at the nightclub. I'd be mortified if this is just my own paranoia."

"Why would someone be gunning for you, Gina?"

"Maybe because I saw the man who drove the van. And I recognized him, too. I mean, I don't know his name, but I've seen his picture in the newspapers a few times. I think he's Russian, or Ukrainian, or something East European."

Venus reached for her gun, holstered it. "Lock your door. Stay down low," she said. "I'm on my way."

OLSON HAD GONE HOME with a headache. Venus pulled Louie Song off watch at Bella's house, and from the office, drafted Mike Maguire and Eric Sweetwater. The four agents beat a path across the West Seattle Bridge and arrived at the dingy complex in record time. Lucky, too, because the gunmen were already kicking down Gina's front door.

Venus ran behind the complex, broke a window in Gina's bedroom, opened the window, climbed inside. Song, weapon drawn, went in behind the three gunmen, and when one of them turned and fired at Song, Sweetwater put two bullets in his chest. That left two inside Gina's apartment. From the bedroom, where Gina lay in her bed paralyzed with fear, Venus heard the gun battle in the living room. She grabbed Gina by the arm and dragged her out the window and across the parking lot into a wooded area. In a few minutes the gunfire stopped, and through the sudden silence Venus heard Gina's sobs beside her, and then saw Song and Sweetwater come outside and wave the all-clear sign. Then Maguire appeared, and Venus sighed in relief.

They found the dark blue van in the parking lot. Inside, they found enough arms and ammunition to supply a small army. They found communications devices, and they found a bomb detonator. The thing that most interested Venus, though, was the English-Russian language grammar, bookmarked at "Important Shopping Phrases."

The three corpses carried no personal identification. There wasn't much to go on, but one look at their dental work was enough to tell Venus they weren't Americans.

FOURTEEN

MIDNIGHT MASS

DR. RAYMOND WONG celebrated Christmas more enthusiastically than most Zen Buddhists. The holiday's spiritual aspect appealed to Ray Wong's sense of serene simplicity, particularly the aspect of the peasant virgin giving birth to the Universal Savior. The concept of virgin birth struck Dr. Wong as supremely elegant, uncomplicated, and without either the burdensome accoutrement of passion or the cold sterility of petri dishes.

Sex was untidy, and petri dishes lacked soul. If Ray Wong were the Creator, his chosen way of reproducing all species, including humans, would be a similar method, Nature sans sex. No spawning salmon, no promiscuous lizards, no messy bridal beds. No bland petri-dish habitats. Just a responsible nuptial contract, and *presto!*—a baby. What could be more Zenlike? Of course, such a major change in the natural order would require Divine Intervention. And this was the reason and purpose behind Ray Wong's honoring the non-Buddhist holiday. Maybe if he prayed to the Christian God, He or She would hear his humble petition and remodel Nature's reproductive processes.

Dr. Wong's office door wore a fresh green cedar Christmas wreath tied with a crimson satin bow, the festive article partially obscuring the sign that hung there, but Venus had it memorized: *When you lose your Song, call Doctor Wong.*

The same tiny Asian woman offered to take Venus's leather jacket but Venus declined, feeling a need for the extra layer of protection, as if an additional pelt could conceal her tormented soul from the doctor's piercing intuition. The woman vanished. Venus stood in the chilly anteroom, rubbed her hands, and blew into them. The eerily Arctic temperatures had persisted, now plunging into the mid-twenties. Rain froze, forming slick black ice on the city's steep streets; hoarfrost coated the naked trees, tricking the budding camellia sesanqua into shock. Global warming at its quirkiest.

On the wall of Dr. Wong's anteroom hung a portrait of a woman. She was not beautiful in the conventional sense, but a mysterious light emanated from her flesh. She was seated at a table, and on the table was a washbasin. The woman held a length of white cloth and appeared to be in the process of bathing herself. She looked up and out at the viewer, as if caught in the act. Her expression seemed to mock the viewer, because even while she stared outward, her vision focused inward at a sight she apparently found eminently more appealing. On the lower edge of the frame, an engraved brass label gave the painting's title, *Virgin Reflecting*. The picture must have revealed something about Dr. Wong, about his tastes and sensibilities, but Venus didn't dwell on this for long because the little woman came back and waggled a finger at her, beckoning.

Dr. Wong folded his hands into a church with people inside, leaned his chin on the roof, and listened to Venus describe the recent events that had transformed her life. Richard's hasty journey to Ivory Coast. The Zanzibar's fire, and Hannah Strindberg's death. NASA's invitation to join the *Earnest* crew. The stolen ark. The elusive pregnant cats. Concluding her report, Venus said, "So now the excitement has returned, along with considerable frustration, of course, but once again, my life is full. The SAD's gone."

Wong gazed at her, a penetrating stare that made her nose itch. After a while he said softly, "So...have you found your soul?"

She shifted uncomfortably. "That's not funny."

"It is not supposed to be funny. I have asked you a serious question."

Venus leaned forward. "Maybe I should explain. Last week, before I went back to work, I learned that my husband was going away on business for a few months. At the time, I was still under the influence of SAD, and I thought that this situation might meet your condition..."

"My insistence that before I treat you, you move out of your husband's house?"

"Right. I figured that since Richard would be gone, you would accept our separation as equal to my having moved out—and then I made another appointment with you, but..."

Wong waved his hand. She didn't need to elaborate.

She continued. "But then as soon as I got back to work, I began feeling better. The depression hasn't bothered me since things started popping. I'm over my SAD, or whatever it was. So I don't need therapy. I kept this appointment today because it was too late to cancel when I realized I don't need your help."

"And you believe," said Wong, "that this...remission of your former condition is a result of your returning to work?"

"That's right." She shifted around under his gaze.

Dr. Wong said, "You do not think, for example, that this lifting of the depression may be related to the physical separation from your husband? Abstinence, for example, from sexual relations?"

"Please, Doctor, I really just came by to tell you that I'm feeling much better and that I don't need your services. As I said, it was too late to cancel my appointment, so I came to tell you in person. Of course, I'll gladly pay for this visit."

Dr. Wong smiled. "Ah. So you have located your soul."

From the anteroom came the little Asian woman's voice. The woman was singing softly, in Japanese.

Dr. Wong said, "Well?"

"Well, what?" She looked at him. He was handsome—gorgeous, in fact. If she weren't a married woman... Now, where did that thought come from?

"You haven't answered my question."

She stood up. "I don't have time for introspection; not anymore. And you know what? I think introspection is overrated. Just forge ahead, get on with life, that's my philosophy." She strode confidently to the door.

"I am sorry to hear that," said Dr. Wong, bowing his head. "I was rather looking forward to working with you."

"That's very kind of you to say, but..."

He raised a hand, stopping her. "Not kindness; the truth. I

was hoping to help you find what exists beneath all your suffocating layers of trivia.''

She opened the door. "Thanks for your time," she quipped coolly, and went out. Behind her, Wong smiled blandly.

"No charge for today," he called out to her.

She turned around. "Gee, thanks."

"Don't mention it," Dr. Wong said pleasantly.

She was closing the outer door, entering the chilly hallway, when she glanced up and noticed mistletoe hanging over the doorway. She mumbled, "Merry Christmas, Dr. Wong"; then her digital phone rang. It was Olson.

Olson said, "How's Gina?"

"Rattled. Staying with her mother in Oregon."

"Any breaks yet?"

She shook her head, as if he could see her. "Nothing."

Olson said, "I got the Russian Mafia list from Interpol. We're checking the three gunmen's identities against it. Like you said, they're probably just nameless paid assassins."

"I want to talk to Chekhov," Venus said.

"Not until we've more to go on."

"Like what? Another naphtha fire?"

"We have to be careful. Chekhov's powerful in this town. Anyway, he was Hannah's friend. You shouldn't jump to conclusions."

She was spinning a snide retort, when a gloved hand gripping a gun appeared around the stair banister. She heard the gun go off, but by then she'd already thrown herself backward into the doctor's office—technically speaking, straight into the doctor's arms. It didn't feel bad.

The Asian woman crept up behind Dr. Wong and said, "Are you okay?"

Venus dropped the phone, pulled out her gun, and ran down the stairwell, but the assailant was gone by the time she reached the street.

Wong came up behind her in the street. "Any luck?"

"No, he got away—or she did."

Wong shook his head and strolled away.

She called out to him, "Hey, Doc!"

Wong turned, looked at her.

She said, "I know a great feng shui consultant."

"RICHARD? Is that you?" Venus sat on her bed, the telephone pressed to her face. A small boy sat beside her. He had café au lait skin and straight, chocolate-brown hair. He was Asian, about ten years old, though no one knew his exact age. He was petite, bright, precocious, and, lately, not so trustworthy. He was Venus's stepbrother, Timmy, an orphan Bella had adopted in one of her magnificent gestures. Lady Bella Winsome-Diamond might be rich and famous, and somewhat psychically repressed, but she had a compassionate heart, though she usually kept it under wraps. British prerogative.

Bella had gone out for the evening, to one of her galas, and Venus was babysitting Timmy at the Taj Mahal on Alki Point. At the foot of the big bed, a flat-screen television hung on the wall, the sound turned down low. Timmy was watching *Return to the Planet of the Apes* for the fifteenth time, and shoving popcorn into his little mouth, making noise when he chewed. Venus made a motion at him and he stopped chewing. Once again Venus said, "Richard? Are you there?"

The sounds coming across the telephone line reminded her of a recording of whale songs she'd heard once. She pressed some buttons on the phone, tried calling Richard's hotel again, and again heard only the whales. She tried twice more, then Timmy said, "He's probably out fighting fires."

"Sure," she said. "I'll bet."

Timmy turned his head and looked at her. She looked worried. Timmy said, "He's okay. Just because he hasn't called doesn't mean he's in trouble."

She said, "He might be okay, but I'm not."

Timmy crunched more popcorn. "Depressed again?"

She stared at him. "Who says I was depressed?"

Timmy shrugged.

"Come on, Tim, who told you that?"

Timmy put a finger to his lips. She started tickling him. He rolled over, spilled the popcorn everywhere. He laughed wildly and pleaded for her to stop.

"Then talk," she said.

"Okay, okay," cried Timmy. "It was Mother."

"Bella?" She let Timmy go. "Bella said I was depressed?"

Timmy scooped up the spilled popcorn. "She said that ever since you got married you've been acting weird. Like, depressed."

"That's funny. The mater never mentioned anything about it to me."

Timmy said, "Mother doesn't want you to know that she's worried about you. She says it's not in her character to show her feelings."

"Then why did she tell you?" Venus narrowed her eyes. "Did you make this all up?"

Timmy waved a little hand. "Hey, no way. I don't lie anymore, remember? It's true, Mother's very worried about you. So is everyone. Dagne told me she's worried, and Rex says you've gone to the dogs. Even Echo and Bliss—I mean, Carlos—have remarked about how you've gone downhill."

"'Gone downhill'?" She was almost screaming. "What's that supposed to mean? And why is everybody talking about me behind my back?"

"Hey, it's how family stuff goes," said pragmatic Tim. "Calm down. All Mother said is she wishes you would get some help."

"What kind of help?"

Timmy shrugged and reached for the channel changer. "I don't know. Maybe she wants you to see a shrink. Like she made me see that lady psychiatrist. God, I hate psychiatrists."

"They're not all bad, Tim. Some psychiatrists actually save lives."

"She was one of the bad ones."

"Why do you say that?"

"Because she made me take my pants down and then she fondled my private parts," Timmy said matter-of-factly.

Venus stared. "Are you kidding?"

Timmy tossed popcorn into his mouth. "Yup."

"That wasn't funny," she said. "You shouldn't talk like that."

Timmy was watching a commercial for panty liners. With the channel changer, he pointed at the television screen. "You wanna hear dirty talk?" he said. "Listen to them talk. Now, can I have some more popcorn?"

"You pop it. I'm going to try reaching Richard again."

She pressed buttons on the telephone.

At the door, Timmy turned around and said, "This is one hell of a Christmas Eve, huh?"

TIMMY INSISTED on attending midnight Mass at St. James Cathedral. She bundled him up and drove downtown through a gentle snowfall. At the cathedral, amid the standing-room-only crowd, Timmy magically produced two tickets to the reserved section, where they could actually see the altar and, if they turned around, the choir loft. As they settled in the pew, she leaned down and whispered, "Where did you score these excellent seats?"

Timmy grinned. "Mother gave me her tickets."

"I should have known."

"And now she owes me fifty dollars."

"What for?"

"Mother said she'd give me fifty bucks if I could manage to drag you to church."

"Congratulations. I get half."

"Hey, hear that? It's the silver trumpets."

As a trumpet chorus was announcing the gospel, a man entered the church from a side door. Venus noticed him because the door was only a few yards from where she stood in the pew. He wore dark sunglasses, a black trenchcoat cinched at the waist, a wool cap pulled down over his forehead, and black leather gloves. He walked to the center aisle, turned, and walked toward her. He kept glancing up at the choir loft. She looked over her shoulder at the choir loft, saw a line of silver trumpets; then she saw a woman wearing a black trenchcoat appear between the trumpeters. She had a gun and she was aiming it at Venus.

Venus grabbed Timmy, shoved him down onto the kneeler and crouched on top of him, then she felt an obscenely phallic object—metal—poke her in the side, then heard a low voice with a thick accent say, "Come with me, or the boy dies."

She leaned down, told Timmy to stay put, and accompanied the man to the rear of the cathedral where a lifesize Nativity scene reposed among cheery poinsettias. The man kept the gun pressed into the small of her back until they reached the double doors. An oblivious usher opened the doors for them and they passed into the snow-covered street, now deserted. He gripped her arm, walking fast. The frigid air hung still and heavy, and above the cathedral a waxing moon shone silver beams over the church spires and cast grotesque shadows on the snow. In the distance, Venus heard the silver trumpets playing "Hark! the Herald Angels Sing." When they reached the corner, he placed the gun at the back of her head. She let out a kung fu cry, distracting him for a split-second, reached behind her back, grabbed his arm, bent over, swung around, and flipped him to the ground. His head struck the pavement with a dull crack. He lost his grip on the gun and it flew through the air, landing yards distant in a snowdrift.

From the cathedral, the choir's angelic voices rode the fresh night air as the man raised his hands in surrender. She shoved her boot underneath his chin and pulled her own gun from its holster. The man lay panting on the ground, but he was smiling, unafraid, only temporarily foiled.

At the cathedral doors, Timmy stood framed in lamplight, watching. He called to her. She yelled for him to go inside and get help, and he instantly disappeared. She kept her attention focused on her captive, while an usher came out of the church, mulled over the scene, then ran back inside. A few minutes later, a police squad car screamed up the hill and screeched to a stop in front of the cathedral.

During the hubbub, no one noticed the inebriated young man who happened to stagger upon the pistol lying on the snow, pick it up, and weave off into the darkness. He'd scored a piece, and to hell with the trouble down by the cathedral.

The man on the ground gave his name as Sergei Petrovich; his identification, a Russian passport. In a convincing Russian accent, he told the officers he was a mere tourist. He'd been walking to the cathedral to attend midnight Christmas Mass, when this woman had assaulted him, pulled a gun, and thrown him to the ground claiming she was a federal agent or some such nonsense. It must be a case of mistaken identity. Timmy tried to defend her, but in the end, the officers let the man calling himself Petrovich go. "We have nothing to charge him with," explained an officer. "Unless you produce the elusive weapon."

She tried explaining about the woman in the choir loft, but no such individual could be flushed out either in or around the cathedral. Petrovich grinned triumphantly, walked across the street into the cathedral, and disappeared among the worshipers.

She stood outside, listening to the silver trumpets, and wondering what Richard was doing. When the service ended, she watched for Petrovich and the woman as the cathedral emptied, but apparently they had left by the side door. "Anyway," Timmy declared, "Russians don't celebrate Christmas when we do."

She and Timmy were walking down the steps when she saw Ray Wong leaving the cathedral. Passing her, Wong smiled and tipped his hat. She said, "Merry Christmas, Doctor Wong."

Timmy said, "Is that your shrink?"

Ignoring Timmy, Venus said, "I've seen that Russian before."

Timmy said, "Where? In some nightmare?"

"No, really. I've seen him before. Only, then he didn't have the scruffy chin."

"Who is he?"

Venus took Timmy's hand. "Come on," she said. "We need to make a phone call."

BACK AT THE Alki pad, Venus located the phone number she wanted through Information. When a woman's voice answered, Venus said, "Good evening, this is Rosemary Poole speaking. Is your husband home?"

"He is not at home," the woman's voice answered frostily. "Should I take a message?"

"Tell him he can run but he can't hide. And, Merry Christmas, Mrs. Chekhov."

She hung up. Timmy stared at her in respectful awe.

FIFTEEN

FLOATING

THAT CHRISTMAS EVE, a heavy snow fell over Helix Island, blanketing the landscape, purifying and softening the contours of the rugged cliffs, and driving farm animals into their barns. Even the native deer took cover in among the thickets. At Breedhaven, on Christmas morning, Gordon Mantle worried over the survival abilities of the exotic species.

AT MERCY on the Rock Cloister, Sister Pontifica pulled her snow boots on and trudged out through the snowdrifts to the old barn. Milk cows don't take snow breaks.

Pontifica tromped into the barn and hollered, "All right, Maybelle, let's have some ice cream."

MORRIS FLUKE woke his wife, Teensy, pointed out the bedroom window, and said, "Just look at that purty white stuff." Teensy sat up in bed and shrieked delightedly, "Oh, Morris, the drought's over." Morris grunted and allowed that as beautiful a sight as it was, a little snow didn't mean the drought was over.

Just as quick as Morris said that, Teensy thought of something else. "Oh, Morris, poor Pearl is out there in that weather. Oh, Morris." And Teensy began sobbing. Morris said, "Don't worry, pumpkin, I'll go out and find her." He got dressed, pulled on a pair of knee-high rubber boots and trudged into the woods behind the house.

WHEN SLEEPER SEXTON'S phone rang, Sleeper lurched out of fitful dreams. The caller identified herself as Doris somebody—Sleeper didn't catch the last name, barely caught the first. "I am

Edna Furbank's supervisor," said Doris. "I need to speak to Edna."

Sleeper said Edna wasn't at home just now, and offered to take a message.

"Tell Edna to call me right away," said Doris sharply. "I need to know if she's planning on coming to work this morning. She's an hour late. Already the first boat had to leave without her. We had to call in a substitute at the last minute, and even then, the first boat out was short one crew member. Maybe it's the snow, but she could have at least phoned in. She agreed to take Christmas Day."

"I'll tell Edna to call you," said Sleeper. "Just as soon as she comes home."

"And tell her she better have a darn good reason for walking off the job halfway through her shift last Wednesday. That sort of irresponsibility won't be tolerated in a Washington State Ferry System employee. We have a long waiting list of job applicants for plum positions like what Edna has, in case she needs reminding."

Sleeper sat up straight. "You mean, Edna didn't show up for work on Wednesday?"

"She worked the first morning boat. But when the *Klikitat* made its noon stop at Friday Harbor, she got off. It was her lunch break, but she never came back on the job. She was supposed to be back at work today." Doris paused, then added, "Are you her life partner?"

Sleeper said he was, and asked Doris to call him back if she heard from Edna. "I'm afraid something might have happened to her," he said.

"Why do you think that?"

"Because Edna didn't come home Wednesday night. I haven't seen her, or even heard from her since early Wednesday morning."

"Uh-oh," said Doris warily. "I'm staying out of this. Just have her call me once you two get things worked out."

Sleeper said, "It's not what you think..." then realized suddenly that it might be exactly what Doris was thinking. Edna might have left Sleeper once and for all. Sleeper experienced that shameful thrill that comes with tragically realized personal freedom.

"Good riddance," he said out loud after hanging up with Doris, but as soon as the words escaped his lips, Sleeper regretted them, for he was basically a kindhearted man with a weakness for the Ednas of the world.

Sleeper drew back the curtain and peered out the window at the swirling snowflakes and the white landscape. Not his favorite kind of weather, but he couldn't deny the beauty of freshfallen snow. He showered and dressed and then called over to Mercy on the Rock cloister. Sister Ramona answered. No, the nuns hadn't seen Edna. She didn't show up for Friday night's pinochle game, only the Flukes, and they said they didn't know where Edna was. Sister Ramona said she hadn't seen Edna for over a week—except, now that she recalled, she had seen Edna last Wednesday morning at the ferry landing. The cloister dining room offered an unobstructed view of the ferry landing, Sister Ramona explained, and she had been looking out the window and saw Edna loading vehicles onto the Wednesday-morning ferry. First boat of the day. It might have been the *Klikitat*. But as far as seeing Edna since then, no. Sister Ramona wanted to know if Sleeper and Edna had had another one of their quarrels. Edna's loud mouth.

Sleeper growled, "That's private, Sister. Call me if you hear from Edna, will you?"

Sister Ramona said she'd do that.

Sleeper then called Jean Teaweather at the little post office/grocery store near the ferry landing. Even on Christmas Day, Jean had to open up for emergency grocery runs. After they talked about the snow, Sleeper said, "Merry Christmas, Jean."

"Oh, same to you, Sleeper," said Jean. "George is cooking the bird this year, so I'll just kick back and pig out. How about you?"

Sleeper said, "Kinda quiet. Say, Jean, has Edna been by this morning?"

"No, I haven't seen Edna since, let's see…last Wednesday morning," said Mrs. Teaweather. "She came in here to buy her gum and mail a letter. To Congressman Butler. I happened to notice the address when I was sorting the mail. Then she bought her Dentyne chewing gum, like she does every morning, and went to work. Come to think of it, that's the last time I saw Edna. I know she has Thursdays and Fridays off, and today, being Christmas... Strange, now that you ask about her, I usually see Edna getting off the *Nisqually* at the three-thirty p.m. landing. Isn't that when her shift ends?''

Sleeper said yes, it was.

''Well, I don't recall seeing her after Wednesday morning.''

''Is Edna's car parked in the usual spot, Jean?''

''Yes. To be honest, I was wondering why she didn't drive it home, and I've been annoyed with it sitting out there taking up space night and day. I thought maybe it wouldn't start up and she just got a ride home.''

''Would you mind checking the car? See if it's unlocked, or anything's, you know, wrong with it?''

''Just a minute. Let me go check.''

Jean Teaweather went to check in the parking lot.

Sleeper caught a glimpse of himself in a window reflection. He looked haggard, drawn, not at all healthy. He brushed his hair from his forehead, hoping that would improve his appearance, but it just made him look more like a cadaver.

Jean came back and said, ''It's locked up, but it seems okay. Mercy, you don't suppose something's happened to her?''

Sleeper thought he detected a hopeful note in Jean's voice. Jean had never been inordinately fond of Edna Furbank. Sleeper said, ''I don't know, Jean, but I'm starting to worry. I'd better make a few phone calls.''

''Well, let me know, will you?'' said Jean. ''Now I'm all flustered.''

Sleeper knew Jean Teaweather was just trying to be charitable, but he told her not to worry, and to take the edge off her anxiety, he said, ''Edna was talking about spending the Christmas holiday with her brother in New Orleans. She might have just decided to up and go home for the holidays.'' Edna had said nothing of the kind, but the fib might help defray any suspicions in Mrs. Teaweather's mind, hold down the gossip a little longer. Not that Jean Teaweather was a gossiper, but things did have a way of getting around the island. Like when Lois Blakey was arrested for murdering her husband. That gossip had spread like a wildfire and Jean Teaweather had done her share of repeating the story, in her inimitable folksy manner.

The fresh snowdrifts made the island roads treacherous. Sleeper put chains on his truck tires and they provided enough traction to get up the dirt road from his house to the main road. But the island's main north-south road had been little traveled since the snowfall during the night, and Sleeper drove cautiously because of the possibility that beneath the snow covering lay a blanket of slick black ice. He had the heater blasting and the radio tuned in to the emergency band, and as he navigated the north-south road, feathery snowflakes wafted in the chilly air, melting when they landed on the truck's windshield. Sleeper might have thought it a lovely sight except that all he could think about was Edna, that Edna might have come to harm. He drove slowly not just out of caution, but so he could study the snowy terrain for any sign of Edna. Rounding the loopy bend at Libb Lufkin's orchard, Sleeper saw the Lufkin boy out in front of his family's farmhouse. He had built a snowman and now was decorating it with bits of branches from a crabapple tree. He'd given the snowman antlers, and a tail. The snowman stood five or six feet tall, life-size, and the Lufkin boy was small for his age. The boy's creation towered over him, casting him in eerie shadow.

The Lufkin boy was one of eight children who lived on Helix Island, and they all attended the same one-room schoolhouse that Sleeper had attended as a boy. The schoolhouse hadn't changed much over two generations, except that now they had a computer, and some of Luther Lufkin's classes were conducted by telecommuting. As it was Christmas, the island's schoolhouse was closed.

Sleeper slowed down and blinked his headlights. Luther glanced up from his work on the snowman, saw Sleeper's truck, saw Sleeper blinking the headlights, and came trudging up a snowbank to the highway. Sleeper rolled down the window, and when he spoke, his breath came out in clouds.

"Nice snowman, Luther."

Luther said, "Not a man. A minotaur. He needs eyes."

"I see you used that big old cedar stump for a base."

Luther said, "Yup. Made a good one, too."

"That was real smart, Luther." In the distance, Sleeper saw a black-and-white cat come plodding through the snow. "So Minnie's come back?"

"She came back this morning," said Luther. "I found her under the house. She's going to have her kittens pretty soon."

Sleeper smiled. "Mine's expecting, too. My Dundee. But she hasn't come home."

Luther whistled. "That's sure tough, Mr. Sexton."

Sleeper said, "You having a nice Christmas?"

"Sure. Got a new iMac. And a pager." Luther leaned down and scratched Minnie behind the ears. Minnie purred, then turned and plodded back toward the house.

Sleeper said, "That's nice, Luther. You seen Edna around?" He tried to sound unconcerned, but he heard his own voice quaver and felt the anxiety in his chest.

Luther didn't seem to notice. "Not this morning," he said. "Care to come down and meet the minotaur, Mr. Sexton?"

"No." Sleeper shook his head. "No, not just now, Luther. I'm looking for Edna."

"She lost or something?"

"I don't know. In fact, I'm worried about her." Why was it easier for Sleeper to be honest about his feelings with a ten-year-old boy than with grown-ups?

Luther said, "Want me to come along and help you look?"

"Thanks, no, son. You just get back to work on that..."

"Minotaur."

"Yeah." Sleeper rolled up the window and drove off, leaving the boy standing beside the road. The tire chains crunched over the crisp virgin snow. In the rearview mirror, Sleeper saw Luther Lufkin slide down the snowbank and run back to his snow creature. He thought how nice it would be to have Luther's problems. The frozen minotaur needed eyes.

Sleeper noticed Minnie peeking out from under the Lufkin house. Sleeper wished Dundee would come back, but he wasn't too worried. Cats have a way of fending for themselves, especially pregnant cats.

There was no central town on Helix Island, never had been. As far as the islanders were concerned, there never would be a town or even a village on Helix Island, just the little post office/grocery store at the ferry landing. In the parking lot, Sleeper found Edna's Saturn in the space where she always parked it, beneath a soaring Douglas fir. That was Edna's spot, and if anyone dared park in it during weekdays, she made sure they'd only do it once, by letting the air out of their tires. Sleeper walked over to Edna's car. He didn't have a key to the Saturn. He peered inside the driver's-side window and didn't see anything unusual, just Edna's stuff: a pile of rented videos she should have returned to the Anacortes video store a week ago; her rain galoshes on the floor of the backseat; a carton that Sleeper recognized was from the cloister (no doubt it contained God's Watchers underwear, which Edna not only wore herself but also bought and mailed to her friends in New Orleans). But no sign of foul play, nothing suspicious in the Saturn.

When Sleeper entered the post office/grocery store, Jean Teaweather glanced up from reading the newspaper and saw snowflakes melting on his coat. So it was still coming down. Sleeper said, "Any sign of her yet?" Trying to sound casual.

Mrs. Teaweather said, "Why, no, Sleeper. I haven't seen her yet. You know, I thought maybe she was sick when she didn't show up for work this morning. The first boat left without her." Mrs. Teaweather stared at Sleeper. "You mean she hasn't come home yet?"

Sleeper shook his head: Not hide nor hair. Hadn't even phoned. Sleeper confessed that he was confused, and a little worried.

"Oh dear," said Mrs. Teaweather. She was too tactful to say what she was thinking. She was thinking that Sleeper and Edna must have had one of their doozies again, and maybe this time Edna had actually carried out the threat she had so often made. Maybe Edna had finally left Sleeper for good, left Helix Island, gone back to where she came from. Well, hurray and good riddance was what Mrs. Teaweather thought, but she wouldn't say it out loud. Instead, she frowned and said, "Oh dear," again, and added, "Is there something I can do?"

Sleeper said no, unless, of course, she happened to hear from Edna—then he would appreciate a telephone call. Mrs. Teaweather went into the little kitchen behind the post office and fixed Sleeper a skinny latte, which Sleeper sipped thoughtfully as he stared out the window at the deserted ferry landing. Gulls circled the snowcapped wood pilings, waiting for the snow to melt off their perches. The water sparkled silvery gray, and whitecaps broke the surface out in the deep waters of the strait. In the distance, a ferryboat ploughed the choppy surface, heading toward Helix Island. The ten a.m. ferry from Anacortes. She might be on it.

Why the hell did he care, anyway?

From where he stood at the window in the little post-office kitchen, Sleeper could see the ferry landing and beyond that, a steep shoreline of solid rock plunging into the saltwater strait. Above the shoreline, a thick sylvan curtain hid Mercy on the Rock Cloister, but Sleeper knew it was in there somewhere, and he knew—because Sister Ramona had told him just this morning—that if anyone was looking out the cloister's dining-room window, she or he could see the ferry landing and the little post office/grocery store. Sleeper tried to pick out the cloister's outline but the snow had softened all the forest's contours, blending the trees and buildings and land together into one billowy pillowscape, and he soon gave up.

Mrs. Teaweather came over, stood beside Sleeper, looked out the window, and said, "Stopped snowing, has it?"

Sleeper grunted.

Mrs. Teaweather said, "You don't think she's over there, do you?"

"The cloister?"

Mrs. Teaweather nodded.

Sleeper shook his head. "Sister Ramona told me they haven't seen Edna since Wednesday morning when she boarded the *Klikitat.*"

"*Klikitat,* or *Evergreen State?*"

"Well, I think it would be the *Klikitat,* Jean. *Klikitat*'s the first boat of the day, isn't it?"

Mrs. Teaweather said yes, and added, "The *Klikitat.* Don't know what made me say the *Evergreen State.*"

"Old age," said Sleeper drolly, trying to make light of things. Jean tittered. "Don't know what I was thinking when I said *Evergreen State.*" She went back to reading the newspaper.

Sleeper watched until the ferryboat sailed into the landing and docked, then he went outdoors and stood near the landing and watched as the vehicles debarked. Gordon Mantle drove off the ferry in the Humvee, no doubt returning from the mainland. Gordon parked and went inside the grocery store. Then came Rick Turner's pickup, then a minivan from the cloister, driven by Sister Pontifica, one of the God's Watchers. Although the nuns all wore the same outfit, Pontifica's sumo-wrestler shape was unmistakable. Next off came a familiar Volvo driven by the Breedhaven scientist, Ted Vigil. Dr. Vigil saw Sleeper standing beside the ferry landing, but he didn't bother to nod, or wave, or anything. Vigil never acknowledged the islanders. He came to work on Hella Island but he rarely stayed overnight, and had little interaction with the island population. But then, Sleeper thought whimsically, neither were the islanders particularly cordial back to him. Sleeper watched Vigil drive up the hill, turn left, and head south on the island's main road. He wondered why some people would go to work on Christmas Day, unless they absolutely had to, like Jean Teaweather.

More passengers drove off the boat. Sleeper saw Andy and Lynette Dorlup, Libb Lufkin, Jenny and Ted Stanley—all coming back from church services on Dot Island. Sleeper felt his heart pounding as the ferry emptied.

No Edna.

Without taking on a single passenger, the boat tooted, preparing to sail. Suddenly a deckhand signaled to the pilothouse and the boat's engine throttled down to an idle as the skipper responded to the deckhand's frantic gestures. The deckhand pointed at the shoreline, near the wood pilings, hopped off the deck onto the dock and jogged toward the wood pilings. Sleeper suddenly had an awful feeling about the hubbub he was seeing.

He crossed the road, and broke into a run behind the deckhand. At the same moment, a speedboat packed with God's Watchers roared into sight, heading straight for the wood pilings. One of the Watchers held binoculars up to her eyes and another had a megaphone at her mouth and was yelling but Sleeper couldn't make out what she was saying.

The deckhand waved to the God's Watchers and shouted, "Get out of the way!" The speedboat reversed gears, but instead of backing off, it puttered up toward the wood pilings. The two men arrived at the same time at the edge of the water, and the deckhand, seeing Sleeper, pointed and said, "There."

It bobbed like so much billowy riffraff on the water's choppy surface, but when Sleeper got closer to the water, he saw what the other man had seen: a floating body, its arms outstretched like wings. The body floated facedown, and you could see bare legs and buttocks. A God's Watcher screamed, "It's Mother Beatifica!"

She wasn't wearing God's Watchers underpants, thank the Lord for small favors. But even so, Sleeper thought he recognized her, because he had Edna's backside committed to memory.

Sleeper plunged into the frigid water, swam out to the floating corpse, and with the *Klikitat*'s deckhand, dragged it onto land. The God's Watchers came ashore and created general chaos and confusion, and Jean Teaweather, seeing a medical emergency, called Libb on her car phone. Gordon Mantle came outside, saw all the commotion, shrugged, as if to say, *"What good could I do?"* and drove away.

Sleeper bent over the corpse and saw something shocking. It wasn't Edna, after all. It was Frances "Fanny" Faber, the Breedhaven trustee.

SIXTEEN

ONE DOWN, SIX TO GO

SLEEPER HAD NEVER performed mouth-to-mouth resuscitation, and when he tried, he got all confused, so the deckhand shoved him aside and took over. The deckhand labored over Fanny until Libb Lufkin came screeching up to the scene in her car. Libb, a registered nurse, took over, but it wasn't long before she looked up at Sleeper and the deckhand and shook her head. "Sorry," said Libb. "She's a goner, I'm afraid."

The deckhand stayed onshore with Sleeper and Libb, and the ferry set sail. The God's Watchers, relieved it was only Fanny Faber and not Mother Beatifica, puttered back to their private marina. Libb Lufkin went into the post office/grocery store and called the sheriff's office. Sleeper again knelt over Mrs. Faber lying on the cold snowy ground. He placed his jacket under her head—as if she needed a pillow. He took her pale, withered hands in his and rubbed, as if that would warm them, but they refused to respond. When the emergency medical helicopter came, Sleeper and the deckhand helped load Mrs. Faber's body, and as the chopper lifted off, Sleeper thought back to the day Sally had drowned. He wondered if Helix Island could bear any more trouble, any more heartache.

GORDON WAS DRIVING near the cliff where Elmer Poole had dug up old Captain Blakey's bones when he saw something glinting on the ground. He stopped the Humvee, let the engine idle, got out, and walked over to the glinting object. He had to dig to bring the whole piece up out of the soil. Gordon held the silver revolver up to the daylight and studied it. If he wasn't awfully mistaken, Gordon had seen this very same revolver before.

Gordon screwed up his mouth and thought about what he

should do with this discovery. What was it doing here? Dare he speculate? He set it carefully in the Humvee, and after he had finished laying out feed and fresh water for the species, Gordon drove back to the main compound.

Dr. Vigil was on site, working over the Christmas holiday, but Gordon and Dr. Vigil didn't communicate well. Miss Poole was off on Christmas holiday, and none of the other interns were around. Gordon went into Dr. Strindberg's vacated office, picked up the telephone, and called Agent Diamond's office. When he got her voice mail, he took down the forwarding phone number and called it. When Venus came on the line, Gordon described what he'd found and where he'd found it.

Venus was at Bella's, for Christmas Day brunch. Gordon's phone call didn't come as a complete surprise. She said, "Have you told anyone?"

"No. Just you, miss. I wasn't sure who's in charge here lately. I wanted to do the right thing."

"Keep it to yourself. I'll pick it up. And, Gordon?"

"Yes?"

"Has the cat—Purim—returned?"

"No. No, she hasn't. Not a trace of her."

"What about the other cats? Have you located the surrogate cats?"

"Er, no, miss. We've checked all over the island, but so far, no sign of any of them. That's how cats are, you know, when they're ready to drop a litter. They hide."

"Have you noticed anything else unusual on the grounds?"

Gordon thought for a minute, then said, "Not really. Everything's pretty normal around here. Except the weather. The cold has caused problems for several of the species. But I'm feeding them and leaving out extra water, and we've installed those heaters in their shelters, so I guess they'll be okay until the weather turns nice again. There was one more thing, though."

"What's that, Gordon?"

"We had a body wash up here on the island this morning. One of Breedhaven's trustees."

"Who was it?"

"It was Mrs. Faber. The sheriff has already been here. I saw the helicopter come over from the mainland. I reckon they took her away. But she was found in the marine-sanctuary waters. I guess that means it's a federal case and not the sheriff's?''

Venus was already strapping on her gun. She said, ''Did she drown?''

Gordon said, ''Don't know. Maybe. But the queer thing was, Sleeper Sexton, one of our island council members? He was there when the body washed in. Mr. Sexton at first thought it was his lady friend, Edna Furbank. Said Edna's been missing for a couple days now. You might know Edna. She was the island lady who complained to your office when Breedhaven opened.''

''Sure, I remember the name.'' Walking toward Bella's front door.

Gordon said, ''Lot of rumors swirling around. Everybody likes Mr. Sexton, but now, there's some rumors circulating. Edna being missing and all. I don't know if that's at all relevant. It might just be a lovers' quarrel for all I know. Just thought I'd mention it.''

Who says men aren't gossips? Venus said, ''Thanks, Gordon. I'm on my way up there right now. Keep an eye out for those cats.''

''Oh sure, miss—I mean, Agent.''

Gordon set the phone down in its cradle. He went to the bathroom door, opened it, peered inside. The two serval kittens were napping on their bed. They opened their eyes and stared at Gordon. He shut the door.

Gordon drove out to the Hawaiian Nene goslings' feed station. He got out of the Humvee, reached into the back and took out a large piece of canvas. He placed the canvas over his head. Two holes had been cut out for his eyes. The canvas fell to his feet, completely covering him. He pulled on a pair of fingerless canvas gloves, took a bucket of feed out of the Humvee, and a stick with a replica of a goose's head on one end. He went inside the feed station, looked around. The first thing he saw was the rhino scat.

''Damn,'' he said to himself. ''That rhino's been in here again.''

The goslings gathered around the big canvas bird. Being careful not to make any sound, Gordon poured the feed into the geese's trough. He held up the stick with the goose head on it and bobbed it up and down in the feed. The goslings honked and came over to the feed trough. Gordon backed out of the feed station and shut the door. When he reached the Humvee, he slid behind the wheel. He didn't take off the canvas cover until he was far out of sight. It wouldn't do for the youngsters to imprint on a human. They had to think their provider was one of them. A goose. Or a gander.

Gordon was driving back into the compound when he spotted Purim near Hannah's cottage. He parked the Humvee, peeled off the canvas sheet, and approached the cat slowly. "So you've come back, Purim," he said gently, and, making sure no one was watching, he bent down to the ground where the mother-to-be had made a soft bed in leaves near Hannah's bedroom window. Gordon approached Purim cautiously, whispering, "Here, Purim. Come to Gordon." Finally, Purim came to Gordon, and he swept her up in his arms and ran into the forest.

Gordon ran half a mile into the habitat, along a path he could travel blindfolded. When he reached the edge of the marshy wetlands, where a flock of New Zealand Takahes were feeding on vitamin pellets he'd left out earlier that morning, Gordon chased them away and went inside their heated shelter. Carrying Purim into a corner, he found some hay and made a soft nest for Purim. As he placed her gently into the nest, he noticed some animal droppings. "Damn," he said aloud. "That stupid rhino's been in here, too." Gordon placed Purim in the soft hay bed, patted her head gently. Purim purred softly and licked his hand. Gordon smiled at the cat.

"There now, Purim, there now."

Gordon went outside the shelter and kept the fat Takahes at bay while Purim dropped her litter. It seemed forever before Gordon heard Purim's mewing. He rushed inside the shed and saw the mother cat licking four of the strangest kittens he'd ever seen.

"Oh dear God," cried Gordon. "This will never do."

MR. FREDERICK FABER, Fanny's husband, was dumbfounded upon learning of his wife's death. He found little consolation in hearing that the case had been turned over to the federal authorities, since Fanny's corpse had been found floating in the protected marine sanctuary off Helix Island. Leave it to Fanny, Mr. Faber had remarked to Venus, somewhat wryly and with bittersweet remorse, to make a federal case out of her own death. Of course, he blamed himself for allowing Fanny to visit Breedhaven that morning. He never should have allowed her to go.

Venus flew with Mr. Faber and the corpse to the Ashland lab. USF&W's forensics chief, Claudia Paganelli, placed a comforting hand on Mr. Faber's trembling shoulder and told him that, because of the suspicious circumstances surrounding Mrs. Faber's death, Fanny's body would not be released until she was autopsied. He said okay, he'd wait, so Venus sat with Faber in the waiting room.

Mr. Faber wept. He said, "I told Fanny not to go up there this morning. She insisted. Late last night, she had a telephone call from a lady up at Breedhaven. I don't know her name. The lady said it was an emergency, that Fanny needed to come to Breedhaven. When I tried to stop her, Fanny said if Breedhaven was having an emergency, she needed to come to their aid. And she rushed up there on the first ferry this morning." Mr. Faber moaned. "But why did she have to die? And on Christmas Day?"

Venus couldn't offer a reasonable answer.

It was late afternoon on Christmas Day when Claudia came out, sat down between Mr. Faber and Venus.

"I am very sorry, Mr. Faber. Your wife was murdered."

Faber covered his face. "What happened to her?"

"She was beaten quite severely, maybe tortured," Claudia said gently. "And then she was put in the water, too weak to save herself. She drowned."

Why did Fanny Faber have to die?

All anyone could say for certain was that Mrs. Faber had at some point been bound hand-and-foot, pistol-whipped, and then probably dropped into the strait off Helix Island. They had more tests to conduct on the corpse, but they already knew that she'd been dumped into the strait almost immediately after being beaten.

Claudia offered some small consolation. Mrs. Faber hadn't been sexually assaulted.

"But why?" cried Mr. Faber over and over again. "Why Fanny?"

Claudia said, "If you want my honest opinion, I think whoever did this is mentally disturbed."

"Must be," said Mr. Faber behind his tears. He turned to Venus. "Have they found her car?"

Venus shook her head. She wanted to say something to comfort Mr. Faber, but she couldn't think of anything. All she could think about was Hannah Strindberg, and, too, she wondered who would be next on the murderer's hit list.

Mr. Faber said, "Is there some kind of trouble on Helix?"

Venus nodded and said, "I'm afraid your wife got caught up in this terrible business. I'm so sorry."

The chopper flew back to Seattle in a thickening snow flurry, and landed on the roof of the Bumbershoot. Venus was running through the snowfall when her phone rang. She ducked inside the building where it was dry and warm, and answered. It was a police officer in Anacortes. He had seen a man matching Petrovich's description walking along the ferry dock at Anacortes. He didn't actually see the man board a ferry, but two ferries had been loaded: the *Klikitat,* headed for Victoria, British Columbia, via the San Juans, and the ferry headed for Sydney, B.C., the *Nisqually.* Both ferries had sailed from the Anacortes dock within the past hour. The police officer had seen an all-points bulletin issued from Fish and Wildlife. There was a telephone number, so when he saw the man matching Petrovich's description, he called it. She thanked him and raced to her car. Christmas dinner would have to wait.

SEVENTEEN

CRAPE AND HACKER

AN ENGLISH PIG determined the San Juan Islands' fate on June 15, 1859, when during an altercation between British and American farmers over jurisdiction of the islands, a furious American farmer named Lyman Cutlar shot dead a very British tusker, and the Pig War was declared. On March 21, 1860, British Royal Marines sailed through Mosquito Pass and landed at Garrison Bay on the northwest coast of San Juan Island. English Camp was established there, while on the same island's southern tip, American Camp was fortified at Eagle Cove. A twelve-year standoff culminated in a truce, and on October 21, 1872, Kaiser Wilhelm, Monarch of Germany, made the final determination of the islands' governance, deciding for the United States. During the entire twelve years, Lyman Cutlar's was the only shot fired in anger, but that English porker's violent and untimely demise sealed the fate of the San Juans.

Not surprisingly, the Britishness of many islanders never waned; afternoon tea is still served in numerous San Juan Islands households, and lots of islanders say "draft" for "draft," and "eh" for "yes." The British hung on to the North and South Penders and Saturna Island, and, to the south of the San Juans, Discovery Island; eventually all their islands joined Canada. Whales may know the difference between Canadian and U.S. waters in the Haro Strait, but evidently don't much care, for they frolic on both sides of the imaginary line that in a wiggle-waggle fashion intersects the strait.

Customs and immigration officials honor this dashed-and-dotted line scrupulously, and none are more scrutinizing of personal identification than Canadian immigration officers. If a U.S. citizen wishes to cross into Canada at, say, Victoria or Sydney,

British Columbia, Canadian immigration officers will ask to inspect a valid photo ID, such as a driver's license. Persons of neither U.S. nor Canadian citizenship must present a valid passport; otherwise, entry will be denied. Canadian officials are tough, eh? Some might call them paranoid, especially near midnight at the border.

Venus parked the Aston Martin at the Immigration gate, got out, and showed her badge to a Captain Ian Hacker of Her Majesty's Royal Canadian Immigration Service. Hacker, a thread of a man, pursed a pair of dry, chapped lips half-hidden by a snaky mustache, scrutinized the badge, worked the parched lips some more, and made the snake dance. He scratched his chest a couple times, blew imaginary bubbles, and let one word fly.

"Why?"

"Pardon?" Venus wasn't sure what he meant.

"I said, 'Why?'" Hacker barked.

"Why what?"

Hacker bristled. "Why do you wish to enter Canada? We have our own wildlife cops. We don't need any of you Americans."

Venus said, "I'm following a suspect who may be armed and dangerous, who assaulted me last night, or rather, early this morning, and who may have committed a terrible crime down in Seattle and a murder over on Helix Island."

Hacker's cute lips parted insincerely. His teeth were little white pegs. He said, "You're the first passenger off this boat. How can you be following anybody?"

"He crossed earlier today. At least, I'm fairly certain he did. He came through here, or at Sydney. But he's probably in Victoria now. I think he's hiding out here. Also," she added, for effect, "the guy's a thief. He may be carrying some valuable contraband. He might be connected to the Russian Mafia."

"Drugs?"

"Frozen embryos."

"What?" Hacker squinted.

"Embryos. Animal embryos. Genetic material from endangered wildlife species."

Hacker sucked his thin cheeks. "Is that a fact?" He might

have been amused, but she couldn't tell for sure, so she just nodded.

Hacker said, "This is going to be fun," then took the badge and ID and went away. Venus stood at the waist-high iron bar that divided her from Canada and watched a couple of Immigration officers paw the Aston Martin. The least they could have done was to wear soft white gloves, but they had no respect for sleek curves. In a few minutes, Hacker came back with another Immigration official who was scowling at a fax sheet.

"You're Diamond?" asked the second officer, not friendly.

"That's right." She smiled insincerely. "I'll bet that's a fax from my agency, confirming my identity."

The second officer, whose name was Arlo Crape, frowned noncommittally. "You carry a weapon?"

Venus showed them her .38 Smith and Wesson.

Hacker guffawed. "You call that a weapon?"

"Shut up, Ian," snapped Arlo Crape. To Venus, he said, "Who's the suspect?"

"That should be in the fax."

Crape barked, "Answer the question."

"He's calling himself Sergei Petrovich. He claims he's a citizen of the Russian Federation. Whatever his name is, he might be a mass murderer. He probably stole a lot of genetic material, and maybe kidnapped some cats...."

"All right, all right." Arlo Crape held up a gloved paw. He studied the fax sheet some more, then nodded and said, "Stay right here. I have to make a phone call."

Venus pulled out her digital phone, offered it to Crape, but he rolled his eyes and went away. Meanwhile the two officers persisted in mauling the Aston Martin, and in the queues on either side, the occasional visitor passed swiftly through into Canada. Venus said to Hacker, "How did I get so lucky?"

Hacker squinted. He didn't understand.

She explained. "I mean, to get in this particular line."

Hacker understood now. He grinned meanly. "You're just one of those people who always ends up in the wrong line. I can see your kind coming a mile away."

"How about kilometers?" she said, sneering. "Can you see us in kilometers, too?"

"Shut up," Hacker said.

She was making a face at Ian Hacker's back when Crape returned, breathless, earnest.

"We've got your man," Crape announced proudly. "Move aside, Ian. Let the agent through the gate."

THE MAN who called himself Petrovich was locked up in a phone booth-sized room, and had been there for three hours since the last ferry from Anacortes had docked at Victoria.

"We were holding him pending confirmation of his passport information," said Crape. "Like you said, Russian citizenship. He's also holding a temporary residence visa from the Sultanate of Lumbai. Claims to have business connections there." Crape scratched his head. "I didn't know anyone lived in Lumbai besides the sultan and his concubines."

"Oil riggers," Venus offered. "And several thousand servants."

Arlo Crape led Petrovich by the elbow, steered him down a long corridor, around a few corners, into a fastidious little office where he made Petrovich sit in a folding chair facing them.

Petrovich didn't act pleased to see her, but then, she wasn't ecstatic either. She curled her lip at Petrovich and he averted his eyes.

He had the same passport, and it still said he was Sergei Petrovich, a citizen of the Russian Federation, and that he was a forty-six-year-old product of Minsk. The passport said he was five feet, ten inches tall, weighed one hundred sixty pounds, give or take a kilo, had blue eyes and black hair, which was cut short but still managed to curl around his ears. In his passport photo, Petrovich wore a shiny business suit and rumpled white shirt, and his hair was longer, slicked back. Right now, he was dressed like a cat burglar and his right hand clutched a black wool watch cap. Somewhat apologetically Petrovich said, "I'd look more like my passport photo if I could shave."

Venus snarled, "You'd look more familiar lying on your back with my boot up your Adam's apple."

"Here now," said Crape. "Stop intimidating him."

Petrovich made a little-boy face that she wanted to slug but didn't, because Crape wouldn't stand for any crapola from her or from Petrovich. If they wanted to slow-waltz, they'd have to wait until Arlo Crape had finished his act.

Crape said, "Mr. Petrovich, please tell me why you wish to visit Canada."

Petrovich offered that he was a simple tourist on holiday from his job as an accountant for the Bank of St. Petersburg. He had visited America just to see what all the fuss was about, left the United States without being very much impressed, and intended on seeing Canada for the very first time—and wasn't it just so inhospitable to treat an innocent tourist this shabbily?

"It makes me very sad," whined Petrovich, more melancholy than bitter, "this boorish treatment. Is this your Canadian brand of hospitality?"

Crape explained that under normal circumstances, tourists didn't arrive so late at night and try to vault over the Immigration gate, and when Petrovich had done just that, Crape had felt a need to detain him. Petrovich replied that he was merely stretching his legs after falling asleep on the long ferry ride, during which time his right leg had taken on needles and pins.

Crape rubbed his chin and eyeballed Petrovich's right trouser leg, like he thought Petrovich was hiding something.

Venus said, "Where's your vehicle?"

Petrovich pointed at Crape. "Inspector Crape can tell you. I walked off the boat. No vehicle. Just a foot passenger. With daypack, which this other fellow takes away from me."

"Hacker?"

Arlo Crape nodded. Venus asked Crape what he'd found in the daypack. Crape got up, went behind the desk, lifted the daypack, turned it upside down, and dumped its contents on the desk. Crape said, "Help yourself."

She pawed through the contents, obviously enjoying violating Petrovich's privacy. To make him even more ill-at-ease, she recited the contents aloud. "Two pairs of boxer underwear, neatly folded, apparently ironed. Made in Estonia. Two pairs of

black silk socks, apparently brand-new. Shaving kit packed meticulously with toiletry items. Huh! Nice cologne.''

She held it out for Arlo Crape to sniff.

''Postcards, still blank, from Seattle: Space Needle, and a
strawberry sunrise over Mount Rainier. Book of American post-
age stamps. First class. Two missing.'' She looked up. ''That's
it?''

Crape pointed to a small paper bag on the desk. ''In there.
What came from his pockets.''

Fifteen U.S. $100 bills, a couple twenties, and some coins.
Two packs of Players rope-cut filter tips. Book of matches from
Ray's Boathouse at the Hiram Chittendom locks in Seattle.

That was all.

Venus said to Petrovich, ''Why don't you tell Customs Inspector Crape how you put a gun to my back during midnight
Mass at St. James Cathedral in Seattle while your girlfriend in
the choir loft tried to plug me through the brain?''

Petrovich grinned affably at Crape and said, ''The lady is
mistaken, Officer. No doubt she has confused me with someone
else.''

Crape seemed unsure. Venus said, ''He's lying. Ask him what
his real name is.''

''Is the lady authorized to interrogate me?'' Petrovich asked.

Crape sighed. ''When did you arrive in Seattle, Mr. Petrovich?''

''*Tak!*'' Petrovich said irritably. ''What difference does it
make? My passport is good, yes?''

Arlo Crape said, ''Answer the question.''

Petrovich said, ''I arrived in Seattle from St. Petersburg yesterday morning, on Christmas Eve—that is, *your* Christmas Eve.
Anyhow, I spend Christmas Eve doing nothing much in small
hotel in downtown district. Last night, I visited nearby cathedral,
and this is where this lovely lady first assaults me. Of course,
local officers came to my rescue. Then this morning, I rented a
car and drive to Anacortes. I leave car at Avis in Anacortes and
I board the ferry to Victoria, intending to spend a peaceful day
seeing sights. Now here I am, Sergei Petrovich, the prisoner,

and a very happy holidays to you, too.'' Petrovich sucked his cheeks.

Venus said, ''What about a credit card? Do you carry a credit card?''

Crape nodded at Petrovich.

Petrovich sighed, rolled up his trouser leg, slid his hand down a black silk sock, and extracted a platinum Visa card that bore the title, *Bank of St. Petersburg*. The name on the card was *Sergei Petrovich*. Expiration date was July, two years distant. Crape took the credit card and went away. When they were alone, Venus said, ''Where are they, Chekhov?''

''My name is Petrovich.''

''The hell it is. You are Larry Chekhov. I saw you at Hannah's lawyer's office. I never forget a pretty face. Now, where are they?''

Chekhov pursed his lips. ''Where are what, my dear?'' Glibly.

''Don't call me that,'' she growled. ''You tell me where the ark is, and where you stashed the cats, Chekhov, or I'll make borscht with your Estonian boxer shorts.''

Chekhov laughed—not harshly. He went, ''Ark. Ark-ark''; then he laughed mockingly.

She grabbed his shirt collar, pulled his face up close to hers and whispered, ''Don't you ever try that jackass stunt again, Chekhov—I'll shoot you next time.''

Petrovich laughed louder. ''You are fun,'' he said. ''I like the plucky woman.''

She had an acidic response on her tongue when Ian Hacker came in and spoiled their good time by standing around pretending relevance. ''Inspector Crape told me to keep my eyes on you two,'' he announced importantly.

She glared at the Russian and he smiled back, infuriating her, but since Hacker had barged in, she decided against making trouble. Instead, she studied Petrovich's false passport. She'd never seen a forged Russian passport.

Petrovich was gazing thoughtfully at his fingernails. ''Chekhov?'' she said, short, fast. He looked up inquiringly. ''Gotcha,'' she said.

"Tak!" the Russian remarked hotly. "I do not understand your English."

"You speak excellent English. Where did you learn your English?"

Chekhov shrugged. "Leningrad, of course—I mean, St. Petersburg. When I studied English, it was still called Leningrad."

Venus said, "How do you say 'endangered species' in Russian?"

Chekhov showed no surprise at the question. If the query startled him, or bothered him in any way, he didn't show it. Coolly he said, "Zanesti v krasnuju knigu."

"Zanesti v Krasnuju Knigu," Venus repeated aloud.

"Literally translated," Chekhov said, "it means, 'put it in the Red Book.'"

Silence.

"In Russian, how do you say, 'Fanny Faber was murdered for what she wouldn't reveal'?" Venus asked.

Chekhov blinked. "Eh, pardon?"

Arlo Crape returned then, all smiles and efficiency. "Everything's in order," he chirped brightly, handing Chekhov the credit card. "Mr. Petrovich, please accept my apologies for this inconvenience. I do hope you understand that our job requires a bit of extraordinary caution. Your passport has been processed, and we sent a fax off to St. Petersburg. The mayor's secretary himself replied." Crape smiled ingratiatingly. "You are apparently highly thought-of in Saint Petersburg."

Chekhov stood up, accepted his passport and his daypack from Crape.

Venus took Crape aside and said, "You can't let him go. He's using a false passport. His other name is Larry Chekhov. He's a gangster and a drug smuggler, and he murdered a woman just yesterday."

"I can't detain him," said Crape.

"But he's a suspect in this case down in—"

"That is your government's concern, not mine. Unless you have an international arrest warrant."

"I don't, but—"

"Then you will have to take up the matter when—and if—

Mr. Petrovich reenters the United States.''

Chekhov grinned broadly as Crape led him over the threshold, into Canada's safe embrace.

EIGHTEEN

CANADIAN SUNSET

IAN HACKER GRINNED.

Venus said, "I'm all clear, right?"

Arlo Crape said, "You're free to go."

She leaped over the gate before Hacker had time to open it, and raced to the Aston Martin. The maulers had abandoned it. Chekhov was walking fast along the pier that led to shore. Venus hung back until Chekhov reached the end of the pier and stepped onto Broughton Street, then she drove slowly along the pier, turned onto Broughton, prowled behind Chekhov. There was snow on the ground, and a clock chimed midnight.

Chekhov walked faster now, headed uphill beneath the street-lamps toward the provincial capital building, and the massive Victorian-era Empress Hotel. She found a parking space on Broughton Street, waited, watching, as Chekhov entered the hotel lobby. Then she got out and followed him inside. She counted eighty-six steps from the Aston to the Empress Hotel.

The posh lobby was decked out with holly boughs, fragrant cedar swags, and a monstrous Christmas tree. Venus picked her way around the lobby's majestic columns and found Chekhov near the newsstand, studying headlines. She moved into a dim corner and watched as Chekhov paid for a copy of the *International Herald Tribune* and a cigar. Chekhov carried his purchases across a wide corridor to a double door under a sign: Smoking Room. He glanced around as if checking to see if he was being followed. She hung back in the shadows. Chekhov went inside the Smoking Room.

Venus went over to the newsstand, bought her own copy of the *Herald Tribune* and a stick of barley sugar. She tucked the newspaper under her arm, popped the barley sugar in her mouth.

The attendant gave her change in Canadian coins, which she stuffed in her jacket pocket. She found a chair that offered a clear view of the hotel's entrance, the elevators and the Smoking Room entrance. The lobby was deserted. While she glanced at the *Herald Tribune,* she watched the elevators. Nothing but bell-hops. Time passed, and the lobby held nothing of special interest. What was Chekhov doing in there? Was he waiting for someone? Just smoking? She had an idea that Chekhov might be looking for something in the *Tribune,* and she perused the newspaper, but nothing popped out at her until she turned to the classifieds. There she found a small ad: *Lady M., Where smoking is permitted, Pro-Gen takes stock.*

A family entered the hotel, Gen-X types trying to pass as rebels, with two bawling children. Dad wore faux leather and a clip-on lip ring. Mom had on a retro rayon frock and a nice pair of Doc Martens. Venus watched them check in. They paid cash, causing a stir. The two kids fought viciously in the sedate lobby, nearly detaching a teddy bear's limbs. Nothing else happened for twenty minutes, then at exactly one o'clock, a woman entered the hotel, paused in the lobby, turned right, and walked toward the newsstand.

She wasn't tall, but statuesque, with perfect posture. She wore a tailored red wool suit that left some room for the imagination, but just a little. She wore sheer stockings and black high-heeled pumps. She wore a lot of gold jewelry around her neck and wrists, and a gold ankle chain below a slim, well-formed calf. Her jewelry decorated all the right places, and the only visibly pierced body parts were her earlobes, from which hung two rubies the size and color of ripe bing cherries. She had pale, camellia-petal skin and her blue eyes glittered behind thick black lashes. She wore tan kid gloves, and when she peeled one off her right hand to count coins for the newsstand attendant, Venus saw the bings' big sister, but she didn't need to see the rubies, or the Ungaro suit, to recognize the woman. It was Rosemary Poole, looking ever so chic and mildly subversive. Venus ducked behind a festooned pillar.

Rosemary said something to the newsstand attendant. The attendant, a portly lad in a hotel staff uniform, blushed and handed

her a copy of the *Herald Tribune.* Rosemary paid him, tucked
the newspaper into a large shoulder bag, glanced around, then
crossed the wide corridor and sat down on a small tapestry
bench. She opened the *Tribune,* scanned it, went straight to the
classifieds. As she read, a small grin curved her mouth. She
folded the newspaper and casually perused the lobby, then stood
up, walked back over to the newsstand, and said something to
the blushing attendant, making a hand gesture like a person
smoking. He pointed behind her and to the right. She turned
around, saw the sign: Smoking Room. She nodded to the attendant, then walked over to the entrance of the Smoking Room
and disappeared inside.

Venus went over to the newsstand. The attendant was surrep-
titiously watching a wrestling match on a little four-inch portable
TV. "Pardon me," Venus asked. The portly lad glanced up.
"That woman who just bought the newspaper. Is she a guest at
the hotel?"

The attendant shrugged. He didn't know. He jabbed a finger
at the reception desk. "Over there. Maybe they can help you."

"Have you ever seen her before?"

The attendant sniffed. "First time. A real babe, eh? Who are
you, anyway?"

She went over to the reception desk, where the night clerk
was very sorry to inform her that hotel policy forbade revealing
guests' names, and anyway, they had over one hundred fifty
rooms in all, and constant turnover, and he didn't know from
squat.

"How about checking your roster for a guest named Petrovich?" She showed him her badge.

The clerk studied it, then said, "What's that? A badge or
something?"

She said, "I am a United States federal agent."

The clerk blinked. "Like, an undercover cop?"

"Like, yes."

"Cool."

The clerk went away and came back a few minutes later with
his manager. The manager studied the badge the way people
window-shop, then said, "U.S.?" rhetorically.

Venus beamed insincerely.

The manager shook his head. "We do not assist foreign police."

"So, if I bring a Mountie in here with me, then you'll help me out?"

The manager didn't reply. He huffed off and disappeared into the executive offices. Venus strolled back across the lobby, this time toward the Smoking Room. She was halfway there when Chekhov and Rosemary Poole came out of the room and turned right, in the direction of the guest elevators. Venus stepped behind a potted palm and watched. Chekhov and Rosemary were having a heated discussion, maybe an argument. Her brother Rex had taught Venus to lip-read, but now she couldn't make out the words coming from Chekhov's and Rosemary's lips.

Maybe they were speaking Russian.

Something cold touched her neck. She felt warm breath in her ear and heard a gruff voice whisper, "House detective. Don't move."

He wore a tweed sportscoat and the hand that held the steel knuckles to her neck had freckles and pale ginger hair on it. He wanted to know who she was and why she was prowling around the Empress Hotel lobby in the wee hours, spying on innocent guests. She turned to explain, showed him her badge, and the distraction was just long enough for Chekhov and Rosemary to disappear.

"Now look what you've done," she hissed.

The house dick said, "We don't want the likes of you making trouble for our guests."

"Who said I was?"

He gripped her arm, led her across the lobby. "I got a call saying you were bothering a couple of our guests. You a divorce dick?"

"I showed you my badge. I am a United States federal agent."

When they reached the revolving door at the hotel entrance, he waited for a space to come around, shoved her in. She went around once, stepped out beside him. She said, "I used to stay here as a kid. Every summer. With my family."

He pushed her into the next space. She went around again, stepped out beside him. "Maybe you remember us. There were five kids. My mother was very beautiful, and my father was a famous aerospace designer. We had a big food fight in the dining room. That was about twenty-five years ago..."

"Here now. Be on your way." He shoved her back into the revolving door. On the third time around she would have stepped out into the lobby again if he hadn't pulled a revolver and aimed it at the twirling door. She went around another half-revolution and stepped out into the street.

She walked a little way down the hill toward Victoria Harbour, then turned and looked back up at the Empress Hotel. Who was Lady M.? Maybe Rosemary had a middle name. Or, like Petrovich, a pseudonym.

Louie Song, on Christmas phone duty, came on the line. Louie said Olson had come into the office, received a phone call around ten p.m., then left immediately for Ashland. "He flew the chopper himself," Louie added.

"What's he doing in Ashland?" She was standing at the foot of the hill, at the seawall on Victoria Harbour. The cold air felt heavy, and when she exhaled, a cloud formed.

Song said, "He wanted to check on some DNA sample."

"What DNA sample?"

"Don't know. He didn't say."

"So, who's watching my mother's place?"

Song said, "Nobody. Olson ended that detail."

"Why, Song?"

"We have other priorities."

Irritated, she said, "Why are you being so damn circumspect?"

"Not," Song said coolly.

"Terse, then. You're being terse. Why, Louie?"

Song said, "I'm in a foul mood. It's been raining too much. Maybe I have seasonal affection disorder."

She said, "It's seasonal *affective* disorder. So what's the SAD all about?"

Song said his current life partner, Dottie, wasn't speaking to him. He said, "I gave her the wrong Christmas gift."

"Don't tell me you got her that beat-up old Honda Gold Wing?"

"No. Not that."

"That was junk. You should get her that Harley she wants. After you sell me mine back."

"Never. A deal's a deal. And that bike Dottie wanted was too big for her."

"So what did you get her? A tricycle?"

"I got her a ticket to Hawaii."

"One ticket?" She yawned.

"Yeah."

Silence. Then, "You mean, you gave Dottie a ticket to Hawaii, but didn't get one for yourself?" She yawned again, checked her Swatch. Two a.m.

Louie said, "Right."

"Let's see. The message here is...?"

Louie laughed ironically. "That's what Dottie said. Before she threw me out."

"That was stupid, Louie."

"Yeah, well. It's a blue, blue Christmas."

"Sorry to hear that," she said. "Have you consulted Dr. Wong about your troubles?"

"Er...no. Why do you ask?"

Venus said, "Because when I was suffering SADlike symptoms, you recommended I go see this Dr. Wong person. I figured you'd follow your own advice."

Song laughed self-consciously. "Oh. Ha ha. Oh, no. It's not that bad. Just a temporary setback in the relationship. Dottie blows up all the time, actually."

"Well, listen here, Louie. I don't have time for SAD. Yours or mine. Furthermore, I know that you've never even met the venerable Raymond Wong. So why did you steer me to him? He's nuts, Louie. A real wacko."

Song hesitated, then said, "He has a brilliant reputation in the International District. Maybe you just aren't enlightened enough."

"Ya sure, you betcha. Now, I need to speak to Olson."

"So try his digital phone," Louie said, and hung up.

Olson answered right away. "I can't talk now," he said. "I'm in the lab. I'll call you back in an hour." The line went dead.

She called her voice-mail service. Two messages—one from Claudia, called in late last night from the Ashland lab. "You were right," said Claudia. "It turns out that the Borneo Bay has an unexplained anatomical anomaly. Its first upper premolar is smaller than normal, and it only has one root. This upper premolar was normal-size, and it has two roots. So it wasn't the Borneo Bay cat that died in the fire. Olson is on his way down to see the evidence for himself. Of course, he's very excited to learn that the Bay cat might still be alive."

The second message was from a Mr. Fuss.

Fuss?...Fuss?

"...from the Swedish consulate..."

Oh, yes, Fuss, Axel Gornall's private secretary.

Fuss said, "I received confirmation from Martine Olaffson's husband. The sandal had been left at Helix Island during one of Dr. Olaffson's visits to the scientific research center there. She had remarked about losing a sandal on her return to Stockholm." Fuss continued. "Also, we have secured all of Dr. Olaffson's research documents. I found one, in particular, which might be of interest to you. I hope you receive my message soon. You see, I have discovered a connection between Dr. Olaffson and that Pro-Gen you were talking about. I found out that it's a privately owned genetics-engineering firm that manufactures genetically engineered animals. All I could get from my source was that they insert human genomes into pigs. They use the pigs' organs and so forth in human transplant surgery. It's enough to make you sick.

"And here's something funny. They are based on the island of Lumbai. It's a Sultanate somewhere in the Pacific. That's all I know. My source is a Swedish biologist who was fired by Pro-Gen for refusing to assist in a transplant experiment. She won't talk to anybody else. She's afraid. She said they tried to kill her when she left her position. She said Martine Olaffson also worked for Pro-Gen, but also quit in protest of company policies. So that's all I know. I hope I didn't use up all your voice-mail space. Please contact me at your earliest convenience. After the holidays, of course.''

End of message. She tried the Swedish consulate's number. No answer, not even a service.

She leaned against the seawall and watched the front entrance of the Empress. What were Chekhov and Rosemary Poole doing at the hotel? Did they have the ark with them?

Nothing happened for half an hour. Then a gray cloud moved in, bringing rain. Rain fell in driblets first, then the temperature dropped and the rain froze into little balls of ice. Hail. It hailed for about ten minutes, then rained again. Under the street lamps a few nightowls scurried about beneath umbrellas and billowy coats, clutching mittened hands to their chests. In car headlights, the raindrops glistened like crystals. The roads were slick black ribbons. Even the noble firs shivered. A gull with a tattered wing searched the seawall for shelter.

Chekhov and Rosemary still hadn't come out of the hotel, unless they'd slipped out the back way. She began walking back toward the hotel. She felt chilled, soaked to the skin. She glanced at her Swatch. Four o'clock. She'd been standing there longer than she thought. She was walking uphill behind the hotel when her phone rang. That would be Olson calling back. She pulled her phone from her jacket pocket. Her thumb was poised over the power button when some hard, heavy object struck her skull. She felt her body go limp, and saw the fireworks shower, then nothing.

NINETEEN

SNOWLITA

ONE GOOD THING about captivity is that it affords a person time to ruminate on life. Edna had spent the last three days and nights alternately lashed to a chair and a bed, and she'd had more than sufficient time to reflect on Sleeper and a few other men she would have rather forgotten. On what Edna had figured out must be the day after Christmas, tied to the straight chair in a dingy cabin somewhere on—she was pretty sure—Helix Island, Edna's dark thoughts turned to her Helix Island neighbors. Her captor had gone out somewhere, so what else could Edna do for entertainment?

If there was one thing Edna despised about the islanders, it was their petty provincialism. More than any other facet of island life, the local prejudice against "mainlanders," which included Edna Furbank, prompted Edna's defiantly friendly attitude toward the island's other "outcasts." Lois Blakey, for example—the widowed proprietor of Blakey's B&B on the island's northwest side—had, like Edna, immigrated to Helix and was never really accepted. So, after San Juan Man was discovered by old Elmer Poole, when Lois was arrested for the murder and alleged breakfast-sausaging of her husband, Captain C.Z. Blakey—the purely circumstantial evidence in the case already convicting her in the islanders' insular minds—Edna had taken Lois's side, and even had helped Lois raise bail by finding a mainland bail bondsman who floated a second mortgage on Lois's B&B. Isn't that what friends were for? With Lois out free pending her murder trial, Edna had been helping prepare her defense. The islanders knew about Edna's support of Lois Blakey, but if they thought anything at all, they thought Lois Blakey and Edna Furbank were two peas in the same rotten pod.

Edna knew this, of course, and she knew that if it weren't for her relationship with Sleeper Sexton, she'd have been forced off the island council long ago. She had been tolerated, but never truly accepted.

And yet the hypocrites had already begun to accept Breedhaven.

The nuns of Mercy on the Rock Cloister also suffered the scorn reserved for outsiders, and Edna had immediately befriended them. "We've got to stick together," Edna would tell Mother Beatifica and Sister Pontifica and the other sisters. "Otherwise, these bigoted barnacles will eat us alive." By "barnacles," Edna meant the islanders. She included Sleeper in this definition, though she never called him a barnacle to his face. Edna, Lois Blakey, and the nuns at Mercy on the Rock Cloister had formed their own secret alliance, calling themselves "the Society of Suffering Fools," and this strong bond helped each of them endure the island mentality.

In all honesty, Edna wasn't totally convinced that Lois Blakey was innocent of her husband's murder. Sometimes she would look at Lois and behold a sort of deep corridor in the pupils of her eyes, and when Edna tried traveling down that limpid hall, she'd experience acutely foreboding thrills along her spine. But Lois had been a good friend over the years, and Edna felt sure that if she, Edna, murdered Sleeper (in self-defense, of course), Lois would come to her aid and comfort. Edna had tried convincing Mother Beatifica and her God's Watchers to come out publicly in support of Lois Blakey, but Beatifica had demurred.

"We all like Lois well enough, don't get me wrong," Beatifica had told Edna somewhat evasively. "But none of us is convinced of her innocence."

What Mother Beatifica wasn't saying, but what Edna knew, was that the nuns at Mercy on the Rock fervently prayed for Lois Blakey's conviction, because they coveted Lois Blakey's land. The nuns, Edna knew in her heart, were nothing more sacred than land-lusting grabbersnatchers of the greediest species. Now that God's Watchers Feelgoods had a Web site up and running, undies sales were booming, and they needed more land to support a new pulp-paper processing plant.

Not that Edna would accuse or criticize the Sisters of Mercy on the Rock in public, or—God forbid—to their faces; Edna's negative opinions of her friends remained unspoken, except the one or two comments she had made to Sleeper when her guard was down. Maybe Sleeper had repeated some of Edna's private opinions to other islanders; Edna wouldn't put it past him. Or maybe it was something else. More likely, Edna's captor had heard the derogatory remarks she'd made about Breedhaven, and how that Dr. Strindberg had deserved to burn. Maybe that was why her captor had kidnapped her off the dock at Friday Harbor, driven her to this primitive cabin in the woods, and bound her like an animal. Even the animals on Breedhaven were treated better than Edna was being treated by her captor.

He wasn't exactly a stranger to Edna. She'd seen him several times from a distance, riding the ferries whenever he visited Helix Island. This was the first time she had seen him up close, and she guessed that the earring had thrown her off. She'd never learned to pronounce his name, but she knew that he had some connection to Breedhaven. He might have overheard Edna's back-stabbing criticism of his friends at Breedhaven, might have learned that she, Edna, was the initiator of a petition quietly circulating around Helix Island demanding that Breedhaven be closed. He might have learned that Edna had just mailed a letter to her congressman, asking that Breedhaven be investigated for tax fraud; she didn't have evidence, just a strong intuitive feeling. Or maybe her captor was Sleeper's paid assassin. Edna had always suspected that Sleeper had drowned his first wife. Maybe now Sleeper had the same fate in mind for Edna.

Edna had overheard her captor talking on his cell phone. He kept repeating the words "Pro-Gen." Edna couldn't shake that name out of her mind ever since she read it on that little scrap of paper on the ferry boat. It sounded sinister to Edna, somehow unholy. Maybe it was a Russian word. Her captor, after all, was one—Russian.

At first, he had told her to call him Mr. Petrovich. Edna had scoffed at that and told him what his real name was. Even though she couldn't pronounce it very well, she told him, "There's nothing Petrovich about you. You're that Larry Chekhov, I don't care what kind of beard you try to grow." You have to get up pretty early in the morning to fool Edna Furbank.

AROUND THREE O'CLOCK in the afternoon, Chekhov returned to the cabin where Edna sat tied to a chair, strapped in with a belt for good measure. On the table before her, he set down a brown paper bag from the Stop 'N Go over at Friday Harbor. Pungent, unattractive odors rose from the sack. Across the table, Chekhov rubbed his hands together, reached for the bag, tore it open, and fished out several cardboard containers. Edna watched as he lay slices of what he called turkey on a beat-up tin plate, added what he said was oyster dressing—though to Edna it looked like mashed bread cubes—and jellied cranberry sauce, then set the plate before Edna. He reached into the sack again and fished out some plastic forks, tossing one at Edna.

"Now eat," ordered Chekhov.

"I can't," snapped Edna.

Chekhov looked at Edna. *"Tak!"* he exclaimed, then he freed her hands. More furious than hungry, Edna sat paralyzed in the chair. "Happy Christmas, Edna Furbank," the Russian said cheerfully, between mouthfuls.

"That was yesterday," Edna retorted.

"Whatever," replied Chekhov, ripping food like a vulture at its prey. It made Edna sick to watch him, so she turned her head away, but Chekhov slammed his fist on the table and shouted, "I said, eat!"

Chekhov was far too burly to argue with, and he had that pistol set right up beside his turkey plate, so that if Edna tried anything funny he could plug her full of holes. He'd warned her, and Edna took his warning to heart. She raised a forkful of Stop 'N Go pressed-turkey product to her mouth, and nibbled. When Chekhov dished up the plum pudding, Edna wasn't hungry, and, too, she knew it wasn't real plum pudding, but artificially sweetened fruitcake. Still, she ate, out of sheer trepidation.

Chekhov smacked his lips over the pudding. Privately, Edna wished he'd choke to death. Hope springs eternal, especially when death looms large.

Later that night, as usual, Chekhov let Edna use the outhouse while he guarded the door. Then he tied Edna to the filthy bed, went over and slouched in a chair, and dropped his head on his chin. Edna lay on the bed trying to make sense of her imprisonment.

Edna was normally too stubborn to interrogate an enemy, but she had to know if Sleeper was behind this. Now, after three days of captivity, she finally broke.

"Mister?" she said from where she lay in the darkness.

"Huh?" said the Russian sleepily.

"Are you a communist?"

He chuckled. "Depends who you ask."

"I'm asking you."

Chekhov reached into his pocket, pulled out a worn leather wallet, and fished out a filthy, frayed-plastic laminated card. He held this before Edna's eyes. Edna said, "I can't read these damn letters. They're Greek or something."

"*Tak!* Allow me to translate." He cleared his throat and read, "'Sergei Petrovich, Member in Good Standing, Communist Party of City of Leningrad, Member Number 314532724.'" He made a sweeping gesture with his arms, and bowed. He was far too dramatic a man for Edna's tastes.

Chekhov said, "But you see, dear Edna Furbank, that was a long time ago, in a different lifetime. I only keep this little card as a souvenir. Today I am a capitalist, and a very successful one, too."

"Why are you holding me here?"

Chekhov shook his head sadly. "Oh, my dear, you are far too—how do you say?—snooping."

"I haven't seen anything."

Chekhov wiggled his finger in her face. "You cannot deny it."

"Are you going to kill me?"

"Have to." Matter-of-fact.

"But why?" Edna's heart pounded. "I told you I didn't see anything."

Chekhov said, "You saw something with your own eyes. Then you had to talk about it. No, it's too late for you, Edna. You know too much."

"But...what are you talking about?"

"You know very well, Edna Furbank. You know what you saw."

"Because I saw you on the *Klikitat* before you kidnapped me? That's all I know. I don't know anything else. I haven't seen anything else. That—that paper? I didn't see what it said—really, I didn't," she lied. "You have no reason to kill me."

Chekhov said, "You're a poor liar, Edna. Your snoopings get you into deep troubles."

"You've held me for three days. Why haven't you killed me yet?"

The Russian smiled, a bit too sweetly. "All things must be done prudently, each in its own time."

"I'll bet Sleeper's behind this somehow."

Chekhov said, "Why, Edna, such a nasty thing to say about your life partner." He chuckled, dropped his chin, and fell into a stupor. Edna lay fuming, thinking of ways to get even with Sleeper once she had escaped. *It just goes to prove, you can't even trust your own life partner.* Then suddenly, Edna had an extraordinary idea. Maybe she and Chekhov had something in common after all.

"Mister?"

Chekhov opened his eyes again and grunted. Edna said, "Have you ever been to New Orleans?" Chekhov shook his head, but a wishful expression came over his face, and a glint dropped into his eye. "One day, I want to go to Big Easy," he sighed wistfully.

Edna said, "I've got some great connections in New Orleans. Know what I mean?" Chekhov woke up fully then, and he and Edna talked into the wee hours.

Later, Chekhov fell off to sleep, and night swallowed up Edna Furbank. As she lay across the filthy bed in the rundown cabin, her mind flashed back to the Carousel Lounge at the Monteleone Hotel in New Orleans, where Sleeper Sexton had lured her off that pinto-pony barstool. Now she saw the carousel turning, could hear the carnival music, could taste the sweet Sazerac.

ON BOXING DAY, Bella always threw a party for her household staff. Because this year's frigid weather precluded the use of

outdoor decks and terraces, Bella held the fête in her living
room, a vast cavern overlooking the Cascade mountain range,
from Mount Baker, along the rugged, snowcapped range to
Mount Rainier. The foreground of this panoramic vista encom-
passed a wide swath of Puget Sound, downtown Seattle, and
Queen Anne Hill, crowned by the ubiquitous Space Needle. Like
all Seattle-ites with views, Bella had the mandatory high-
powered telescope on a tripod, aimed out the windows. Bella
never spied on the neighbors, but her adopted son, Timmy,
thrived on such prurient activity.

So powerful was Bella's Bushnell that Timmy could even spy
two hills distant, on diners at the restaurant on top of the Space
Needle, and he often did so. One of Timmy's favorite tricks was
singling out a particularly romantic pair of diners. Timmy would
ring up the Space Needle restaurant and start bawling, describing
the woman of the couple as his mother, claiming she had locked
him in the house, and now the house was on fire and he was
trapped—or some such tale. Timmy possessed a vast collection
of tall tales and intrigues, and what better way to pass a boring
evening at home than to terrorize the diners in the Space Needle?
So far, Timmy had managed to evade discovery by using Bella's
non-IDed, secured cell phone.

On this particular Boxing Day afternoon, during the house
staff festivities, Timmy was perched at Bella's Bushnell, the cell
phone on his lap ready for speed-dialing, and was zooming in
on a couple of prospects, when Burden, Bella's house manager,
approached him.

"Here now, Timothy," said Burden reproachfully. "Come
away from there. I know what you are doing."

Timmy waved a tiny hand at Burden. "No thank you, Burden.
I don't care for dessert."

"That is not what I said, young man." Burden, to whom the
mistress of the house had granted certain discretionary powers,
grasped Timmy by the earlobe and pulled him away from the
telescope.

"Now, what am I supposed to do?" Timmy fumed. "This
party's a flop."

Just then Stephen materialized with a plate of turkey and trimmings, handed it to Burden, and said, "Leave him to me, Burden." Stephen grasped Tim by the arm and marched him into the foyer. When they were alone, away from the party scene, Stephen leaned down and said, "Now, young man, kindly tell me where Trouble got off to in such a hurry."

"Her name's Venus," snapped Timmy. "And I promised not to divulge that information." Timmy didn't have the foggiest idea where Venus was, but, just for effect, he pressed his lips together and folded his arms across his chest.

Stephen leaned in closer to Timmy's resolutely sealed lips. "You tell me, or I'll report you."

Timmy glared at Stephen with no small disgust. "Report me for what?"

Stephen said, "I found this in your bedroom," and produced a heavily thumbed paperback volume of *Lolita*.

Timmy grinned defiantly. "Go ahead. Report me. I dare you."

"Very well." Stephen straightened up and marched into the dining room where Bella was holding court. Stephen approached Bella, whispered in her ear. From the foyer, Timmy watched Bella's eyes widen and her brows lift simultaneously, not at all in the individually arched manner in which they rose in disapproval, but more in genuine surprise. When Stephen finished whispering, he showed Bella the volume of *Lolita*.

Bella glanced at the book, exclaimed, "How lovely, Stephen darling. Timothy is reading the classics."

Grinning victoriously, Timmy grabbed his coat and mittens from the hall closet, and escaped out the front door. An unusually tenacious snowfall coated the expansive front lawns, the fountains were frozen, and it was simply too cold outdoors to have any fun. *Unless,* Timmy thought, *I build Snowlita.* He immediately applied himself to the task.

Within a short time, Timmy had fashioned a reasonable replica of a naked Lolita astride a prone young man. He was working on the nether regions—or what he imagined the nether regions to be—when a car drove up, a man got out and peered through the gates. The security guard had gone inside for the festivities, so Timmy temporarily abandoned Snowlita and friend and walked down to greet the stranger. The one thing Timmy would remember later was the man's perfectly shaped earlobes, and, too, his eyes reminded Timmy of soaked teabags.

"Can I help you?" Timmy asked when he reached the gate. The man said, "Is your mother home?"

Timmy said, "Yeah, but she's busy. She's having a party."

"That's lovely," the stranger said. He handed Timmy an envelope. "Would you give your mother this letter?"

Timmy accepted the envelope, stuffed it inside his jacket. "Sure." He was heading for the house when the stranger said, "You ought to be spanked."

Timmy turned around. "What for?"

The man pointed at Snowlita. "For that. It's dirty."

Timmy tossed off an expletive, and the stranger disappeared down the street.

BELLA READ the message with alarm; any mother would have. The message, in bold print on cheap paper, said:

Lady Winsome-Diamond.
We have your daughter. Unless you come immediately to Breedhaven and bring the ark's decode material, we will kill her. If you notify the police or anyone else, we will immediately execute your daughter.

Stephen said, "Is something wrong, ma'am?"

Bella looked up from the message and stared at Stephen. "Oh. No. No, nothing at all, Stephen darling. But I'm afraid that I must go somewhere right away. Will you kindly take care of our guests?"

TWENTY

ARDITH

EXHAUSTED FROM WORRY, unable to shake the image of Fanny Faber's battered, bloated corpse from his mind, Sleeper Sexton decided to take a few days off from work, and from island council business. He had asked Morris Fluke to take over island council duties for a while, but Morris had spent the past few days searching all over Helix Island for Teensy's cat, and Morris was tired, too. Ordinarily, Morris said, he'd have been glad to help Sleeper out, but right now Pearl was his first priority. "I've searched all over this rock," said Morris. "And I can't find hide nor hair of that cat. Teensy's having conniption fits, afraid Pearl's been catnapped, of all things."

"Sorry to hear that, Morris."

"What about Dundee?" Morris asked Sleeper. "You found Dundee yet?"

"No, Dundee hasn't come home. And I haven't seen Pearl. But cats are resourceful. I'll bet they're safe somewhere. They'll eventually turn up."

In the end, Sleeper and Morris decided to ask Jean Teaweather to hold the council reins. The two men remarked on Jean's resourcefulness, how Jean could handle anything that came along, no matter how dim the skies or bleak the spirit. Sleeper told Morris to convey his regards to Teensy, then he turned off his telephone ringer and made up his mind to do nothing for the rest of the year except read the classics. A man has to find solace somewhere.

THE NEXT MORNING Libb Lufkin stepped out the back door of her house carrying her French-press coffeemaker, and walked over to the edge of the woods. On the way, she passed Luther

working on his snow minotaur, which by now was more ice
than snow. Luther had spent hours sculpting the minotaur, and
when the snow began melting, Luther had experimented with
hot water and freezing temperatures until he had perfected an
ice sculptor's formula. He'd managed to keep the minotaur alive
for four days now, and was determined to prevent it from melting for as long as he could.

Libb smiled at Luther and flung the coffee grounds from her
French press into the woods. "Helps fertilize the ferns," Libb
remarked, but Luther didn't hear his mother, so absorbed was
he in his task. Libb clucked her tongue proudly at the sight of
her industrious son. Some mothers are just plain blessed with
Good Boys. Libb went on inside and got back to her household
chores.

Luther had formed a beautiful set of ice antlers on the minotaur, and as the noontime sun peeked through a gray cloud
cover, the creature's antlers glistened. Luther watched ner-
vously. Sooner or later the creature would melt, and then what
would he do? As he watched the sun warm the minotaur, Luther
thought he heard a mewing sound in the woods nearby. The
sound continued for some time, and got Luther's curiosity up.
On the one hand, he wanted to keep an eye on the antlers'
reaction to the sun. On the other hand, the mewing sound interested him. Minnie tended to stay underneath the house most of
the time, but Luther hadn't seen Minnie all day, come to think
of it, and that sound in the woods might just be the reason why.
Luther shot a last glance at the minotaur's melting antlers and
ran into the woods.

He found Minnie and her newborn kittens inside a fallen cedar
log that time and creatures had hollowed out and softened. Minnie had brought in some grass and made her own birthing bed.
Now she lay inside the log, protecting her newborns, which Luther could hear but couldn't see. Luther got down on his knees
and peered inside the cedar log. Minnie looked out at Luther
and hissed.

"It's okay, Minnie," said Luther gently. "Good girl, Minnie."

Minnie hissed again, but Luther wouldn't be discouraged.

"Let's see those kitties," he said and reached an arm inside the log. Minnie hissed, and with one paw lashed out at Luther's hand. "Ow! That hurts," cried Luther, and he removed his hand.

"Whatcha got there, Luther?"

Luther looked up and saw Gordon Mantle. Gordon was standing with his legs kind of spread; he reminded Luther of a bow-legged cowboy. Luther said, "It's my cat, Minnie. She's had kittens."

"Is that right?" Gordon came forward, pushed Luther aside. "Let me have a look-see."

"Be careful," cautioned Luther. "She scratches."

"Aw, Minnie knows me," said Gordon, and he got down on his knees and peered inside the cedar log. "Well, I'll be," he said, and then he reached one arm inside. Luther heard Minnie hiss and howl, and then Gordon said, "Ow," but he kept his arm inside the log until he got hold of something. Then Gordon said, "Gotcha," and pulled his arm out.

Gordon held up a tiny kitten, unlike any Luther had ever seen. The kitten had golden red hair, a bright white stripe across its brow, and a long black stripe along its tail. "Gosh," Luther exclaimed, "That's a funny-looking kitty."

Gordon nodded solemnly and said, "You go home, boy."

"But I have to help Minnie with her kittens—"

Gordon said, "No. These kittens are deformed. They won't live long. You go home and let me take care of things here."

Luther was worried now. "They're going to die?"

"They're very sick, son, and I am going to help them out."

"You're going to kill them?" Luther stared, unbelieving.

Gordon said firmly, "You go on home. Go on now."

Luther wasn't convinced. "But, these are Minnie's kittens," he argued. "Maybe Minnie can help them, if you just leave them be—"

"I said, go on." Gordon sounded angry.

Luther couldn't decide what he should do. He didn't want to abandon Minnie and her kittens, especially if they were ill. But Gordon Mantle sounded very upset, and he was a grown-up and probably knew what was best for the cats. Luther said,

"Couldn't I just stay here and watch while you help the kittens?"

The kitten Gordon held in his big hand mewed softly and searched for its mother's milk. Its golden coat looked nothing like Minnie's white fur, and the shape of its head and its face reminded Luther of a bobcat. It wasn't ugly; in fact, Luther thought the kitten was adorable. He reached up. "Let me hold it, Mr. Mantle."

Gordon almost shouted, "I told you to get out of here—now, Luther. There are some things you don't understand. Now git, before I have to swat you one."

"Will Minnie be okay?"

"I'll bring her on home to you in just a little while."

Luther wasn't entirely convinced, but he finally turned and walked out of the woods toward his house. He wanted to consult his mother. She was a nurse, after all.

Inside the Lufkin house, Luther found his mother in the kitchen, peeling apples for a pie. Luther said, "Mom, Minnie had her kittens up in the woods. But Gordon Mantle said they're sick, and he's going to take care of them."

Libb dropped the apple and the knife into the sink and exclaimed, "My God! Where is Minnie?"

"Up in the woods. I'll show you."

But Libb was already out the back door, running past the minotaur, across the field into the woods.

Luther caught up with her. "Over here," he shouted, and Libb turned and followed him. When they reached the cedar log, Minnie lay on the snowy ground beside four dead kittens, crying and licking them with her tongue. Gordon was gone.

"Oh, God, no," cried Libb. "Oh my God, no!"

Minnie looked up at Libb and mewed. Luther said, "I guess Gordon couldn't save them." Forlornly.

TEENSY FLUKE was tossing stale breadcrumbs out to the birds when a strange cat pounced onto her back porch, narrowly missing her. Teensy dropped the pan of bread and ran into the house where Morris was watching television. "Morris, come quick," she cried. "There's a wildcat out there on the porch. He pounced at me. Hurry, Morris."

Morris rose wearily from his chair and went outdoors. He couldn't see the cat Teensy was talking about. He walked around the yard, just to satisfy Teensy that it was safe. Then he saw something he had hoped he'd never see. Over beneath a holly bush, Pearl lay lifeless on the ground. Scooping up the dead cat, Morris turned and saw Teensy standing right behind him.

"Oh, Pearl," Teensy cried. "My poor Pearl."

"God, I'm sorry, Teens," said Morris. "And she's lost her litter, too."

Teensy reached up and touched Pearl's neck. "Why look, Morris. I believe Pearl was strangled."

VENUS'S HEAD throbbed and when she tried to move her arms and legs, they wouldn't budge. A cloth gag had been drawn taut against her mouth. She opened her eyes but saw only darkness at first. When she breathed, she could taste salt air, but she detected a distinct odor of animals along with it. She couldn't tell what time it was—if it was night or day, or how long it had been since someone had knocked her silly at the Empress Hotel.

Her back hurt something awful. She wanted to shift her position, but even though her brain had returned, her body wouldn't budge. When her eyes became accustomed to the dim light, she saw that she was seated on the ground on some hay, lashed to a wood post. How long had she been unconscious? Hours? Days? Weeks?

The space around her was pitch-black and cold. She could hear the wind blowing, but she didn't feel it, so she must be indoors. When she heard the honking, Venus thought at first that her own voice had made the sound, but then realized that something else, very near, was making the noise.

Honk. Honk, honk, it went.

"Erghh..." went Venus.

Honk.

"Erghh."

She felt something soft brush against her arm, where her arm was bare at the wrist. It pressed into her, and she knew it was alive. It butted up against her, as if rooting. She tried pushing it off, but it wouldn't budge. Then she sneezed and the thing flew off into the darkness. In the distance, an owl hooted, and she decided it must be night.

When daylight finally streamed through cracks in a wall, she saw that she was in a barn, or outbuilding structure. The streaming daylight shone across bales of hay, and a wooden stall, where Venus perceived a strange tail wagging. Whatever it was attached to was lost in the darkness. Nearby, some goslings were pecking at seed that had been placed on a low feeder. Venus looked around and decided that, except for the baby geese and the strange animal in the stall, she was alone.

Her gun was gone, and so was her digital phone. It took half an hour and extreme patience to work the ropes off. When she stood up, she swayed dizzily and had to hang on to the post. Gradually her sense of balance returned, and after a cautious inspection, she located the barn's door on the opposite side of the hay bales. She'd have to pass the stall with the odd tail poking out of it. She stared at the tail for a long time, trying to identify it. It didn't belong to a cow, nor a horse. Nor a mule. A donkey? No. If she really let her mind go wild, she'd say it looked like a rhino's tail....

Of course. The white rhino. She must be at Breedhaven. She had been taken to one of the feeding stations on the habitat, held there as a prisoner. Whose prisoner? Chekhov's? Rosemary Poole's? Who had smuggled her back across the Canadian border? Why hadn't they just killed her? Why hold her? As a hostage?

Cautiously she moved across the barn. The rhino made grunting sounds, but Venus kept moving, and eventually reached the other side. She was pushing the door open into the cold bright morning light when she felt a smooth, cool object rub against her. She looked down and saw the great horn, the tough gray skin. She looked straight into the bull rhino's eyes, but she lacked hypnotic powers, and when she flinched, the rhino grunted, pawed the snow-covered ground, and bending his head, he scooped her onto his back, and took off. She clung to his hide as the rhino tore headlong into a wooded thicket, where they parted when Venus slipped off into the frozen marsh, landing headfirst among a gaggle of the strangest geese she had ever seen. The rhino, apparently as terrified as she was, lumbered off into the forest. She stumbled to her feet.

The air was frigid, the gray dawn sky hung low, and fog vapors poured through the woods. She heard gulls cry, a bell buoy, and the sound of a passing vessel's foghorn. Thrashing through densely packed snow, she ran breathlessly, then stumbled and fell to the frozen earth. Crawling to her feet, she lost her balance again, fell against a bramble bush, its sharp bracts tearing the flesh on her legs. As she stanched the bleeding, she heard a thrashing sound behind her. She turned around and saw Gordon Mantle thrusting through the fog.

"Oh, dear God," cried Gordon, obviously alarmed. "Where did you come from?" He fled into the woods. She didn't bother chasing him. But why had Gordon run away when he saw her? Had he recognized her? She thought so. Was he tearful, or was it guilt that had caused Gordon to flee?

Slowly she picked a path through the woods, keeping an eye out for the ubiquitous rhinoceros. Sooner or later, she'd reach civilization, or what passed for it on Helix Island. She was cold and tired, but energized by a gut feeling that she was close to the habitat's main compound. Then she saw it through the woods.

Vigil's Volvo sat in the parking lot, beside a black Mercedes sedan. She moved cautiously along the wooded path toward the main lodge, but her soft footfall struck a stone and she fell, landing on top of Ardith Pierce—or what was left of her. Mrs. Pierce was very dead. Beside her lay a set of car keys: Mercedes-Benz.

Mrs. Pierce still wore her diamond jewelry, and her handbag was strapped across her shoulder. This hadn't been a robbery. A single bullet hole to the head—this was an execution. The body was still warm; she hadn't been dead long. She closed the corpse's eyes.

Through the trees, Venus saw the compound yard was deserted. She listened. No sounds of activity, but the air crackled electrically. She felt a presence, but it felt like death. More death.

When she reached the main lodge, she forced open the rear door and slipped inside.

Silence met her. She moved from one room to the next, cautiously. In the kitchen, a pot of coffee sat on its warmer. On the counter, a plate of butterhorns, and, beside the plate, some linen napkins. In the main hall, she found overnight luggage belonging to Ardith Pierce, Fanny Faber, and Stan Rowe. Besides Mrs. Pierce's Mercedes, no other cars were outside except Vigil's Volvo. Had the three trustees arrived together in Mrs. Pierce's car?

The foyer and living room were deserted. She picked up a telephone. The line was dead. The bedrooms hadn't been disturbed. She walked down a long corridor to the last room. She opened the door and went in. Inside, she found a conference room, and a table set up for a meeting...of trustees? No; a stockholders' meeting. Pro-Gen stock certificates lay on the table before each place. At one place, Stan Rowe's body slumped over the table. She checked his pulse. Dead. Bullet through the head. Near his cold hand on the table lay a piece of paper that said Mr. Stan Rowe now was the proud owner of one thousand shares of Pro-Gen stock. A lot of good it would do him now.

From all appearances, Breedhaven's trustees had been offered Pro-Gen stock, but at least some had refused. That may have made them witnesses to a crime, not coconspirators. And surely they were being pumped for the decode materials. Which trustee had been given possession of this vital information? Chekhov needed to know, if Chekhov had stolen the ark.

She walked around the table, reading the stock certificates at each place. Frances Faber. Stan Rowe. Larry Chekhov at the head of the table. Tina Medina seated beside Chekhov. Rosemary Poole. Ardith...

She heard a car drive up outside, its wheels grinding against the gravel. Venus peered out the window, but couldn't see the car, or its driver. She heard the car's door shut, then footsteps crunching on the gravel moving toward the lodge. She looked around the conference room. There were no closets, no decent hiding places. Someone was walking into the lodge, heading down the corridor toward the conference room. She ducked under the table just as the door opened. From her hiding place she looked up and out at the intruder. She saw the legs first, the unmistakable Lloyd's of London legs.

"Mother," she cried. "What are you doing here?"

Bella shot back, "Good heavens, Venus, you nearly scared the life out of me. Now come out from under that table and explain this ransom note."

"What ransom note?" Venus stood up, brushed off.

Bella thrust the letter at Venus. Venus read the note. "But I haven't been kidnapped. That is, I might have been, but now I'm not—"

"Oh yes you are," said Chekhov, appearing in the doorway. He pointed a gun at her. "And now, so is Lady Winsome-Diamond."

Bella turned around. "Why, Larry!" she cried. "Put that gun down, or I shall speak to Ilona."

Chekhov grinned. "Lady Winsome-Diamond, what a lovely sight. Have you brought the decode material?"

Regal, composed, Bella sniffed, "I refuse to be blackmailed."

Venus said, "But, Mother—"

"Shut up, you dimwit," Chekhov snarled. Herding them into the hall at gunpoint, he ignored Venus's protestations. "I'll have to split you two up." He locked Bella in a hall broom closet, then dragged Venus farther down the hall. "So you escaped from me, did you?" he said to Venus. "Well, don't try it again, little pussyfoot, or I'll shoot your mama."

"Leave Bella out of this," said Venus. "I'll come along with you, but leave Bella alone. She's not involved in this. She doesn't have the decode."

"Then who does?" demanded Chekhov.

"I don't know, but my mother has nothing to do with this," Venus insisted. "And you didn't have to shoot out her plate glass window trying to kill me."

Chekhov shoved Venus into a coat closet. Before he shut the door, he said, "But I wasn't trying to kill you, my little pussyfoot. I was trying to scare your mother. And now I am going to scare both of you. That is, unless you agree to tell me what I want to know."

"What do you want to know?"

"I want you, or your mother, to tell me where the decode is."

Venus said, "I don't know. Neither does Bella."

Chekhov shook his head. "I can see this is going to be a long and gruesome night."

He shut the door, locked it, and went away.

Venus was locked in a closet containing several overcoats, probably meant for the trustees or other guests to wear when they visited Breedhaven and wished to walk the grounds. Methodically, she went through the pockets of each coat. She came up empty, until the last coat. In its pocket, she found a pair of woman's gloves, and a corkscrew. With the sharp edge of the screw, she jimmied the lock in the doorknob. When the door popped open, she ran down the hall and forced open the broom closet door. The closet was empty.

Venus raced to the window. Bella's Town Car was gone.

Had Bella been taken away? Had she escaped? Did Bella know that Venus, too, was locked in a closet? Had Bella escaped and left her daughter behind?

From the rear door of the lodge to Ardith Pierce's corpse, Venus counted one hundred and eighty steps. The leaden sky threatened rain or more snow—at the very least, a storm. She heard the wind howling through the trees. She bent over Ardith Pierce's corpse and reached for the key to the Mercedes-Benz. The metal key was cold to the touch, like Ardith. She clutched the key and trudged back to the lodge, counting her footsteps as she went.

The parking lot was deserted. Vigil's Volvo was gone. The Mercedes sat alone in front of the lodge. Where was Chekhov? Venus would have to cross the gravel drive, about fifty feet from where she stood at the side of the lodge to where the Mercedes was parked. She started walking, her breath tight, her heart pounding. She heard crows cawing as the storm moved overhead. She counted her steps...ten, eleven, twelve...fifteen, sixteen...she reached the Mercedes, unlocked the driver's-side door, slid behind the wheel. She fit the key in the ignition, turned it. The engine turned over, purring. She backed out of the parking lot, gravel flying under the squealing tires. She floored the gas pedal. The Mercedes sped down the road, through the compound and into the habitat.

The sky grew blacker, and though it was afternoon, she should have used headlights, but couldn't risk attracting attention. She drove fast, her heart pounding. She was halfway through the marshlands when she felt the deceleration and heard the engine sputter. The car came rolling to a stop.

Venus got out, started walking. The ground was frozen and snowy patches made a treacherous path. She heard noises coming from the marsh, stopped, listened.... Grunting. *What creature is that?* Then she saw the rhino. Wallowing. She stood very still, waited, hardly breathing. The rhino rolled over in the mud, moaning ecstatically. She took a chance, moved without sound, but slipped on a patch of snow, landing with a crash against some low branches. The rhino sat up and listened. She held her breath. He was about thirty feet from where she crouched beside the low bush. She could see him looking around, sniffing the air.

She knew this much: Rhinos are herbivores. They don't eat meat, but they'll attack any red-blooded animal that threatens them. They'll kill, but they won't eat.

She held very still, hardly breathing. Finally the rhino resumed his wallowing and moaning. She crouch-walked out of the march, then ran into the forest. She knew that if she headed west, sooner or later she'd reach the rocky ledge above the wooden dock that Gordon had shown her. At the dock was the little boat.

The air grew colder and the howling winds increased. She ran swiftly through the woods, finally reaching the rocky ledge above the dock. She stopped to catch her breath, and that's when she heard a voice say, "So there you are, pussyfoot."

Chekhov pointed his .44 Magnum at her head and led her back into the woods, to a small cabin nearby. From the cabin, she could see the dock. In the distance, she could see a boat passing. If she yelled, someone might hear her, might go for help. But Chekhov would have shot her before they came. As Chekhov took her behind the cabin, she heard the boat putter into the distance. Then Chekhov smacked her over the head.

TWENTY-ONE

NIRVANA

SHE WASN'T UNCONSCIOUS, but dazed. She went limp, but Chekhov knew how to play the game. He heaved her slack body off the ground, flung her over his shoulder, and began walking. As he walked, she counted the steps. When they had gone a little way, she heard Chekhov's feet on a different surface. Not earth. Wood. She heard a ferry boat toot in the distance. She heard the wind blowing, the water slapping against rocks.

She wanted to fight him, but her body felt listless, her brain fuzzed. She kept counting...fifteen...twenty-five...thirty...forty-five...fifty-one. Fifty-one steps, then Chekhov stopped walking.

She opened her eyes. It was too dark to see anything, but she felt hands peel her off Chekhov's shoulder and she had the sensation of falling, then realized that someone was holding on to her, and pulling her downward. She heard water lapping against a solid surface, and felt a rocking sensation. She was being carried along the deck of a boat.

She heard a door slide open, felt the hands let go of her, and then her body landed in a heap on something soft. She heard a door slide shut, felt the crisp night air disintegrate, and she breathed in an exotic perfume. She felt warm, comfortable. The night air had vanished. And in here, the lights were on. At first, her eyes blinked and watered profusely, but gradually they focused on the face of a beautiful woman.

ROSEMARY POOLE was dressed all in black like a cat burglar, like Chekhov's twin. She was crouching over Venus, her face so close that Venus felt her breath, and that exotic perfume was hers, a pungent, spicy fragrance full of sensual promises that she probably kept. Her eyes were limpid blue pools, reflecting some

inscrutable light, and her full mouth was painted deep scarlet.
She frowned and her two caterpillar eyebrows joined for a split
second, then the worry left her expression and her face smoothed
out. She smiled and said, "Have a headache?"

Venus glanced down, saw she had landed on a mountain of
silk cushions. She moved her arms, flexed her wrists and said,
"Whose party boat is this?"

Rosemary smiled and said, "We are guests on the *Nirvana*.
Would you care for some juice, and something to eat?"

Venus looked around. They were in the boat's stateroom. A
ship, if you wanted to get technical. The vessel rocked roughly,
but nothing in the room shifted or moved. The room was a shrine
to the real Taj Mahal (not the Alki Point pad), with gold gilt
furniture, sleek silk couches, huge silk cushions piled everywhere. Overhead, crystal chandeliers glittered like Rosemary's
eyes. The couch on which Rosemary now reclined had arms and
legs dipped in gold. On a jade coffee table, a solid jade cigarette
box was engraved with a circular crest.

Rosemary reached behind the couch, pulled on a silk tassel,
and a small boy in pajamas materialized. Rosemary addressed
him in English, which the boy apparently understood. The boy
bowed, whispered something to the carpet, and backed out of
the stateroom through a tall door that he gently but firmly locked
behind him. Rosemary stretched out lazily. "Just behind you is
the powder room. There's aspirin in there, for your headache."

Venus went in, tried jimmying the lock on the porthole window, but it wouldn't open so she went back to the stateroom
where Rosemary was reclining like an odalisque on the persim-
mon couch, only now she was holding a book up to her face
and apparently absorbed in reading. When she heard Venus, she
glanced up.

"We can't set sail in this storm," Rosemary announced. "So
we'll just spend the night here." Her eyes sparkled, her gaze
traveled briefly around the room, came back to the book, and
she resumed reading. Venus went over to the door that led onto
the outside deck, tried sliding it open. It didn't budge.

"It's locked," explained Rosemary. "We are locked in. It's
for our own protection."

"Oh yeah?" Venus growled. "You call this being protected? I call it being shanghaied."

"Shanghai? No, we're not going to Shanghai."

"Then where?"

"Someplace warm and sunny. That's all I care about." Rosemary went back to her book. Venus tilted her head, read the title on the book's binding. *Gone with the Wind.*

Oh great, Venus thought to herself. *Another Scarlett wannabe.*

As if reading her mind, Rosemary looked up and said curtly, "I am not reading this of my own volition."

"So then, why?"

"My grandfather, may he rest in pieces, is requiring me to read it. As a condition of receiving the trust fund he left me."

When she pivoted onto her side, Rosemary's trim waist formed a gentle valley to her hips, a landscape Venus guessed Chekhov had traversed a few times. Venus said, "Is his real name Chekhov, or Petrovich?"

When Rosemary smiled, her eyes shut for a split second. She opened them and said, "Larry Chekhov has several identities. He's a master of disguise."

"What about you, then? Are you the mistress of disguise?"

Evasively she said, "Chekhov and I are...collaborators of sorts."

"I'll bet you are." To Venus, Rosemary and Chekhov were a couple of criminals trying to steal a caseload of rare genetic material and some rare cats.

The boy in pajamas was named Cuckoo. He came back carrying a lacquer tray piled with fruit and cheese and flatbread. He set the tray on the table in front of Rosemary, bowed prayerfully, and backed out of the stateroom once again, locking up behind him.

The seas grew rougher and the boat rolled. The door opened again, and Cuckoo returned with a fancy thermos filled with what Rosemary insisted was hot poppyseed tea, which the boy poured for the two women. Then he bowed prayerfully again, backed out, and locked up. Rosemary went to work on the repast, urging Venus to join her.

"You must be hungry," Rosemary said. "Are you afraid we'll poison you?"

"As a matter of fact, I am," sneered Venus.

Rosemary frowned. "But just look. I have eaten. I have drunk. I'm fine. See? You can trust me. I don't intend to poison you, or drug you. I don't wish to harm you in any way whatsoever." She was friendly as a puppy. She behaved nothing like the bright but circumspect doctoral candidate Venus had encountered at Breedhaven. Maybe this was Rosemary's doppelganger, a clone gone wrong.

Rosemary said, "About Chekhov and me. Our relationship is entirely professional."

"As if I asked." Sarcastically.

"Is your mother all right?"

"How the hell should I know? The last time I saw her, Chekhov was stuffing her into a broom closet and locking the door. Then she disappeared."

Rosemary seemed surprised. "He didn't hurt her, did he?"

"As if you care."

The poppyseed tea apparently hadn't affected Rosemary, so Venus poured some into a small round cup and drank. It tasted more bitter than she'd expected. She swallowed and said, "How unique."

Soothingly Rosemary said, "Settle down. In time, you'll understand everything."

TIME PASSED SLOWLY and understanding did not come. The ship rolled and pitched and the weather grew surly and so did Venus. She tried again to elicit information from Rosemary.

"Where are the cats?" Venus asked.

Rosemary appeared to consider. "Which cats?"

"The pregnant female cats carrying Borneo Bay litters. You know what I'm talking about."

"I wish I knew. If we could answer that question, we'd all be very happy."

Cuckoo came in and rattled the tea things. Venus said, "Where's the ark?" Rosemary blinked. Venus growled, "Answer me, Rosemary. And quit batting your eyelashes. It makes me nauseous.''

Rosemary opened her eyes wide. ''Is this better?''

''Much. Now, where are you stashing the ark? And don't give me this guff.''

Cuckoo looked up inquiringly. ''What is an ark?''

''Like, Noah's ark? Get it?'' Rosemary said sweetly.

Cuckoo thought it over. ''No. I don't get it.''

''What part don't you get?'' Venus, slightly acid.

''Who is Noah?''

''You never heard of Noah, the biblical figure?'' Even Rosemary was surprised.

Cuckoo shrugged. ''I haven't read the Bible.''

Venus said, ''What about the Koran? Have you read the Koran?''

''In Lumbai, we are discouraged from reading religious material of any kind. It is against the rules,'' Cuckoo answered.

Lumbai? Of course, now it made sense. The Sultan of Lumbai had tried to buy the Borneo Bay, but Hannah got it. So, the sultan was still after the Bay cat. Maybe the ark, too.

To Cuckoo, Venus said, ''So not only are you in servitude, you also are forbidden to practice religion. What a delightful kingdom.''

Cuckoo said, ''You were going to tell me what is an ark, and who is Noah.''

''An ark is a vessel that holds something sacred, something precious,'' Venus told him. ''Noah was a biblical figure who supposedly lived some four thousand years ago. When a great storm came and an enormous flood threatened the world, Noah built a big boat and placed two of each animal species in it, a male and a female, in order to save all the earth's species from extinction. Noah's boat was called an ark because it protected life.''

Cuckoo smiled. ''Thank you for telling me about Noah. Now, tell me, please, is it fact or fiction?''

''It's biblical fact, which means it's a story passed down through time. Oral history, you know? The way history was recorded before people wrote things down.''

"Still, is it fact, or fiction?" Cuckoo was insistent.

Venus sighed. "Why don't you just go back to fixing tea and locking people up?"

This remark did not please Rosemary, who snapped, "Don't be rude to Cuckoo. He is the sultan's personal servant, and is due respect just like any other individual."

Venus said sarcastically, "No, hey, no disrespect intended." To Cuckoo, she said, "Nobody really knows whether Noah actually existed, or if he is just a figment of some early post-limbic fantasy."

"Limbic?" Cuckoo frowned.

"The brain stem. The part of the brain that formed first and controls our basic needs and desires." Venus yawned.

"Oh, I see." Unconvincing.

The boat pitched sharply. Cuckoo went out and locked up. Rosemary stood up and walked to a large window. The silk blinds were down. She raised a blind and peered out. "Nothing but blackness out there. We're in a bad storm."

Venus didn't say anything.

Rosemary turned from the window. "Are you frightened?"

"Of what?"

Rosemary said, "Of being anchored out here offshore in this storm. Are you afraid we'll drown?"

"It hadn't crossed my mind. From what little I've seen, I'd guess this is a pretty large vessel, pretty stable. As long as the captain knows what he's doing, we're probably okay."

Rosemary smiled. "Oh, Chekhov knows what he's doing."

Venus stared. "Chekhov's driving this boat?"

"Of course. Chekhov is an experienced skipper."

"What about the crew? Do we have a crew?"

Rosemary laughed. "You really are scared. Yes, of course we have a crew." She counted silently on her pretty fingers. "You've already met one of them."

"He who walks backwards?"

"I'll bet you want to know how Cuckoo got his name."

The boat listed hard, throwing Venus off the cushions. She caught herself before hitting her head on the jade coffee table, then rolled back onto the cushions and lay on her back, staring up at the shivering chandeliers. She said, "Okay, how did Cuckoo get his name?"

"When he was only four years old," said Rosemary, who now clung to the couch so she wouldn't fall off, "the boy was given a beautiful bird. Most little boys would love a bird and treat it as a pet. This little boy cooked the bird and ate it. Ever since, he is able to sing like a bird. Some even say he can fly. I don't know about that, but I know that he sings like a bird. When the Sultan of Lumbai heard about Cuckoo's talents, he bought the boy from his parents and made him a servant."

Venus sat up. "So this is the sultan's boat?"

Rosemary frowned. "I thought you already knew that."

Venus said, "If this is the sultan's boat, and Chekhov is the boat's captain, what does that make Chekhov?"

Rosemary smiled demurely. "The sultan's skipper, of course."

"More like assassin. The sultan's paid assassin."

The boat rolled steeply. Cuckoo struggled through the door, approached Rosemary and whispered in her ear, then backed out onto the stormy deck. Rosemary sighed contentedly. "We are to sit back and relax," she announced. "The captain has advised us that we shouldn't worry about the storm. He has everything under control."

"I'll bet." Dryly.

Rosemary ignored the sarcasm and added, "I'd suggest you get a good night's sleep."

"Why? So I'll be easier to drown tomorrow?"

Rosemary smiled, not unpleasantly, and said, "Tomorrow we'll all be very busy."

"I can hardly wait." Venus yawned again.

Rosemary settled back on her couch. "Just remember one thing," she said. "I may be a slut, but I'm loyal. Pleasant dreams."

Squalling gales lashed the vessel. It pitched and rolled, but Rosemary fell off to sleep almost immediately. Venus crept off the cushions and stole across the room. If she could just get to the dressing room without waking Rosemary. The shrieking bluster outside shrouded the sound of her footsteps, but the boat pitched hard and she lost her balance several times, crashing against furniture. Once, Rosemary stirred and half opened her eyes. Venus froze. Finally Rosemary fell back into a deep sleep. Venus grabbed the jade cigarette box and slipped into the bathroom.

She used the jade box to smash the porthole window, opened it, crawled up, squeezed through, and let herself down the other side, landing on the storm-ravaged deck. She grasped a brass railing and held on. The storm pounded the boat, and out here on deck she had no protection from its merciless assault. She might have done better to stay indoors, but now it was too late to turn back.

Struggling, she made her way along the deck, moving just inches with each step, and finally reached a ladder. She looked up but the storm was so thick she couldn't see where the ladder led. She climbed anyway, the howling winds lashing at her back, her bare hands gripping the wet iron bars. When she reached the top of the ladder, she threw herself across a flat surface and hung on. Through the squall, she saw the upper deck, and she saw the pilothouse. She crawled in that direction, not knowing what she'd do if she encountered Chekhov, but desperate now to escape the storm's brutal assault. Rain pelted her and the vessel rolled to starboard, throwing her off balance. She slid halfway back down the deck, caught herself on a lifeboat, narrowly avoiding rolling overboard into the sea. She lay still until she regained strength, then once more slow-crawled across the deck. At the pilothouse door, she pulled herself upright, struggled with the handle. It turned, and with fierce energy she slid the door open.

Chekhov stood with his back to her, his gloved hands gripping the ship's wheel. When the raging storm howled through the opening, he turned in surprise. She fell inside, slid the door shut, and clung to the cabin wall, breathing hard, but her hands lost their grip and the strength in her legs dwindled. She said, "Chekhov, you son of a..." Then she collapsed.

SHE REMEMBERED fragments at first. A storm, a heaving ship, a woman named Rosemary, a boy slave named Cuckoo. Chekhov.

She remembered that it was—or had been—the day after Christmas, what the English call Boxing Day. When she opened her eyes, she saw daylight streaming into the room, creeping across her body. She was lying on a bunk, in a room she didn't recognize. Slowly she sat up and felt her head pounding.

Had it been in the tea? Some strong potion had knocked her loopy. Had Rosemary drugged her? Or Cuckoo? She eased off the bunk, stood up, tried standing, but she toppled over. Residual hangover imbalance. She was locked in a small bedroom, on the ship's starboard side. There was a single window with bars across it, and she could see the salt water, some gulls perched on its glassy surface, and in the distance, the San Juan islands; the storm had blown over. She saw the cable attached to the ship's anchor. They were still moored near Helix. She was thinking about what to do next when she heard Chekhov's voice. It came through a wall, from the next room, maybe the pilothouse. He seemed to be on the telephone.

"Let me speak to Tina." Another pause, then Chekhov said, "Why haven't you contacted me?"

Venus couldn't hear the other voice.

"Why do I think you are lying, Tina? Now listen, the weather out here is hideous. In fact, it sucks. I am risking life and limb, and I expect to hear from you... Yes, yes. We have the ark down below. It's fine. But we've got problems with Rosemary. She's too friendly with my prisoner.... What? No, not the mother. The other one. I'm telling you, Rosemary is being too nice. She's not trustworthy.... What? Yes, I mean that Fish and Wildlife agent. I don't know what she was thinking.... No, I do not find it amusing, Tina, not at all."

A long pause, then Chekhov said, "Are you saying that I should kill both of them? Hey, Tina, I'm a businessman, not an assassin. You want bombs, I give you bombs. You want Uzis? I give you Uzis. But I don't personally kill with bare hands.... What? Well, first I want to know who's got the decode materials. Now, the ark is with me, so don't think you can double-cross me. If you even try, I'll make you a miserable death."

Venus lay still as Chekhov paced, muttering to himself. Then he got on the phone again. "Hello, this is Mr. Petrovich speaking. Is Mrs. Medina still there? Well, can you put me through to her voice mail?'' A pause, then, ''Tina, it's Larry. I've decided you were right. I don't know what I was thinking. It must be nerves. I'm very tired of all this bad weather. So, everything's status quo. Just forget what I said about Rosemary. See you on Lumbai.''

Silence.

Was Rosemary one of them? Should she tell Rosemary that her life was in danger? That Chekhov might be double-crossing her? Maybe Rosemary wouldn't believe her. Or maybe she already knew, and was planning to double-cross Pro-Gen. And what about Vigil? Did he fit into Chekhov's scheme?

Now she knew that at least two of Breedhaven's trustees were involved with Pro-Gen. Larry Chekhov and Tina Medina. Who else? Maybe someone on Helix Island. One thing was certain; she was trapped in the lair of double-crossing thieves, and if she didn't escape, she, too, would become extinct. She had to take a chance.

Chekhov unlocked the door and slipped inside. ''How is my little pussyfoot feeling this morning?'' he asked from behind the barrel of his gun.

She said, ''Where is my mother?''

''Do not worry about your mama,'' he said. ''She will live longer than you.''

''So where's this barge going?''

''Soon as weather permits, we sail to Lumbai,'' Chekhov said matter-of-factly. ''It is a five-day journey, but you won't be alive for most of it.''

She noticed how relaxed he seemed. Some people thrive on evil. Evil deeds relax them the way free weights relax an athlete. She glared at Chekhov. ''Where's the ark?''

''Is that all you can say?'' He pouted.

''It's all I care about.''

''What about your mama? Have you already forgotten your mama?''

''Don't play with me, Chekhov, or I might have to break that ugly nose of yours.''

Chekhov, wide-eyed, exclaimed, "And I thought you were attracted to me—physically, I mean."

"I'd rather wrestle a pit of vipers."

"But, when you placed your boot up against my throat, I had distinct feelings that you wanted me to make love to you."

"You were hallucinating."

"*Tak!* Then, why do you insist on chasing me around the world?" Chekhov pressed his lips together and shook his head. "And me, just an innocent banker from St. Petersburg." He made a sad little face.

"Oh," she laughed shrilly, "so you're still riding that hobbyhorse, are you? Next you're going to tell me that Anton was your uncle. Now where is the ark?"

Chekhov waved a hand. "Please, do not trouble yourself over the ark. It is in ideal conditions, down below in the hold. It is being cared for by an expert. Nothing will happen to it. Not one single embryo will suffer. All is safe. There is nothing to worry about."

She stood up. She still felt dizzy, off balance. Her legs felt weak. She gripped the table. She said, "I want the ark returned to my agency. And the cats. They belong to the United States Government, not to some kooky sultan who thinks he has a right to own every exotic species in the world. Not to some multi-national genetics-engineering firm that sacrifices animals for fun and profit. Now, let's stop kidding around here, Chekhov. I'm a United States federal agent, and I'm going to prove that you have committed grand larceny, destruction of federal property, kidnapping, the terrorizing of private citizens, and probably arson and mass murder."

Chekhov laughed. "What a creature you are. So small and yet so dangerous."

"Go to hell, Chekhov."

"Please, please," Chekhov said. "Don't wish me bad things. I am merely a businessman, taking care of business."

"Who do you work for?"

Chekhov smiled demurely. "I never name names."

She tried another tactic. "I'll bet you're lying. I'll bet you

don't have the ark. That's why we're still anchored out here.
Because you haven't found the ark.''

Chekhov laughed. ''Very clever—but, no, you are quite
wrong. We have had bad weather. That is why we have the
anchor down. And yes, we have the ark. Now, I imagine you
would like to see it, to be assured that it is safe and undama-
ged?''

''That would be pleasant.''

He took her through a narrow indoor passage, down a steep
flight of stairs, through a second elaborately furnished stateroom
on the floor below, then down another flight of stairs to what
appeared to be servants' quarters. He lifted a hatch and a blast
of cold air rushed out. He sent her down first. She climbed down
a steep steel ladder. She looked down, but couldn't see the bottom because warm air from above mixed with the cold air in
the hold, forming heavy vapors. The noise from the boat's en-
gines echoed. At the bottom, beneath the cloud vapors, she could
see clearly. The hold was solid steel, painted gray. Down here,
the ship's motion was stronger, and she lost her balance and
almost fell. Chekhov took her arm and led her across the floor.
She tried shaking him off, but his grip was too strong.

They passed a Sea Sport Cruiser, perched like a fetus in the
womb. Farther on, they passed an automobile shrouded in canvas, stacks of crated goods, some emergency equipment, and
another set of steel stairs leading upward to the boat's deck. She
saw a red beam of light up ahead. She saw two thugs holding
Uzis, and they watched her the whole time. Chekhov pointed to
a huge refrigeration unit. ''In there.'' Chekhov aimed a remote
key. The red beam blinked off, the freezer door opened, clouds
poured out, then gradually cleared, and she saw the ark.

TWENTY-TWO

PRO-GEN

IT WAS A SIMPLE stainless-steel box, with a single latch. Chekhov pulled a pair of gloves from his pocket, slipped them on, flipped the latch, and opened the box. "Come here," he said. "Have a look inside."

She stood on tiptoe, and peered inside the ark. The contents almost disappointed her, because they were exactly what she expected, no more or less wondrous, no magic, no surprises, no dazzling jewels or sorcerer's stone, just several dozen glass vials packed, freeze-dried, and neatly labeled. Chekhov reached in with a gloved hand, pulled out a vial, and held it up for her to see. She read its label.

Borneo Bay. Embryo specimen. H. Strindberg.

She studied its smooth glassy surface. She felt the tiny etched scratches. She glanced at Chekhov. He placed the vial back inside the box, shut the lid, latched it, and closed the freezer unit's door. When it shut, Venus saw the red alarm light come back on. They crossed back to the other end of the ship's belly, climbed the three flights of stairs, and when they were back in the main stateroom, she said, "Was it worth all the killing?"

Chekhov grinned proudly. "The sultan thinks so."

"The Sultan of Lumbai can't do anything with a bunch of frozen genetic material. He'd need a scientist who understands some very complex procedures."

Chekhov shook his head. He thought that was amusing.

She said, "Who's going to perform the surgery?"

Chekhov said matter-of-factly, "Oh that won't be a problem. Our scientists will perform the operations."

"Rosemary and...?"

Chekhov wasn't telling.

She said, "So, you and Rosemary stole the ark for the Sultan of Lumbai, not for this Pro-Gen group?"

Chekhov wanted to boast some more. "The first thing you must know," he said, "is that His Eminence is a pauper. The sultan spent his fortune saving rare creatures from extinction. Personally, I have a different philosophy, but we are speaking of the sultan. Now Pro-Gen is going to save the sultan's country from extinction."

Chekhov lit a cigarette, went over to the door, slid it open. He blew smoke into the cold wind, watched it whirl. The wind tore the smoke to shreds.

Venus said, "So, how do you fit into all this wheeling and dealing?"

"I, Larry Chekhov, am security boss."

"You mean Russian Mafia."

He shrugged. He didn't care what she called him.

Venus said, "Security boss. That's a cute title for mass murderer."

"*Poof.* In the end, we all die. Those people, do you think they were any better than you or me?"

"Why did you shanghai me? Why didn't you just kill me?"

"Oh, don't worry. I will. Not me personally, but one of my boys."

Venus said, "So what are you waiting for?"

Chekhov grinned. "You have hidden the decode materials. I want them. I'm going to make you tell me where you are hiding them. After that, we only wait for the tides to turn. So you wash out to sea, not onto the shore."

Venus said, "I hate to break your heart, Chekhov, but I don't have the decode."

Rosemary came into the stateroom, sat down beside Chekhov, rubbed his knee familiarly. Chekhov moaned softly. Venus looked out the window at the clearing horizon. After a while, Chekhov stood up, handed his gun to Rosemary. "I am going to check on the weather," he said. "Watch her." He went away.

Venus waited until Chekhov was out of hearing range, then said, "Rosemary, what if I told you that the ark you have stored down in the hold is a fake? And that your life is in danger?"

Rosemary stared. "You have a fantastic imagination."

"There's a vial down below labeled, 'Borneo Bay Cat.' Hannah had no more Borneo Bay material left. The collection down below in the hold is a fake. And, Chekhov and Tina Medina are planning to double-cross you."

"Why would they do that?" Rosemary fidgeted.

"Because they suspect that you're double-crossing them. And I agree."

Rosemary seemed to consider. Then she said, "Please mind your own business."

Chekhov came back in, said, "I have to go ashore." He tied Venus's hands behind her back. To Rosemary, he said, "Keep her in here." He went away, and in a few minutes, they heard his skiff putter off the *Nirvana*'s starboard side. When he had gone, Venus said, "So who's guarding us?"

Rosemary said, "Please, keep your voice down. There are three or four crewmen, plus two guys with Uzis."

"Don't forget Cuckoo."

Rosemary nodded. "And him."

Venus said, "You think they'd mind if we went out on deck, for a little fresh air?"

"They'd probably freak. But if you're game, so am I."

Rosemary led Venus out on the starboard deck. The wind had picked up and dusk brought more threatening buffalo clouds over the horizon. On the starboard side, they stood against the deck railing where the winds could blow their conversation out to sea. A thug with an Uzi leaned over from the upper deck. Rosemary called up to him, "She's seasick. I didn't want to mess up the cabin." The thug nodded, squinting through the twilight as Venus faked seasickness. The thug went away.

Venus said, "Now it's your turn to spill your guts, Rosemary."

"Your mother is fine. I let her out and sent her away in her car. Chekhov came before I could let you out. I told him your mother escaped by herself, but I don't think he believed me."

"I'm having a little trouble myself." Irritated.

"Where should I begin?"

"Let's start at the Empress Hotel. You went there to meet Chekhov. Why?"

Rosemary said, "Chekhov wasn't expecting me. He was expecting Tina Medina. She's a Breedhaven trustee, and she's involved in this thing with him. And they're lovers, too, I belatedly discovered. Anyway, Chekhov was expecting Tina at the Empress, and I'm sure they met after I left, but I went there before Tina arrived. I pleaded with Chekhov to stop killing people. Chekhov got furious with me. I was supposed to be on his side."

"His side against whom?"

"The Fish and Wildlife Service. You guys."

"Go on."

Rosemary put out her hand. "All along I've been pretending to cooperate, but actually I'm working against them." Rosemary lowered her voice. "Before Hannah went to the conference, she constructed the fake ark, just in case Larry would try to steal the ark while she was gone—"

"Wait. Is Ted Vigil in this, too?"

"Of course. Ted *is* Pro-Gen. Ted, Tina Medina, and Chekhov. Ted founded the company. He's the brains."

"Go on."

"Hannah hid the real ark somewhere, I don't know where. But she confided in me about her fears, and she told me that she'd substituted a fake ark for the real one. After she died, and the plan to send the ark into space was revealed, I played along with Ted and Larry, helped them steal the fake ark. I wanted them to think they had what they wanted, then sail off to Lumbai with the fake. Meanwhile, I would turn the real ark over to you. As soon as I figured out where Hannah hid it."

"But why didn't you just notify us, Rosemary? Why all the secrecy?"

"I have been constantly watched by Vigil and Chekhov. All my phone calls outside the habitat were monitored. I'm followed everywhere. I was even followed to the Empress Hotel by these thugs of Chekhov's. I couldn't risk contacting you without being caught."

Venus said, "How about untying my hands?"

Rosemary untied her hands and said, "Chekhov really means to kill you."

Venus said, "Can you swim?"

"Not in forty-degree waters. But listen, I have to carry this thing through...."

"Sooner or later, they'll discover the ark in the hold is a fake."

"I know, I know," Rosemary said. "But what else can I do?"

Venus said, "Play along with them. Give me a chance to escape. Then, right before they lift anchor, you could say you just discovered the ark is a fake."

"What will that accomplish?"

Venus said, "They'll come back ashore, looking for the real ark. We'll be waiting for them."

Rosemary sighed. "I don't know if I'm that good an actress."

"Believe me, you are."

The gusts died down, and overhead, the clouds parted and a fat moon revealed its pits and valleys. Venus looked up. Uziman was leaning over the deck railing, smoking a cigarette, staring at the moon. Venus said, "Where's the real ark?"

Rosemary shook her head. "I honestly don't know. Hannah hid it before she left for the conference. That's all I know."

"On Helix?"

Rosemary nodded. "I think so."

"Oh great," said Venus. "So while we're drifting toward some *über*mecca on a repossessed barge with a fake ark, the real ark is in danger of being discovered—or, worse, destroyed by the elements, on Helix Island. And who knows who else is out there looking for the ark."

She heard an engine throbbing, then Chekhov's boat pulled up against the *Nirvana*'s starboard side. Cuckoo came out and helped tie up the skiff.

Chekhov came aboard. "The storm is clearing off," he said to no one in particular. He looked at Venus. She kept her hands at her back.

Rosemary said, "Seasick. I didn't want her making a mess inside."

Chekhov nodded and went up a flight of stairs to the pilothouse, Cuckoo in tow. Passing Rosemary, Cuckoo said, "Chekhov says to put her indoors. Now."

"Okay, okay," Rosemary said. "Soon as she finishes throwing up."

Leaning over the rail, Venus heard a sound off the starboard side. In the distance, she saw a small craft, and heard its engine. The vessel seemed headed in their direction. She watched it approach through the moonlight. When it got close enough, Venus read its name: *Sally*. The *Sally* pulled up close to the *Nirvana*. A man's voice called out, "Ahoy. Anybody home?"

Rosemary said, "That's Sleeper Sexton. I know his voice."

In a shaft of moonlight, Sleeper pulled the *Sally* starboard aside the *Nirvana*.

Chekhov's voice came from the *Nirvana*'s upper deck. "What do you want?"

Sleeper called out, "I'm looking for a woman. She's disappeared."

Venus whispered, "It's now or never. Get ready."

Venus unstrapped her Swatch, tossed it into the water toward the *Nirvana*'s stern. The guard went over to see what flashed in the moonlight.

"What are you doing?" Rosemary whispered frantically.

"Either you swim now, or you play along with my plan."

Rosemary said, "I'll play."

Venus slipped over the side of the boat, down into the cold black morass. She heard Chekhov and Sleeper Sexton shouting back and forth. She duck-dived and swam beneath the surface toward the *Sally*.

"Well, we haven't seen anybody like that," shouted Chekhov.

Sleeper thought the voice sounded familiar, but he couldn't place it. He said, "Who am I talking to?"

Chekhov shouted, "Not your business. Now, go away."

Underwater, Venus grabbed the *Sally*'s swim ladder. Sleeper revved the engine and puttered off. She stayed beneath the water's surface until the *Sally* passed out of the stream of moonlight. Once in darkness, she climbed aboard the *Sally*. Sleeper stood at the boat's helm, looking worried, aiming the *Sally* toward Helix Island. Venus came up behind him. Sleeper turned around, saw Venus, and nearly fainted.

Venus said, "It's okay, Mr. Sexton. I'm a federal agent."

On the way in, Venus told Sleeper the story, and Sleeper offered his sad tale about the missing Edna. Venus said, "Do you think this is connected?"

"I don't know," Sleeper said mournfully. "I'm beginning to think so."

Venus said, "Did Edna know Chekhov?"

Sleeper wasn't sure. "Maybe she'd met him aboard a ferry. They've both been around the islands for several years. She might have known him."

The *Sally* headed for Sleeper's little dock. In the distance, they saw the *Nirvana*'s lights go out; darkness engulfed the sultan's ship.

TWENTY-THREE

A HIGHER LAW

THAT EVENING, Sleeper put down his copy of *Lord Jim*, drew a hot bath, soaked, shaved, and dressed in his best sports coat and trousers, and went out to meet the public at the annual Helix Island holiday gala. The snow had begun melting, baring the fragrant freshness of the evergreens, the roads were clear and almost dry. As Sleeper drove past the Lufkin place, he marveled that Luther Lufkin's snow minotaur had not yet melted. Sleeper made a note to ask Luther about Minnie. No doubt Luther would show up with his parents at the island gala. Everyone would be there, except, of course, the nuns. Not that they weren't invited; the sisters were cloistered, after all.

Edna wouldn't be there. Everyone knew by now that Edna Furbank had disappeared. Sleeper didn't look forward to the pats and cluckings of sympathy, but he went on inside the little post office/grocery store, and he endured the consolatory shoulder pattings and the calculated expressions of regret. It was bad enough accepting sympathy when a loved one passes, Sleeper thought to himself, but so much worse when the person wasn't even dead—just missing—and when the person was despised. Only Gordon Mantle seemed truly sympathetic, but then, Gordon had never been in a relationship, as far as Sleeper could recall. No one mentioned Fanny Faber's murder; no one made note of the fact that Sleeper, in his heroic effort to save Mrs. Faber, had surely mentally revisited Sally's drowning in the Haro Strait. Sleeper was glad of that because he didn't want Sally's memory dragged up and mixed up into this ugly Breedhaven business.

Luther Lufkin was gorging on pumpkin bread when Sleeper

came up to him and said, "I heard about your Minnie, Luther. I'm awfully sorry."

"Yeah," replied Luther sadly. "Me too. I'm pretty sure they were murdered."

"Oh," said Sleeper, "I see." But he didn't, and he didn't know what else to say to Luther, so he walked over to Gordon Mantle and said, "I hear you've had some trouble over there at Breedhaven, Gordon."

Gordon made a face. "I guess you mean that lady trustee drowning? Yeah? So what did you hear, Sleeper?"

Sleeper repeated to Gordon what he'd heard after Fanny Faber's death, mostly rumors.

Gordon listened, nodding his head, and when Sleeper finished, Gordon said, "It's a mess, alright."

Jean Teaweather came over bearing a plate of cookies and held it out to Sleeper. Sleeper thanked Jean but said he wasn't feeling like sweets just then. Gordon took two cookies, bit into one, and said, "These are nice, Jean. What do you call them?"

"Drip-grind cookies," said Jean proudly. "I made them with the coffee grounds in my drip-grind coffeemaker." She shook a finger at Gordon. "Simplify, simplify. That's my motto."

After she went away, Sleeper said to Gordon, "What about this federal agent they say is missing up here? You know anything about that?" Testing him.

Gordon thought it over. "Maybe. I might. Was it a small blonde lady who wears black leather and talks real clipped-like?"

Sleeper nodded. "She's looking for Fanny Faber's murderer. And, well, the ark too, I guess, and she disappeared around here somewhere."

Gordon nodded. "That would be Agent Diamond. I met her when she came up here investigating the situation. After Dr. Vigil called in the theft, Agent Diamond came up here with a couple other agents and they searched the habitat. I drove her around in the Humvee. They didn't find anything. Even I can't find it, and I know that habitat like the back of my hand."

"Are you looking for it?"

Gordon smiled slyly, and nodded.

Sleeper said, "Now, Gordon, what would you do with a bunch of endangered-species embryos?"

Gordon said, "I'd destroy them, that's what. What they're doing over there on the habitat is sinful. You shouldn't mess with God's plan. When I find the ark, I'm going to destroy all those embryos. It's for the moral good."

Sleeper was mildly shocked but knowing Gordon like he did, he wasn't totally surprised at Gordon's way of thinking. And to be honest, he didn't take Gordon's threat seriously. Still, what Gordon was suggesting was clearly illegal. Sleeper felt bound to say, "Well, you be careful what you do, Gordon. You don't want to break the law, and then get caught and end up in prison."

"Don't worry. I have a Higher Law on my side."

"Well, you be careful."

Sleeper was turning away from Gordon, heading for the coffeepot, when the sheriff came in with his two deputies. Sheriff Buzz Cone walked straight up to Sleeper and said, "Sleeper, I hate this, buddy, but I need to place you under arrest for murder."

The whole place went silent then, and if a pin dropped it would have echoed as Buzz Cone put the handcuffs on Sleeper and recited his rights under the law. Jean Teaweather rushed forward and said, "Buzz, you can't do this to Sleeper. He didn't kill Mrs. Faber."

Sheriff Cone looked at Jean Teaweather and somewhat sorrowfully said, "I don't know about Mrs. Faber, Jean. All I know is, Sleeper has been charged with the murder of old Captain Blakey."

"Captain Blakey?" exclaimed Jean Teaweather. "But they got Lois Blakey on that charge."

Sheriff Cone shook his head sadly. "New evidence."

"What new evidence?" demanded Morris Fluke, pushing himself forward.

Sheriff Cone said, "You tell them, Gordon."

Gordon shrunk back behind the sheriff. Jean Teaweather glared at Gordon and said, "What's this all about?"

Gordon didn't answer. The sheriff sighed and pushed Sleeper

gently toward the door. Morris Fluke grabbed Gordon and shouted, "What do you know about this, Gordon?"

"Nothing, nothing. Leave me alone," Gordon said, whining.

"You tell us," demanded Morris Fluke.

Gordon, in Morris Fluke's grip, finally blurted, "Okay, okay. Leave me alone." When Fluke let go of him, Gordon said meekly, "I found Sleeper's gun on Breedhaven. It was buried over by where old Elmer Poole dug up Captain Blakey's bones. It's Sleeper's gun for sure. It's that pretty silver pistol Sally gave him for his fiftieth birthday. Y'all remember that? When I took it to the sheriff, he said that was curious, because the bullets in Sleeper's gun matched the bullet in Captain Blakey's skull."

Sheriff Cone said, "I hate this as bad as anyone."

When the sheriff had taken Sleeper away, and Gordon had slinked out, Jean Teaweather turned to her fellow islanders and announced, "This party's over." In a lower voice, she said to Morris and Teensy Fluke, "Next thing you know, they'll charge Sleeper with Edna's murder."

"Oh dear me," said Teensy Fluke, her eyes still swollen from crying over Pearl, "what about Sleeper's cat? Dundee's expecting any minute now. I guess I better go over there and see if she's come home."

"That's nice," said Jean Teaweather. "Why don't you do that for Sleeper."

ROSEMARY CHOSE two a.m. for her wake-up call. Chekhov rolled over in bed and mumbled, "Who's there?"

"It's Rosemary, Larry. Open up. I have some terrible news."

Chekhov got up, went to the door of his stateroom, peeked through the peephole, then unlocked the door. Rosemary came in, all agitated.

"The agent escaped. I don't know how. I had locked her up in the cabin. She broke free somehow. She must have gone overboard."

Chekhov cursed.

"And we've been tricked," said Rosemary, sounding alarmed.

"How do you mean, 'tricked'?" Chekhov rubbed his eyes.

"Apparently Hannah Strindberg was a complete and total fraud."

"What?" Chekhov said angrily. "What do you mean by that?"

Rosemary said, "The contents of the ark. It's worthless. I've been examining the contents of the vials. Maybe Hannah's theories sounded plausible, but her practice suffered from many mistakes. Hannah's ark is a worthless collection of decomposed tissue specimens. She had all of us fooled."

"You can't be serious."

"I'm afraid so." She paused, just long enough, then said, "Unless someone is trying to trick us."

Chekhov stared at her.

Rosemary said, "Maybe this is a fake ark. Maybe the real ark is still back at Breedhaven. Oh my God, Larry—you don't think Tina and Ted would try to double-cross us?"

Chekhov was already dressing. "We're going to find out. Find Cuckoo, and prepare to go ashore."

TWENTY-FOUR

SNOWMELT

DAWN CAME SLOWLY to Helix Island, as dawn does at the forty-ninth parallel. Jean Teaweather unlocked the door to the post office/grocery store just as daylight broke across the boughs of the great Douglas fir that draped its wide canopy over Edna Furbank's abandoned Saturn. Jean had meant to speak to Sleeper about removing Edna's car from the parking lot, but what with Sleeper being arrested and charged with Captain Blakey's murder—pure poppycock. Jean hadn't wanted to disturb him with such trifles, even though he was already out on bail. Sleeper had enough problems. Jean *whooshed* her first latte and glanced out the window. The morning broke bright and clear, and if Jean wasn't awfully mistaken, she spied several orca fins cutting through the water's surface just offshore. Yes, there went one, leaping out of the water, soaring into the air, its distinctive black-and-white markings gleaming in the fresh daylight. With a loud crash the giant mammal slammed back down into the water, a spectacular belly flop that made Jean wince, hold herself, and say, "Ouch."

Just then, Jean thought she heard a cat mew. At first she thought it was in her head, wishful hearing, a groundless hope that her poor Abby had survived the murderer's cruel hands. Then Abby leaped up on the window ledge. "Abby," cried Jean Teaweather. "Oh, Abby! You've come home." She opened the window, reached out and lifted Abby inside. After an emotional reunion, she set Abby on the counter and went to work.

LUTHER LUFKIN had given up on the minotaur. It had melted down to half its original size, and already the cedar stump, which

Luther had used for a base, was showing through the ice. Luther was worried, very worried.

When two people drove up in a black limousine, Luther was standing beside the minotaur, watching it melt, but when he saw the woman and Mr. Chekhov coming down the bank toward him, Luther cried, "Mom! Mom! They're here."

Libb came running outside, took one look at the visitors and ran to her son. The woman and Chekhov came up, and Chekhov said, "'Morning Mrs. Lufkin. 'Morning, Luther."

"What do you want?" said Libb, standing close beside her son.

Chekhov nodded at the melting minotaur. "We think the snowman's hiding something."

"He's a minotaur!" shouted Luther. "And you leave him alone."

Chekhov and the woman walked around behind Libb and Luther. Luther ran up to the minotaur and guarded it with his arms. "Don't you touch him," Luther said.

"Step aside now, boy," said Chekhov, pushing Luther aside.

Libb said, "Leave him alone."

Chekhov took out his gun and pointed it at Libb. "Please, my dear lady, don't make us trouble." Chekhov grabbed Luther.

"Don't hurt him," Libb cried.

"Stay where you are," Chekhov snarled at Libb, holding the gun to Luther's head while he kicked away the ice foundations until the cedar stump lay bare.

Then the woman, who was wearing a sealskin coat, stepped forward and peered inside the hollowed-out stump. "Bingo," she said. She held the gun while Chekhov hauled a stainless-steel box up out of the cedar stump, detached it from an electrical cord that led back to the Lufkin house. He opened the refrigerated box, removed a silver suitcase, and hefted it onto his shoulders. Luther fumed as Chekhov carried the ark up the bank and loaded it into the limousine. Then, as Libb screamed helplessly, Chekhov hauled Luther up the bank. Libb came after them, but they drove off before she could stop them. Libb hollered and ran inside to call for help.

JEAN TEAWEATHER saw the *Klikitat* plowing through Haro Strait, headed for Helix Island. First ferry of the day. Jean sipped and tried humming as an antidote to the sickness she felt over Sleeper's predicament, but it didn't help. Some troubles can't be hummed away. The *Klikitat* was docking and Jean was stacking groceries when she heard helicopter blades slicing the air. *Now, what do you suppose has happened out there?* Jean asked herself. She peered out the window, but couldn't see the chopper, so she went back to stacking groceries from their cartons onto shelves.

The door opened and Teensy Fluke walked in, saying, "Goodness gracious, you'd think the marines were landing."

Teensy wanted to buy some staples, and while she shopped, Jean said, "I wonder what went down out there."

"Oh, that wasn't a Coast Guard helicopter," Teensy said. "I don't think anything went down out in the strait. It's that Fish and Wildlife chopper. Remember how it clamored over a few days before Christmas and got everybody's cows off their schedules? It's that same helicopter."

"It's back, eh?" said Jean. "Must be more trouble down at Breedhaven. You know, I haven't seen any of those folks for days now. Except Gordon Mantle, at the gala last night. Next time I run into Gordon, he's the mother of all meat, I guarantee you that. The nerve, accusing Sleeper of killing Captain Blakey."

Teensy eased a package of whole-wheat flour off the shelf and added it to three cans of tomato paste. "Pizza night," she explained to Mrs. Teaweather, who never inquired about people's eating habits. "I know what you mean about Gordon," she added. "I'll bet he's the one who killed Pearl. I tell you, Jean, maybe the island trust is better off without that piece of land. It seems like so much trouble just flies off the old Poole place."

Jean Teaweather concurred, and the two women stood silently as they watched Sleeper's *Sally* dock beside the ferry and a passenger step off and walk in the direction of the post office/grocery store. When Venus opened the door and stepped inside,

Teensy Fluke took one look at her and exclaimed, "Why, hello, Agent Diamond."

Mrs. Teaweather held Abby up for her to see. "My Abby came back," she said joyfully, then added sadly, "But no kittens. I don't know what happened to them."

"Well, I do," snapped Teensy. "My Pearl was strangled to death. And she lost her litter. I'll bet the same scoundrel murdered Abby's kittens, too."

"I heard about Pearl. I'm sorry, Mrs. Fluke," Venus said.

Teensy said, "You heard about Minnie, too? The Lufkin boy's cat?"

Venus nodded. "That, too."

"Mr. Sexton's cat, Dundee, hasn't come home," Teensy said. "Lord only knows where she's hiding. And about to give birth, too, poor creature."

Jean and Teensy didn't care to become involved in anything controversial, particularly if danger might be involved, but when Venus asked to use the telephone, Jean was more than happy to oblige.

Venus called Olson's phone. He answered from the chopper. "We're in position," he said. "Ready to pounce. Are you ready?"

"Send someone now."

"Louie's on his way," said Olson. "Is the *Klikitat* gone yet?"

"It's pulling out now. I've notified the ferry authorities. They won't dock another boat until we've cleaned up here. Anyway, I don't think they're planning to leave by the ferry."

"Why?"

Venus said, "They've got a small cruiser that used to belong to Elmer Poole."

"How do you know that?"

She could hear the chopper's engine. It was setting down somewhere nearby. She said, "I saw it when Gordon drove me to the western shore on the habitat."

Olson said, "We've got the Coast Guard bringing a boat over from Bellingham."

She looked out the window. In the distance, on the flat hori-

zon, she saw a Coast Guard cutter heading toward Helix Island.
"Okay," she said. "And I hear Louie now."

"Be careful," Olson said, then hung up.

Jean Teaweather was holding a fist to her mouth.

"Oh Lordy," Teensy Fluke said. "There's more trouble at Breedhaven."

When the telephone rang, Jean picked it up and heard Libb Lufkin's voice. "What's that, Libb?

Luther's been kidnapped? Oh mercy me."

A familiar Harley appeared on the crest of the hill, Venus's old bike, the one she'd given up for Richard's sake. It belonged to Louie Song now. The Harley sped downhill to the ferry landing. Louie, all black leather and Revos, scooted up on the bike and Venus climbed on behind him. The Harley sailed north on the island's tarry backbone and turned into the meadow behind Mercy on the Rock Cloister, where the helicopter idled in the grassy field behind the nun's barn. Venus clutched Louie as he sped across the bumpy field. A nun came out of the barn and yelled, but they didn't hear her, so sister kicked over a bucket and stomped back into the barn.

Inside the chopper, Venus said to Olson, "They've got Luther and Rosemary. Did you bring the map?"

Olson handed her a sheet of paper, a rough sketch of the habitat. As she studied it, he said, "Most likely, they didn't see our approach. We flew in from the north. Claudia and Mike are bringing in a second unit."

Beside Olson sat Eric Sweetwater, piloting the chopper. Behind them sat Agent Marla Mason, fresh off maternity leave, and Agent Sparks, up from southwestern Washington at Olson's insistence. Long, lanky Sparks didn't like this sort of scenario, but at least he'd shown up.

"Do you have a pen?" Venus asked Olson.

"To hold what?"

"I mean to write with."

Olson handed her a pen. While she made marks on the map, he said, "You look like hell."

"Breedhaven isn't exactly a health spa."

Sparks leaned forward and said, "We didn't bring the hounds.

I thought we should bring them, but Olson said not to bring the hounds.''

"The hounds would spook the animals on the habitat," said Venus. "We can't use hounds."

Marla asked, "Well, then, how are we going to track him?"

"Not 'him,' Marla. *Them.* You're going to meet me on Breedhaven after I've reached their hideout. We won't need hounds. I know where to find them."

Olson said, "How do you know where they are?"

"I've been there." Venus laid the map on the floor. "Now, everybody pay attention. Here's the main compound, with the lodge," she said, indicating a spot on the map. "To the left of the lodge is the lab building, and just beyond that are offices. Can everyone see?"

"Go on," Sweetwater said.

"About a hundred yards from the lodge, down this path"— she marked a spot on the map—"is Hannah's private cottage, and just down a short slope from her cottage is the caretaker's cottage. Behind the caretaker's cottage is a service building that the caretaker uses for maintenance."

She looked up. Everyone seemed alert, paying attention, even the chronically laconic Sparks. She said, "These buildings will probably be deserted, but we can't risk it. Chekhov might have posted guards inside or near by. Probably not, but we have to operate as if he has guards posted there."

"How are we going in?" asked Song from behind the Revos.

"I'll show you in a minute. First I want all of you to notice that the main compound is surrounded on three sides by water, which makes a water getaway the most likely."

"I told you, the Coast Guard's out there," Olson said.

"To the northwest of the compound is thick forest, then rock cliffs that drop about thirty feet into the strait. Right here is a flight of stairs leading to a boat dock down below the woods."

"Where's the entrance road?" asked Marla.

"The habitat is entered at its northeastern end." She indicated the entrance to Breedhaven on the map. "Once inside the gate, you'll cross some hill country, rolling meadows. Several of the African species are kept here. You're likely to encounter some of these species, and they'll be wary. Be especially cautious of the white rhino."

Sparks guffawed. "White rhino? You're kidding."

"No. You may also encounter bongos, a few deer. Also some exotic birds. Obviously you'll use caution if gunfire breaks out. We don't want to hit any of the animals. In fact, if we can avoid disturbing them, that would be ideal."

"Impossible," Olson said. "Now, look here." He pointed on the map. "I've marked seven shelters that Hannah had built. Here's the bongo station, here's the rhino station, here's the Australian emu station, and so forth. These are potential hideouts."

"Right," said Venus. "What other structures are you aware of on the habitat?"

Olson said, "Hannah had feed stations placed in the forest and in the marshlands." He pointed to the northeast of the compound. "These are marshlands. We have two or three small feed stations in the marshes. In the forest, I'd say we have two, maybe three feed stations and a couple shelters. Then, over here, where the meadows front up against the woods, there's a shelter for the emus, and another one up here for the margays and okapis."

Louie Song whistled. "That's a lot of hiding places."

Venus said, "There's a cabin near the dock. I'm guessing that's where they are." She turned to Olson. "Any other dwellings you can recall?"

Olson rubbed his face.

"Hurry up," she said. "Think."

"Don't push me," Olson snapped. "I recall Hannah mentioning one or two old cabins. Run-down places, she said. She wanted them torn down. I don't recall just exactly where they were located, but I think they both were in the forest on the western edge of the habitat. I just don't recall for sure."

Song said, "What we need is an aerial map."

"It wouldn't help much," said Venus. "Anyway, our target is in the forest, under cover of the tree canopy." She pointed to the western edge of the habitat. "There."

"How do you know that?" asked Olson.

"Instinct," she said. "Or, if it makes you feel better, call it an educated guess."

"Just once," Olson pleaded unfairly, "can you please be right?"

TWENTY-FIVE

RHINO POWER

OLSON READ his watch. "It's now eight-oh-three. Let's set a timetable."

Venus said, "I'll need time to get onto the habitat. I'll have to pass the main compound. If I'm lucky, the compound will be deserted."

Song laughed. "That's not luck you're counting on. That's a miracle."

"Then pray for a miracle," she said, tucking a gun in her holster.

The radio crackled. Olson spoke into it. Claudia Paganelli's voice came back. "We're at Bellingham," said Claudia. "Maguire, myself, and six others. Where do we go now?"

Venus snatched the radio. "Do you have ground vehicles?"

Claudia paused, then said, "Several back-road scooters."

Venus frowned.

"She means Hondas," Louie explained.

"Where shall we set down?" Claudia asked.

Venus directed them to the meadow behind the convent.

Before signing off, Venus said, "We need your team to block a land escape; move into the forest from the northern edge, but remember, the habitat is housing fragile species. No unnecessary noise."

Marla handed Venus a cell phone. Venus clipped it on, and pulled on a pair of boots. She climbed on the Harley, and sped off across the grassy meadow, headed for the north-south road that formed the island's backbone. When she reached the main road, she accelerated, and the wind stung her face in a biting caress she hadn't felt for months.

Breedhaven's gate was locked. She backed up onto a high dirt bank, accelerated forward. Out loud, she said, "Here I come." The Harley took flight, landing neatly inside the habitat. She sped along the main road. When she reached the marshlands, the bike's noise roused a dozing fawn that leaped for cover. Now she could see the compound up ahead, and she saw the Humvee. Gordon must be around somewhere. Instead of heading into the compound, she turned and sped into the forest, along the narrow trail she remembered traveling with Gordon in the Humvee. When she reached the trail's end, she stopped. Listened.

Voices. Coming from the woods. She pulled the Harley into a thicket, got off, called Olson, then tramped through the woods. In the distance, she heard the helicopter. Too close, too noisy. Chekhov and his cohorts would hear it, and try to hasten their escape. Through the thickets, she could see the strait now, but no sign of the Coast Guard cutter. Maybe it had sailed to the wrong side of the island. She came up at the rear of the cabin, where it stood on a precipice overlooking the strait. The air was cold and clear and sounds traveled easily. She heard birds singing, tree branches rustling, the salt water lapping against the rocky shore, and the distant sound of the helicopter. No noise came from the cabin. She moved up to a window, peered over the sill.

Nobody home. Had she been wrong?

The sound of the helicopter died out as it landed. She looked down at the water, saw the old boat dock. At the end of the dock sat a float plane. She hadn't counted on this. Then she saw them; two men walking along the dock toward the float plane: Chekhov and Ted Vigil. Chekhov was carrying a silver suitcase. The ark.

Behind them came Rosemary Poole and Luther Lufkin, and behind Luther and Rosemary walked Cuckoo, alongside a woman in a sealskin coat, who held a gun on Luther and Rosemary. Tina Medina. The men's voices drifted up into the crisp, clear air. She heard Ted Vigil say, "Hurry up."

Chekhov, hefting the ark onto his shoulders, growled, "I'm doing my best."

Luther said, "I throw up in airplanes."

Tina Medina said, "Let's just shoot them now."

"We can't do that," said Vigil. "We need hostages."

"We should have taken a trustee," argued Tina. "They were worth more than Rosemary and this island brat."

"We've got what we've got," snapped Vigil. "Now lift."

They lifted the ark into the float plane. Vigil climbed in after it, then Chekhov, who reached down, grabbed Rosemary and Luther, and dragged them up into the plane while Tina Medina held the gun. Then Cuckoo climbed aboard.

Venus picked up a stone, threw it at the water. Vigil was helping Tina Medina aboard when the rock splashed into the water near the plane's left pontoon. Chekhov said, "What's that?"

"A fish jumping," said Tina Medina.

Venus threw another rock.

Splash.

"That's not a fish," insisted Chekhov. He drew his gun, climbed out of the plane and looked around. Vigil peered out.

Into her phone, as quietly as she could, Venus said, "Where's that damn Coast Guard cutter?"

Olson came back: "It went around the east side of the island. I don't know why."

"Hurry," she said. "West side. Now." She slid down the embankment.

Chekhov had climbed back into the plane and was revving the motor. Venus dove into the water. Chekhov saw something but wasn't sure what it was. He started to taxi just as Venus heaved onto a pontoon and climbed aboard. As Chekhov accelerated the engine, they taxied faster along the water's surface. Behind the plane, a dorsal fin circled slowly. Shark. Venus got the cockpit door open, climbed inside. Chekhov pulled back on the throttle and the plane lurched upward, lifted off, and caught a draft. She pointed her gun at Chekhov's head, mouthed the word *Down,* three times before he took her seriously. In the copilot's seat, Vigil sat frozen from fright. Chekhov reached for his gun, which he had laid in his lap, and aimed it at her. She shot at Chekhov's hand. He lost the gun, and he lost control of the plane. Vigil screamed. Panic reigned. "Shut up," she yelled at the passengers. She shoved Chekhov aside and grabbed the controls.

Rosemary, seizing an opportunity, grabbed Tina Medina's gun. Venus fought to bring the plane level. It banked steeply, leveled out, banked again. She pulled back on the throttle, found an updraft, leveled out again as the passengers screamed and clung to their seats. The plane rode the updraft through a cloud bank before she turned it around and aimed it at Helix Island. She let the throttle in gradually and brought the plane down on the water with a loud smack. Belly flop.

They were taxiing up to the dock when Olson's team swarmed down the embankment, weapons drawn. But they were onshore, too far away.

On the float plane's pontoons, Vigil clung to the struts while Chekhov, his hand bleeding, grabbed Venus and shoved her overboard. She grabbed onto a pontoon with one hand, but the pontoon was slippery and she struggled to hang on. Vigil saw her hand, lifted a foot above her loosening grip, started to crush her fingers, but Rosemary fired at Vigil, and he fell screaming into the path of a large dorsal fin. Venus went after Chekhov, but the Russian moneybags dove into the strait and disappeared. The dorsal fin cut a path through swaths of rich, red blood.

MAYBE CUCKOO really could fly. They never did find him. Sweetwater and Mason hauled off Tina Medina and her sealskin coat, while Claudia and Mike climbed uphill to the cabin with their forensics equipment to begin the tedious process of evidence gathering. Rosemary, not one to miss an opportunity, melted into Louie Song's willing embrace and sobbed. Luther watched Olson and Venus haul the ark out of the plane.

On the dock, Venus opened the ark, reached in, fished out a vial. She said, "There are only numbers on these labels. No names." She reached in, fished out another vial. "There's no name on this one, either." She looked at Olson.

He laughed and said, "Do you think Hannah would give away her secrets that easily? Now, let's put this baby on ice."

The Coast Guard cutter was just rounding the bend at the

southern tip of Helix Island when Luther said, "I think Gordon killed Minnie's kittens. And now he's got Dundee."

"Dundee?" said Venus. "Sleeper Sexton's cat?"

"Yes. The last cat carrying Bay kittens," said Luther. "I'm pretty sure Gordon killed the other litters. Dundee's going to drop that litter any day now. But Gordon's got her."

"Where is he?" Venus asked.

"Somewhere on the habitat," Luther said. "When they brought me onto the habitat, I saw him in the parking lot. He had Dundee. He's going to kill her kittens. See, what he does is, he waits for the litter to drop, then he kills the kittens. He's crazy. Gordon says they're 'the product of the devil.'" In a quiet voice Luther added, "And Sleeper didn't murder Captain Blakey."

Olson came over and said, "We've got to get this sucker on ice. Hurry up."

Venus put a hand up to silence him. To Luther, she said, "Go on, Luther. Tell us exactly what you know."

Luther took a deep breath. "I saw what happened. It wasn't Sleeper who shot Captain Blakey. It was Mr. Chekhov."

"Wait. You saw Chekhov shoot C.Z. Blakey?"

Luther nodded solemnly.

Venus frowned. "That was a long time ago, Luther. How old were you?"

Luther said, "I was only four. I was over here at the Pooles'. Rosemary was babysitting me, and I was playing out by the rocky ledge, right up here." Luther pointed to the rock ledge just above the dock. "Mrs. Blakey and Mr. Chekhov were in that cabin up there. I was spying on them through the window. I saw them...you know."

Venus nodded. Olson, interested now, said, "That's okay, Luther. You don't have to say it."

Luther seemed relieved. "While Mrs. Blakey was in the cabin with Mr. Chekhov, Captain Blakey pulled up in his boat, tied up to the dock right here." Luther showed them where. "He came up to the cabin. I hid in the woods, but I could see. I was pretty scared."

"Go on," Venus said.

"Aren't you going to help Dundee?" asked Luther.

"Sure," she said, "just as soon as you finish your story."

Luther said, "Then Captain Blakey called out Mr. Chekhov's name. Then Mr. Chekhov came outside and before Captain Blakey could do anything, Mr. Chekhov shot him. He had Sleeper's fancy silver gun. I don't know how he got it. Then Mr. Chekhov and Lois Blakey buried his body."

Olson said, "What did you do then?"

"I ran away. I never told anybody. I thought if I told on him, Mr. Chekhov would kill me. I heard he smuggles drugs and kills people."

"Who told you that?"

"Edna Furbank. She was in the woods, too, when Mr. Chekhov and Mrs. Blakey were burying the body. She saw them, but I don't think they saw her. Later on, Edna told me that she saw what I saw, and that Mr. Chekhov was a drug smuggler, and that he used Chekhov Meadows up here for his drug operations. Edna said Chekhov might kill me if I told on him."

Venus placed a hand on Luther's shoulder. "You're a brave young man, Luther. And all this time you've been protecting Hannah's ark."

Luther said, "My mom helped. We had to run a power cable from the house."

Venus smiled. "Hannah would be very proud of you."

Venus felt cold and soaked to the skin. Claudia, always prepared, had brought along emergency gear. Venus changed into some of Claudia's dry clothing. It was six sizes too large, but this wasn't a fashion show.

They organized into teams, and set out across the habitat. Maybe they could stop Gordon.

Venus rode the Harley back to the compound. The parking lot was empty, except for the Humvee. In the deserted laboratory, she found nothing unusual. Nothing in the offices. In Hannah's office, the bathroom door was open. The servals were missing. She walked across the gravel path to Hannah's cottage. The door was locked. She looked around for signs of Purim. No servals, no cats of any species. Gordon's cottage was locked up. She peered through a window. Seemed like nobody home. She went behind the caretaker's cottage to the maintenance building. Nobody there. She asked herself, *If I were Gordon, where would I take a cat ready to drop its litter?* As she was contemplating this, she heard an engine noise.

The Humvee. Gordon had come back. She raced out of the building and saw the Humvee heading into the marshes. She leaped onto the Harley and sped after it. The Humvee was rugged and fast. She hadn't ridden the Harley in over a year. She didn't know this terrain, and Gordon knew it like the back of his murderous hand. When the Harley bogged down in a marsh, the Humvee lost her in the wetlands. Under the watchful gaze of the bongo family, she dragged the bike out of the marsh, hopped back on, and sped uphill toward the meadows.

The Humvee had reached the marshlands, and from a distance through the trees, she caught glimpses of Gordon climbing out of the vehicle, carrying a crate. She stopped, leaped off the bike, and moved cautiously after him. He still hadn't seen her, hadn't realized she'd caught up to him. She reached the animal shelter just as Gordon ducked inside, carrying the crate.

Inside the shelter, Dundee crouched and arched her back. She was heavy with the litter that was ready to drop. Gordon sat watching the cat. Venus took out her gun, went in. Gordon looked up and Dundee scampered a little way but then froze, as Gordon grabbed her scruff and pulled her back.

"Put her down, Gordon," Venus said.

"She's carrying the devil's seed," Gordon cried.

Venus moved in closer. "Put her down."

Neither of them noticed the strange tail poking out of a stall, but when Gordon tried to make a run for it, the startled rhino charged out of the stall. The powerful beast moved fast, trapping Gordon in a corner.

A sweat broke over his brow. Gordon said, "Easy, boy, easy now."

The rhino lunged at Gordon, tossed him up into the air. Gordon flew through the door, landing outside on the hard ground. He scrambled to his feet, but too late. The rhino charged out the door and came at Gordon with its horn. Gordon screamed, but the rhino gored him anyway, and when Gordon's body fell back to earth, the rhino poked it inquisitively for a moment, then ambled off in the direction of the meadows. Gordon's dead flesh and bones had nothing to offer an herbivore.

As the cat delivered her litter, Venus sat beside Dundee. One...two...three. Venus was no felid expert, but she knew these three kittens were pure Borneo Bays. She watched as the surrogate mother cleaned her kittens, exactly as Dundee would have done with any litter she carried. She rolled over to expose her nipples, and each kitten instinctively found the nipple that would be its exclusively until weaning. *Not a surrogate,* thought Venus, *but a true mother.* DNA aside, Dundee had carried these kittens and given them life. Two males and one female. Someday there might be more kittens. More Borneo Bays.

Venus was standing in the doorway, watching Dundee and her kittens, when she heard a hissing noise. She froze, listened. More hissing, louder. She had decided to make a run for it when the cat leaped out of a tree and landed on her shoulder, scratching viciously. She fought, but the animal was tenacious. It sunk its sharp teeth into her neck, aiming for her jugular. She felt its claws scraping her skin, felt its teeth tearing into her neck, and the blood drip into her eyes. She struggled for her gun, pulled it out, fell to the ground and rolled. The cat lost its hold on her. She aimed her gun at its head, and then she saw the distinctive white stripe on its face, the golden red fur, the spots on its legs and belly, the black tip on its tail.

He was small, about the size of a large house cat. His forehead was short, rounded, and his jagged teeth were stained with Venus's blood. He hissed threateningly, but didn't move. He stood between Venus and the mother cat with her kittens, a father protecting his own. But how could he know?

Blood dripped into her eyes, but she dared not raise her arm to wipe it away. One move might cause the Bay to attack again. Her torn flesh stung in the frigid air. She could hear her heart beat and in the distance, a gull's doeful lament. The Bay cat hissed louder, and suddenly she recalled Chekhov's words.

"What a creature you are. So small and yet so dangerous."

She didn't want to shoot, but if she didn't, the Bay would torture her again. It certainly knew where to find her jugular—

to the Bay, she was just a big monkey. Meat. The cat hissed louder and arched his back. The hairs on his back stood straight up. Her blood dripped from his mouth. His eyes focused on her. He leaped.

A gun went off, but it wasn't hers. The faraway noise threw the Bay cat off. He turned in midair, his ears following the sound. She scrambled to her feet and ran for the Harley. She was skirting the marshlands when Louie Song, riding a Honda, scooted up alongside the Harley. Rosemary Poole sat behind him, clasping onto his waist. Venus slowed down to cruising speed, said, "You didn't have to shoot at him, Louie."

"I didn't," said Louie. "It was Rosemary."

"I shot in the air," said Rosemary. "Just to scare him off."

"I see you two have bonded," Venus remarked dryly.

Louie said, "The servals are okay. Rosie gave them to Luther's mom to hide."

The Bay cat didn't chase after them, just let them speed away. The danger gone, he returned to the shelter, crept inside, and strolled over to his family. Dundee was guarded at first, then, realizing the male cat wasn't intending to harm her brood, she allowed him to sniff around, but when the Bay tried to nuzzle the kittens, Dundee slapped him with her paw.

TWENTY-SIX

BLAST-OFF

THE COAST GUARD captured the *Nirvana* on the edge of international waters, brought in the crew and the Uzi thugs.

Later that evening, inside the lodge, warming by the fire, Dundee and her kittens luxuriated. The papa Bay cat sat nearby in his cage, hissing, scratching, wanting out. Olson stared alternately at the kittens and the Bay. *God, Hannah would be so proud of these kittens,* Olson thought, *so proud.* Olson fought bittersweet tears.

Song burst into the lodge, hauling firewood, and stoked the fire. On the couch, Venus sat beside Rosemary. In a soft voice Rosemary said, "Hannah came to me the day before she went to the conference in Seattle. That's the first I'd heard of her fears, and of Ted's plan to steal her research. Hannah told me that she was planning to expose Ted and Chekhov and Tina that night."

"The night of the fire?" Venus said.

"Yes. Hannah and Martine Olaffson were planning to expose Pro-Gen's plot to steal the ark. Hannah worried that they might also try to take the Borneo Bay." Rosemary blushed. "Actually, I lied to you about the Bay cat."

"No kidding." Sarcastic.

Rosemary said, "Hannah did load the Bay cat into the crate. But on her way out of the habitat, she set him free. It was her best chance of saving him. She wasn't careless. She never would have taken the Bay to Zanzibar's."

Venus said, "What about the teeth? They found some wildcat teeth near Hannah's body."

Rosemary seemed surprised. "Oh." She considered this, then said, "I'll bet those were the serval teeth Hannah always kept in her purse. They were from her very first wildcat autopsy. I remember she showed them to me once.''

Venus and Olson exchanged glances. Venus said, ''So what was in the crate?''

''A security videotape Hannah and I had made of Ted, Tina, and Chekhov. We caught them on tape, planning to murder Hannah and Martine.''

''But why did they have to murder them? Why not just steal the ark?''

Rosemary sighed. ''Hannah's ark offered enormous potential for financial gain. Hannah and Martine were on the cutting edge of the science, and Ted was intensely jealous of them. When Ted put together Pro-Gen, he hired Martine as a consultant, but Hannah was the real genius, and she wouldn't have any of Pro-Gen.''

''So Vigil was the brains behind Pro-Gen?''

''Of course. And Ted was stupid for a change. He tried to recruit Martine to steal Hannah's ark for them. When Martine refused, and told Hannah about the plot, Ted and Chekhov hired some thugs to terrorize the two women, so they planned to expose Pro-Gen at the nightclub event.''

Venus said, ''Which explains the news reporter who was present and died in the blaze.''

''That's right,'' said Rosemary. ''The reporter didn't know anything, except that if she showed up, she'd get a story.''

Venus shook her head. Something felt loose. ''But why did Vigil locate Pro-Gen in Lumbai?''

''That was Larry Chekhov's suggestion. They needed a neutral country, a country that needed money. Chekhov knew of the Sultan of Lumbai's dedication to endangered animals, to preserving these species. They exploited his impoverished financial position, and his love of animals. Chekhov told him that in exchange for providing a tax-free haven for Pro-Gen, Pro-Gen would pay royalties to the sultan on everything they marketed. Of course, they led him to believe they were developing technology to *save* endangered species. They didn't tell the sultan that they were doing animal experimentation on their farms.

They certainly didn't tell him that they planned to steal Hannah's ark.''

"Maybe this is naive, but how exactly did Vigil, Tina, and Chekhov plan to benefit from Hannah's ark?"

"Ted could have, with Hannah's techniques, re-created these species and then sold them for huge profits."

Venus shrugged. "Not pretty, but at least he would have saved the species."

"But only for financial gain," Rosemary said. "And Ted and Tina had other motives for possessing the ark."

"Such as?"

Rosemary glanced up. "This is the big one." Louie came over and sat in a chair beside his new love interest. Rosemary batted her nice eyelashes at him. Louie winked at her, and lightly touched her double helix tattoo. Venus said, "Don't give me some fictitious, *Jurassic Park* scenario, Rosemary."

Rosemary shook her head. "I'm speaking of human body parts. Ted had already set up shop in Lumbai. He had some junior-level scientists in Lumbai, and he taught them how to genetically alter animals, so that their organs could be utilized in human transplant surgery."

Louie said, "You're kidding."

"No," said Rosemary. "It's a growing and lucrative field. But Ted had gone beyond inserting human genes into animals. They're farm-raising animals on Lumbai for organ-transplant purposes. A client wants a human ear, Pro-Gen slices it off one of their research pigs and provides it, for a very high fee. Ted wasn't working for the advancement of humankind, or to protect animal species. He was greedy and ambitious, and he had Tina's support. They had no ethics, no scruples. They were willing to experiment with any creature, no matter how fragile or endangered. Hannah's ark contained the embryos of several species believed to be potentially good hosts for human body parts. Not wholly human parts, but genetically altered—these animals could serve as surrogates, producing organs, and limbs, possibly for human transplant."

"Which species?" Venus asked.

Rosemary said, "Only Hannah knew that. She didn't tell anyone. She would never allow her research animals to be used like that. Although I imagine that somewhere, maybe in the decode materials, she must have kept documentation of her discoveries. You know, with years of hard work, Ted could actually have re-created what Hannah had already accomplished, but it was so much easier to steal the ark and then try to locate the decode materials.''

Olson came over and said, ''Where are the decode materials?''

Rosemary shrugged. ''Hannah didn't tell me. Honest. All I know is that she entrusted them to a Breedhaven trustee. That's all any of us knew. First Ted and Larry tried bribing each trustee with Pro-Gen stock. Then they tried to torture it out of each one.'' She turned to Venus. ''Your mother was the last one left.''

''MOTHER, this is Venus. Can you hear me?''

Bella said, ''You'll have to speak up, dear. The connection is dreadful.''

''I'm on Helix Island, Mother. I just called to say I'm alive and well. And I need to ask you something.''

Bella sighed. ''In case you are at all interested, Venus, it is quite rude to disappear without a trace, leaving your flesh and blood fretting over innumerable morbid scenarios. And your office has been less-than-forthcoming. We've all been sitting around here worried sick over your well-being.''

''I'll bet.'' Wryly. ''I need to ask you something.''

''Very well, but make it snappy. I have Antonio here and we are discussing a scene.''

''I thought you finished the film.''

Bella said, ''This is my next project. Quite an original story in which everyone believes he or she is a cat. Now, what were you asking me?''

''Mother, we need to know where you hid the decode materials.''

Silence. Then, ''Is this a secure telephone connection?''

Venus said, ''Use some kind of code to communicate it. Something only I will understand.''

"Very well. Here is your hint. Tangerine silk."

Tangerine silk. Tangerine silk. Of course, the *Lady Bella.* The tangerine silk-covered bed. Venus said, "Where, exactly?"

"Taped to the underside."

"Thanks, Mother. By the way, how's Tim?"

Bella sniffed. "Timothy is presently doing time-out in his room."

"What's the crime?"

"Timothy constructed a rather lurid snow sculpture. I have grounded him for the non."

"Tell him I'll come visit him in his cell."

"All right. Now, I am going to ring off. Do be careful up there, dear. Those ferry crossings can be treacherous."

CRIMES OF PASSION are nothing new. It's when you shoot your spouse in cold blood, fillet him, and grind him into breakfast sausage, that people sit up and take notice. Although the gun found near Captain Blakey's skull and bones belonged to Sleeper Sexton, only two sets of fingerprints were found on it, and neither set was Sleeper's. So, while Lois Blakey denied to the very end that she had made C.Z. into sausage, she was convicted as Chekhov's accomplice in hiding Captain Blakey's bones. In the deepest reaches of their hearts, some islanders believed that Chekhov had also murdered Sally Sexton—but why? And how did he get Sleeper Sexton's gun?

One warm spring afternoon, as Jean Teaweather was sorting the mail, she came across a letter addressed to Sleeper Sexton. It was from the Walla Walla Prison for Women, inmate Lois Blakey. Jean called Sleeper and Sleeper raced to the little post office/grocery store and opened the letter. Jean read over Sleeper's shoulder—not that Sleeper had given her permission. In her letter, Lois Blakey told how Sally Sexton had accidentally witnessed Larry Chekhov's drug-smuggling activities from his land on Helix Island. Chekhov had lured Sally around the point to the cove near Elmer Poole's dock and drowned her, making it appear like a boating accident. Lois had been with Chekhov when he murdered Sally. Before drowning her, Chekhov had taken Sleeper's gun away from Sally.

The islanders rarely spoke of it, but often wondered whatever had happened to Edna Furbank. Months later, Buzz Cone returned from a trip to New Orleans—county sheriffs' convention—and swore he had seen Edna riding the carousel bar in the Monteleone Hotel.

Sleeper went home, got rid of Edna's belongings, took out his framed portrait of Sally, dusted it off, and placed it on the bedside table. He immediately embarked upon an American-history reading program, vowing to reach Current Affairs before age sixty-five. In retirement, Sleeper hoped to read nothing but popular fiction.

Once again Helix Islanders were concerned with nothing more stressful than the pesky wasps that spun their nests on the cliffs above the water, and, too, the real estate-hungry nuns of Mercy on the Rock Cloister. Life on Helix Island seemed almost normal again, and if anyone asked Jean Teaweather, she would say that if it weren't for the infernal boredom, Helix might be the idyllic island paradise.

RICHARD WINTERS, home from Kadoudougou on his first leave, found Venus lounging on the sunroom chaise. He rushed to her, lifted her up, swung her around, pressed her body against his, and kissed her fervently. She heard his protestations of love, his vow to never again travel so far away without her. She'd just have to come with him, he declared. She heard his sighs as they made love, and later, as they lay in each other's arms, Richard said, "So, babe, what did you do while I was away?"

"I helped a cat named Dundee deliver her kittens," she said. "Other than that, nothing much." Mentally, she counted the steps from the bed to the closet containing her suitcase.

"That's sweet. Kittens." He patted her derriere. "Hey, look who's getting back into shape. You been working out?"

She sat up. "Richard," she said. "Do you remember before we were married, I told you about a letter I sent to NASA? About becoming an astronaut?"

ON A BRIGHT and clear June morning, as the space shuttle *Earnest* rocketed toward the international space station, Astronaut

Venus Diamond gazed out the window and saw planet Earth far below. Across the cabin, Captain David Dillon gave her a thumbs-up signal. She returned it, and was trying to think of something profound to say when Dillon signaled.

"You have a phone call," he said casually.

"Just let it ring," she said to Dillon.

"We don't do that up here," Dillon replied. "Answer the phone."

It was Olson. "A fellow named Fuss called, from the Swedish consulate."

"Message?"

"He thinks you're sexy. He wants to date you."

Venus said, "You called me to tell me that?"

"I also thought you'd like to know that your job is waiting for you when you return. If you still want it."

"Okay, anything else?"

"Richard called from Kadoudougou. He said Singapore will be fine—whatever that means. And Bella and Timmy have left the launch site. They want to know where the *Earnest* is going to splash down. They want to meet you."

"Somewhere in the Pacific," she said drolly, "maybe near Lumbai."

Dillon signaled that it was time to hang up. There was work to be accomplished aboard the *Earnest*. Venus said to Olson, "Would you mind contacting Dr. Ray Wong? Tell him I need to push my next appointment ahead two or three days. We've delayed our return, and I don't want Wong thinking I stood him up."

"Okay. How's the ark holding up?" Olson asked.

Venus said, "Noah would be proud of Hannah Strindberg."

DEAD AND GONE

DOROTHY SIMPSON

AN INSPECTOR LUKE THANET MYSTERY

During a small and decidedly uncomfortable dinner party, Virginia Mintar, wife of a prominent lawyer, disappears, only to be found hours later, stone dead in the garden well of the rustic estate.

Virginia's scandalous behavior had earned her the rage of family, friends and lovers alike. Who had been finally driven to kill her? As Inspector Luke Thanet and his partner, Sergeant Mike Lineham, begin to unravel the tangled threads of dark family secrets, bitter hatred and devious intent, not even they are prepared for the final, ghastly discovery in what emerges as the most poignant and disturbing case of their careers.

Available March 2001 at your favorite retail outlet.

WORLDWIDE LIBRARY ®

WDS379

maquette for murder

GRETCHEN SPRAGUE

A MARTHA PATTERSON MYSTERY

After a successful career as a New York attorney, retired
Martha Patterson stays busy doing freelance legal research.
It is a life that is proving both fascinating...and dangerous.

Her closest friend, Hannah Gold, is the victim of a break-in.
Hannah survives a blow to the head, but her celebrated new
maquette, a small-scale model of a large piece of artwork, is
savagely destroyed.

While immediate suspicion falls upon another sculptor, Martha
puts her legal mind to work, seeing the fine print in a crime
that leads to the dark places of love, loss and revenge.

Available March 2001 at your favorite retail outlet.

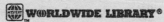

WGS378

THE HIRELING'S TALE

JO BANNISTER

A CASTLEMERE MYSTERY

Detective Inspector Frank Shapiro and his two chief investigators, Liz Graham and Cal Donovan, probe a murderous conspiracy, which may rob Castlemere of more than one of their finest.

A young prostitute is found dead on a boat in the Castlemere Canal. Adding to the puzzle, there's a hired killer on the loose, making target practice of farm animals—before taking aim at the real mark. But the hit misses—and Shapiro takes the bullet. Now it's up to a shaken Graham and Donovan to sort out a complex crime that will lead to another fatal confrontation in the lonely English countryside.

Available March 2001 at your favorite retail outlet.

WJB377